Heroes and Lovers

A Sam Jenkins Mystery

Wayne Zurl

Published by
Melange Books, LLC
White Bear Lake, MN 55110
www.melange-books.com

To Bazzie:

Fiction is fiction. No matter what anyone says, I have an imagination.

Chapter One

The last thing I wanted to do just before Christmas was tangle with a creep like Elrod Swaggerty. Unfortunately, a police officer has little choice of what or who gets dumped onto his lap. Our motto is, "To protect and serve." Humbug.

At quarter-to-eleven on Monday morning, December 18th, I heard an angry voice in the reception area.

"Now looka here, missy. I wanna see the head man, and I want him now. And y'all need ta lock up that no-account, thievin' sum-bich! Ya hear me?"

Calling Sergeant Bettye Lambert *missy* sounded like a bad idea to me. I decided to intervene so I wouldn't find an injured hillbilly in the lobby of my police station.

Years of experience taught me the best thing to do in a situation like that would be walk in on the conversation and do nothing until the tide changed.

I stopped ten feet from Bettye's desk. The complainant, a local specimen who looked to be somewhere between forty-five and his mid-fifties, wasn't alone. A woman around thirty stood in the shadow of the older man. She held a four or five-year-old girl by the hand. None of the three looked like they bought their clothes in Parisian's, but they seemed clean and healthy and were probably in need of legal assistance.

I folded my arms across my chest and began my stoic Chief Pontiac impersonation, trying to look just this side of downright mean.

"Sir, we have every intention of takin' your complaint and helpin' you the best we can." Bettye can usually sooth the nastiest characters with only a few words.

The man stood in front of her desk scowling, hands on hips. His salt-and-pepper hair looked like someone trimmed it with a hedge clipper.

I think Bettye sensed my presence. She turned and looked at me but said nothing. The man stopped talking, and the young woman, who had yet to speak, looked at me with anticipation. I tried to look like Grumpy, the seventh dwarf. I thought my act started well, but the suspense was killing me. I wondered what our visitors thought.

I decided to break the silence. "Good morning. I'm Chief Jenkins, and I'd be happy to listen to your complaint—if we can do it like two civilized gentlemen." I nearly growled, and he blinked first. "Sergeant, would you do the honors?"

Bettye gave a sigh. "Chief, this is Mr. Bunker and his daughter, Lorene. They've had a problem with a local auto repair shop. Mr. Bunker thinks it may be a criminal matter."

Outside our doors, in the lobby of the Prospect municipal building, the colored lights on a tall Christmas tree twinkled in no particular order. The recessed ceiling lamps had been dimmed a little, and the marble halls looked cozy. Bettye, on the other hand seemed tense, and the atmosphere in our reception area was decidedly uncomfortable. Unless I smoothed out our overwrought customer, I assumed asking Bettye to wear a Christmas elf's costume would be out of the question.

"Okay, I'd like to hear about it." I nodded at the two adults. "Mr. Bunker, Miss Lorene, I'll try to help if I can. Let's go into my office and sit down. But first, Lorene, will you introduce me to the young lady here?"

Lorene looked too thin. She wore tight jeans and a hooded sweatshirt. Her mousy brown hair hung straight and below her shoulders. She smiled, looked toward who I thought was her daughter and spoke in a sing-song Smoky Mountain accent. "This is Tonya. Tonya, say hello to the po-leece-man."

Tonya lowered her eyes and remained quiet. I got down on one knee, tilted my head, tried to look friendly—something not always easy for me—and extended my hand.

She was tiny with long dark hair surrounding a doll-like face. Her red dress, white socks and Little Lulu shoes seemed like clothing from

2

another age.

"Hello, Miss Tonya. My name is Sam. I think your momma and papaw might have a problem. Would you like me to fix it?"

Little Tonya invoked her right to remain silent. I shrugged and smiled, thinking big girls responded favorably to a smile, why not a little kid. She hugged her mother's thigh, but finally said, "Yes, sir."

"Okay, I can do that. But first, we need to be friends. Can we shake hands?"

She maintained a death grip on her mom's leg, but extended her right hand toward mine. I took the little paw between my thumb and forefinger and gave a gentle shake.

"Good. Now we're buddies," I said.

Tonya gave me ten percent of a full-size smile. A little progress seemed better than none.

Mr. Bunker and Lorene sat in the two armchairs in front of my desk. I carried a side chair around front and placed it close to Lorene so Tonya could sit with her mom.

"Now, Mr. Bunker," I said, "I know you've already told the sergeant your story, but can I hear it again?"

Bunker clicked his teeth several times before giving me a concise story. "Lorene had took her Taurus to Smoky Mountain Transmissions fer a check-up. The car'd been actin' funny, and I guessed the bands were a-slippin'. She dropped the car off on Monday, got it back on Wednesday afternoon."

He paused to shake his head in apparent disgust.

"Had ta give seven-hunnert-fifty dollar. Man said he had ta re-build the transmission." He stopped again and looked at me.

"Uh-huh," I said. "I'm guessing there's something else?"

"Yes, sir, there is. My son, Leroy, he looked at the car. Leroy had took him some classes on auto re-pair in hi-skoo. Leroy says ain't nobody never even touched that transmission a'tall."

"Does the car drive better now, Lorene?" I asked.

"Yes, sir, it does."

Tonya looked at me with big brown eyes while she twisted strands of hair around her fingers. I winked. She smiled.

"Mr. Bunker, what's your first name?" I asked.

Bunker pulled his head back a few inches, looked at me for a long moment. "Alvin."

"Might I call you Alvin, sir?"

Bunker scowled again, looking a little distrustful.

"Shore. I don' care if ya do."

"Okay, Alvin, let me tell you what I think. I think seven hundred and fifty dollars is a lot of money. Maybe that's how much it costs to rebuild a transmission. I don't know."

Alvin's scowl deepened the crevices between his eyebrows.

"If this repairman never worked on the car, like your son thinks, and charged Lorene for an expensive job, that would be a crime."

Alvin's face brightened a little.

"If it's okay with you and Lorene, I'd like our mechanic to take a look at the car. He knows a lot more about transmissions than I ever will. You have the car here now?"

"Yes, sir, we do," he said.

"Okay. You parked out back?"

"Yes, sir."

"Our garage is in back of the parking lot. Let's get your car on a lift and have the mechanic take a look."

We walked half way to the garage in silence before Alvin Bunker spoke. "They's a bunch o' Jenkinses here in Blount County, but you shore don't sound like you're from Tennessee."

"I'm from New York."

"Our church took us on a bus trip to New York City once," Lorene said.

"Big place, isn't it?" I asked.

"Lord have mercy, yes," she said. "And biz-zy!"

"You with the po-leece up there?" Alvin asked.

"For twenty years. I worked on Long Island, retired and moved down here."

"Lord have mercy. Y'all musta seen a lot."

* * * *

I stood under Lorene's '92 Ford, looking up at about sixty square feet of dirty metal undercarriage.

"A repairman charged the girl seven-hundred-and-fifty dollars to rebuild this transmission," I said. "You see any evidence that the car's been worked on?"

Earl Biggins, the Prospect city mechanic, looked up at the car. He moved a bright droplight this way and that. He turned around in a circle and tilted his head to the right and to the left. He hadn't responded to my question.

I wanted to grab him by the neck, shake him and say, "Yes or no, Earl?" But I waited. And then waited some more.

A Dodge dealer's commercial ended, and the country radio station began playing *The Devil Came Down to Georgia*.

"Sam," Earl said, "this here car's what, fourteen, fifteen years old?"

I nodded. "Yeah."

"Looky here. You drop a tranny, they's a lota handlin'."

"Uh-huh," I said.

"Ain't no way you don't git dirty. Ain't no way you don't mess up all the road dirt that's done built up over the years. My opinion, Sam, ain't no one never messed with this tranny. No sir. Leastwise not from down here."

"Is there any other way to do a rebuild?"

"Course not."

Charlie Daniels was still singing as I next spoke. "She says the car runs better now than before she took it in. What do you figure?" I asked.

"My guess is she was way low on fluid. Shoot, a woman probably don't never check. Man takes a look, tops it off, sees it takes a sizeable lot and test drives it. Car feels okay—end of story. Cost ya what, ten, twelve dollar in transmission fluid—retail?"

"So we've got a scam?" I asked.

"That's what I said, Sam."

"I want to leave the car here and get someone to take photos of the undercarriage and transmission," I said. "Then I'm going to see how many times we can catch this bugger cheating other customers. If you need to use the lift, take the car down. But I can have a county crime scene guy here in half an hour or so. Work for you?"

"Shore does. I ain't goin' nowheres."

"Thanks, buddy. I'll get back to you."

5

Wayne Zurl

I walked back into Earl's office and gave Alvin and Lorene the bad news. She'd been screwed out of seven hundred and fifty bucks.

"You gonna arrest that hairy-faced bastard, Chief?" Alvin asked.

"Not today, Alvin, but soon. Let's walk back to the PD, and I'll tell you what I'd like to do. But I need to keep your car here for an hour or so and have a police photographer take pictures of the transmission. You probably don't want to wait around, so can I get you a ride home after we're finished speaking? If you need a ride back, I can do that, too."

"I'd 'preciate the ride home, but no, sir. I kin drive Lorene back here in m' truck."

I explained to Alvin and Lorene how I wanted to set up the owner of Smoky Mountain Transmissions with a few more opportunities for scamming customers out of their money.

Alvin wanted to take the more direct approach of arresting him immediately for cheating Lorene and then circumvent the sometimes inefficient legal system by dragging him behind a police car. While Alvin's method of corporal punishment sounded innovative, he deferred to my expertise with the criminal justice system to handle the situation with a more liberal approach.

Bettye arranged to have a car take Alvin, Lorene and little Tonya home and promised to call them as soon as the police photographer finished with the Ford.

Thirty minutes later, my favorite county crime scene guy, Jackie Shuman, knocked on the office door.

"Howdy, Chief. Y'all got a job fer me?"

"Have I got a job for you? Yes, an easy one."

Compared to some of the work I've asked Jackie to do, a few simple photos could have been handled by a rookie.

"I've heard that one before." He looked skeptical.

"You won't even get dirty."

"I hope not. This uniform was clean this morning."

We walked across the parking lot to where Lorene Bunker's Taurus sat up high on the lift. Earl pointed to various spots on the transmission where accumulated dirt and gunk would be disturbed if actual work had been done.

Jackie and his trusty Nikon snapped away at the lack of anything to

6

see. I felt like Sherlock Holmes explaining the curious case of the dog barking in the night. The curious thing being the dog didn't bark at all.

After a dozen photos, we returned to my office.

On the way, Jackie said, "Kinda weird, ain't it? You wantin' shots of somethin' that ain't there."

"Welcome to the world of schemes to defraud. I should be calling on you for more before-and-after shots on other vehicles. That work for you?"

"It does. You do git inta some strange stuff, don't ya?"

"I try to make life interesting."

"This the kinda thing you did when you was a cop up in New York?"

"All the time."

"Miss it?"

"Not much."

We walked a few more yards.

"Well," he said, sounding like he wanted to make friendly conversation, "we got us another Smoky Mountain Christmas coming up."

"We do. And don't eat too much. Don't want your snazzy uniform getting tight."

"Don't I know it? Ever since Thanksgivin', I've been eatin' like a hawg. Tween cookies from my momma and mamaw, and the dinners my wife's been makin', I'm gonna weigh a ton by New Years."

"Wait till you get older. Sometimes I just have to think of food to gain weight."

He smiled and shook his head. "Well, I'll be back, but if'n y'all don't need me, I'll hit the road an' see if my real boss wants me. See ya, Sam."

"Take it easy, kid, and thanks."

* * * *

"Bettye, my love," I said, "how about using your gorgeous fingers on that magic computer and find me a name for the owner of Smoky Mountain Transmissions?"

She looked at me over the tops of narrow reading glasses. Her hazel

7

eyes caught the overhead light and sparkled.

"Gorgeous fingers?"

"Sure. I'm trying to woo you into doing a couple of favors so I don't have to use the computer myself. Pretty suave, huh?"

"Suave? Is that what you call it?"

"Well, what it actually is shouldn't be said in polite society. When you know who the owner is, run him through this and that and see what else we know about him?"

"I will. Now take yourself back into your own office while I work on this. And Sam, the word you were lookin' for is bullshit, pardon my French."

"If I had any feelings, they'd be hurt."

"Darlin', it takes more than that to hurt your feelin's."

"Why do I always get tied up with smart women?"

She wiggled her fingers to shoo me away.

While Bettye looked for a pedigree on our dishonest mechanic, I needed a plan to catch him in a sting. Nothing earth-shaking or terribly innovative, just recruit a couple of people he wouldn't recognize as local cops—people who owned cars not in need of serious transmission repair. I'd get Earl to dummy up a problem, and see if our con man charged for major repairs he never performed.

I pondered over whom to charm into being my first operative. I needed someone who looked like they weren't very savvy about cars. I made a quick phone call.

"Hello," she answered.

"Hi, sweetie. How'd you like to do me a favor and be part of an exciting police operation?"

"Sammy, I've lived with you for almost forty years—I've done lots of exciting things."

"See how lucky you are? I'm going to let you in on the ground floor of the greatest operation ever seen at Prospect PD. Something they can make a TV movie about. I'm thinking about writing the screenplay myself. When a studio buys the idea, I'll ask Cheryl Ladd to play you. Or would you rather use Lynda Carter? You in or what?"

"Perhaps, love, you should tell me what you want me to do. And am I going to get paid for this?"

"How can you put a price on a genuine po-leece adventure?" I explained the plan to my wife. "Easy, huh?"

"I could be like Charlie's fourth angel."

"You're my only angel, baby. You have anything planned tomorrow morning?"

"I'm all yours, dahling."

"Good. Plan on being here at 9:30. We'll have sex in the evidence closet like two real detectives, and then you can hit the road."

"Sam!"

"What? You don't want to hit the road?"

"I'll see you tonight." She sighed.

"See ya later, alligator."

"God, some of the things you say make you sound so old." She hung up on me.

A minute later, Bettye walked in and sat down. She no longer knocked, but just took liberties. I needed to tighten up the women in my life.

"The owner of the transmission shop is Elrod Swaggerty," she said.

"No kidding?"

"Could I make that up? Elrod has not led the life of a good citizen. He's got three arrests for auto theft, two for possession of stolen property, two possessions of marijuana and one possession of a weapon."

"And a partridge in a pear tree," I added. "How many convictions?"

"Nine arrests, five convictions and another arrest in North Carolina for reckless driving, but there's no disposition listed for that."

"Good work. We've got a skell in beautiful downtown Prospect. Someday they'll write a book about you and me—the dashing police chief and his beautiful blonde sidekick."

"Oh, stop it! Does your wife know you say things like that?"

"She knows I'm hopelessly in love with you, but since you're already married, I behave myself."

She shook her head and stood up.

"Kate has the patience of a saint."

"I'll check the *Police Chief's Manual*, but that sounded almost insubordinate."

"I've learned one thing in the last six months, Sam Jenkins."

"What?"

"You are impossible."

"Reputation is everything."

"What do you plan on doin' with Elrod?" she asked.

"Catch him in a sting."

"Pretty sophisticated for li'l ol' Prospect."

"Should be a piece of cake."

"Why is it when you say, 'Piece o' cake,' like that, I think about loadin' up the shotguns?"

Chapter Two

The next morning at 8 a.m., I left my wife and dog at home and drove to work.

In the middle of town, incongruous holiday decorations on the low, flat roof of Foothills Mortuary and Cremation Services grabbed my attention. Angled skyward, Santa Claus sat at the helm of an orange sled behind eight reindeer. Behind Santa, a white coffin with orange trim and big UT letters, waited for an interested buyer. I shook my head. You can't make things like that up.

Jackie Shuman promised to meet me at the garage by 9:30 and photograph Kate's Subaru after Earl doctored it up.

At 9:40, only ten minutes behind schedule, Kate walked through the front door and made a quick stop to say hello to Bettye before stepping into my office.

"Detective Kate Jenkins reporting for duty, sir." She gave me something a non-military person might recognize as a salute.

"I can't believe this," I said. "I left home this morning, and you were wearing an incredibly sexy night gown. I sit here and wait for an innocent-looking Mrs. America to show up, and who walks in?"

"What?" She gave me one of those looks women use when they want you to know you said something offensive.

"You look like one of the girls from *NYPD Blue*. The only thing missing is a Glock on your belt and a badge hanging around your neck on a chain."

Kate wore a short black leather jacket, a moderately tight knitted blouse showing a respectable hint of cleavage and blue jeans. She looked

11

like the stereotypical female TV detective.

"You don't like my outfit?" she asked.

"I love your outfit. Remember what I said about sex in the evidence closet? I can't wait. I just hope the shop owner doesn't make you for a cop."

She stuck her tongue out and then said, "Why honey, I'll make him think I'm jest a poor helpless woman beggin' ta be taken advantage of." She can fake a great Tennessee accent.

"That's my girl. Forget what I said. Just remember to bend forward a few times, and he'll be putty in your hands."

Obviously shocked that I'd suggest she show her cleavage to someone other than me, she said, "God, you're a Philistine."

"Yeah, you women make all those nasty remarks, but you can't live without me."

"Watch us, big boy."

"Wait here a minute while I take the car to Earl. After he's finished fooling around, we'll know what you have to say. While I'm gone, tidy up the evidence closet. I won't be long."

Thirty minutes later, a sufficient amount of transmission fluid had been siphoned out of the Subaru's casing and whatever else Earl Biggins did to make the gears slip or slide or do what they were supposed to do to give Kate a reason to be worried about her car. And Jackie had taken enough photos to substantiate the grungy undercarriage was untouched by human hands. All that accomplished, Kate started out on her first undercover operation in Prospect.

* * * *

At 11:30, she walked back into the PD looking quite pleased with herself. I stepped out of my office to find my wife and her friend, a local real estate agent, Glenda Mae Waddell, standing next to Bettye's desk.

"I wondered how you got back here," I said. "Now I see you've got a partner. Hi ya, Mae. You two look like Cagney and Lacy."

"Hello, sugar," Mae said, batting her eyelashes and giving her blonde hair a toss. "Lacy and who?"

I smiled. "Doesn't matter."

Kate told the story of how Elrod scrutinized the transmission, oo'ed and ahh'ed and um'ed, and finally diagnosed the car in dire straits.

She repeated what she heard, "'Lucky y'all got here when ya did, cuzz this'n maybe ready ta blow. Leave it here fer me ta check out, an' I'll let ya know the bad news tomorra.'"

Kate, not wanting to be caught in cahoots with the local fuzz, called Mae at Walking Horse Realty and got a ride back to the PD.

I grinned at Kate. "I love to see a rookie do good work. We'll put this guy away for life."

My watch told me it was11:45. "But it's lunch time, and I'm hungry, and I like company when I eat. Come on, ladies, I'm buying. How about Chinese? Everybody like that?"

Everyone nodded.

"Betts, call in one of those homely male cops to watch the desk. Then you three can visit the girl's room, or whatever you chicks do, while I make a few notes about the case."

"Y'all are such a sexist, Sammy," she said.

Kate and Mae laughed.

If I wanted to appear cool, I would have called a limo to pick up 'Sammy's Angels' on the street in front of the municipal building. But Wah Lum sat just a hundred yards from the office, so we walked. It was good exercise and gave me the opportunity of being seen with three of the best-looking girls in town.

* * * *

After lunch, I thanked Mae, drove Kate home and left Bettye to hold down the fort.

Less than an hour later, I sat at my desk organizing a case file destined to turn Elrod Swaggerty into cat food. Everything seemed to be progressing nicely. I had two cases of smooth-talking Elrod scamming women for unnecessary repairs.

With that under my belt, I needed to think like a defense attorney. I'd protect my client by saying those were only two isolated cases—nothing more than errors in judgment on Elrod's part.

I'd say, "Surely, ladies and gentlemen of the jury, there is no evidence showing my client intended to cheat those women."

I saw some logic in that. I also thought it sounded like a bucket of manure, but it was a good argument, and juries can often be susceptible to an eloquent line of trash.

I needed to establish an undeniable pattern of criminal activity, enough documented cases of swindling distressed car owners so a jury would side with the *cheatees* rather than the *cheator*.

To do that, I needed a few more likely marks. But therein lay my dilemma. With only twelve cops and me in a town where we are all seen quite often, potential undercover agents were scarce. I could ask the county sheriff for logistical support, but that assistance might cause loss of operational control. The case began as a Prospect problem, and I wanted to keep it in-house. So, I looked into my bag of acquaintances.

I dialed a Knoxville number I remembered without looking at my Rolodex. Some critics might ask why I knew it so well.

The phone rang four times, and then a recording played. "Hello, this is Rachel. I'm not at my desk right now, but please leave your name and number, and I'll get back to you. Your call is very important to me. Thank you." The overly dramatic theme music from her 6 p.m. news show played in the background.

"Hello, TV star. This is your biggest fan from Prospect PD. Give me a call, and I'll wish you a happy Christmas and tell you how I can help send your ratings off the Nielsen charts. Thanks a bunch. Talk to you later."

I almost hung up when I heard her voice.

"Sam? Hello? Sam? Are you there?"

"Yes, ma'am, I'm here—your humble and obedient servant."

"Humble, never. Obedient, I doubt it." She gave a short sexy laugh.

"You sure know how to hurt a guy's feelings. How are you doing? You ready for a big Christmas?"

"Not a big day, just family. You know how it is with two teenage boys."

"Actually, I don't. But I do have a teenage dog. She likes to open edible presents."

"Very funny. Hey, I'm so glad you called. I had hoped to hear from you. Can we have lunch sometime before Christmas? I'd like to hear you talk like Humphrey Bogart again."

She chuckled. I wished she wouldn't do that. I'm susceptible to

14

women with great laughs.

"You sure know how to make a guy feel special, doll-face" Bogey said. "But I've been waiting for the phone to ring. I would have gone home crying if you didn't call before Christmas. So, I decided to call you. Strictly on business."

"You are such a liar!" She has a beautiful voice, with a hint of a Pennsylvania accent.

"You have a polygraph in your purse?" I asked. "Policemen never lie."

"Okay, Mr. Policeman, I am happy you called. And we can talk about lunch after we finish our business. What kind of deal have you got for me today?"

"Okay, sister, lunch is on me." I sounded more like Bogey than he ever did. "We'll pick a day when the criminals are sleeping. I'm a real sap for a dame who's a hot number, a dame like you, doll-face. I'll be there with bells on."

"Just bells?" She giggled.

We could have gone on like that for a long time, but I needed to get on with my police work.

"Don't be silly. Okay, here's the deal… Before you got to be the sweetheart of Knoxville weren't you an investigative reporter at another station?"

"How did you know that, Sam Spade?"

"I'm a hard-boiled gumshoe, a world-class shamus. I get around this cockamamie town, and I know everything."

She spent a few more moments laughing. "Oh, really?"

I switched back to my normal voice. "Actually, I Googled you."

"Oooo, that sounds sort of kinky."

"Stop that. Don't let this conversation go astray."

"A girl can daydream, can't she?"

"I know I'm irresistible, but let's stick to business."

"Okay, if we must." She giggled again.

"Right. Why did I call you?"

"Something about investigative reporting and big ratings?"

"Sure," I said. "I remember now. Why do I always need a cold shower after we speak?"

"Steady, big feller."

"Easy for you to say, lady. Okay, I'm back on track and can behave like a professional."

She laughed again. I think she knows it only encourages me.

I explained Elrod's scam and my plan to stop him.

"That sounds promising," she said. "What do you have in mind for me?"

"What I need, partner, is a couple of non-cops who aren't recognizable like you and won't mind dealing with this creep."

"Are you sure your creep is being dishonest?"

"Do you think you're dealing with an amateur?"

"I didn't say that."

"Of course you didn't, but have faith. I want two or three more people cheated, so he can't claim he just made a mistake with his diagnoses. You provide the drivers and the cars, and I'll have my mechanic and photographer take care of the rest. When we finish all these stings, I'll apply for an arrest warrant, we'll lock him up, and you can get it all on film."

"Can I interview him?"

"It would be best not to do that when we pop him. But no doubt, he'll make bail after arraignment. You can follow him to his shop, then walk up and surprise him, just like on 60 Minutes."

"We're better than 60 Minutes." The sexy sound came back into her voice.

"You're sure as hell a lot better looking than Mike Wallace."

"Thanks…I think."

"This thing work for you?

I'd plotz if she said no.

"You're not just kept in the loop, you're part of the loop. An exclusive story. What do you say?"

She paused. "Sounds good to me, but I'll have to run it by the station manager first. You sure this is going to work?"

"Have I ever lied to you?"

"I don't know. Have you?"

"Ug! The second time I'm wounded in one conversation."

"Oh, stop. I'll do what I must on this end, but I have one problem."

"Oh, please, don't rain on my parade."

"No rain, just a short delay. The manager is off today."

"Civilians."

"Hey, I'm a civilian."

"But you're a reporter. At least you have a sense of urgency."

"I'll come in early tomorrow and have an answer for you. I promise."

"Thank you, ma'am. I'll wait with bated breath. And plan on a nice lunch."

"Thanks, Sam. I'll call you."

"Okay, lady, I'll talk to you soon."

I had a good feeling about the investigation. It would be like shooting fat fish in a small barrel. I slipped out of my holiday boredom and began having fun. What could go wrong?

Chapter Three

At nine o'clock, Wednesday morning, December 20th, I walked into our outer office. Bettye sat at her desk reading a field report through her little granny glasses. If I wore a hat, I would have tossed it onto an arm of the clothes tree standing behind her desk—as Sean Connery did when he played James Bond.

Then I'd say, "Good morning Mish Moneypenny. You're looking espechially lovely thish morning." Nevertheless, I had no Trilby, so I settled for, "Mornin', Betts. How's things?"

"Hi, darlin'. All's quiet," she reported.

We spent a reasonable time discussing our respective holiday plans. Having three children, Bettye said more than me.

Even the PD lobby sported a few Christmas decorations. An artificial wreath hung on the wall over the three guest chairs. Garlands of greenery framed the glass room divider behind Bettye's desk, and three-foot illuminated candles stood on either side of our double doors. Sergeant Lambert refused to let me hang mistletoe in my office doorway.

Just before ten o'clock Rachel Williamson called. We spent a few minutes engaged in chitchat and then got down to business. Everything on their end was a go, and I could coordinate with two of their assistant producers and orchestrate their visits to Elrod. All this would start on Thursday and be filmed from afar by a clandestine cameraman hiding in an advantageous spot.

At 3 p.m., Katherine called saying Elrod finished work on the Subaru. Luckily, he kept the cost of re-building the transmission to only $975.00. I assumed his sliding scale of rates varied with the value of the customer's wardrobe.

I grabbed one of my city credit cards, issued in an assumed name for such occasions, and drove home to pick her up.

Kate was ready to go when I got there. I put on an old Army field jacket, the new Brooklyn Dodgers ball cap Kate found on some nostalgia web site and a pair of aviator shades. Sam Jenkins, master of disguise. We used my truck and drove back to Prospect.

Earl Biggins and his assistant, Logan Mapes, laughed at the idea of paying $975.00 for the amount of work done on Kate's car. Elrod, the big sport, expended about $6.95 worth of transmission fluid to top off the reservoir. Jackie Shuman added to his collection of photos, and my wife drove home before cocktail time.

* * * *

Bitsey, my auxiliary K-9 cop, and I headed for work early the next day. It began as a morning to keep a bird watcher busy and happy. All around the house, pairs of cardinals landed and flew off bare bushes, in and out of cedar and Leyland cypress trees. The air felt crisp and cool, with a damp and frosty smell everywhere. As I turned out of the gravel driveway and onto the road, I drove along the perimeter of our property and looked to the right over a railroad-tie guardrail at the pie-shaped pond on the edge of our lot. A stately great blue heron stood in three inches of water less than a hundred feet off the road. I slowed and stopped the car. The engine hum betrayed our presence and caused the big bird to look to his right. Apparently, he perceived no more danger from us than we did from him. He returned his look toward the pond, hoping to spot breakfast swimming close to the mirror-like surface of the green water. Like the crane, herons are considered symbols of tranquility and good luck in many societies. It was a good start to the morning.

After a stop at the Post Office, Bitsey and I headed straight for Prospect. The dog was so accustomed to her days at work, I no longer put her on a leash going into or out of the municipal building. We used the prisoner's entrance rather than the rear public doors, so none of the workers would make a fuss over the cute little black dog. And I didn't want Trudy Connor, the mayor's secretary, to see Bitsey and blow the whistle to His Highness.

As soon as I opened the door, the poster girl for Mighty Dog made a beeline to her Aunt Bettye. I didn't bother to retrieve the mutt since she and Bettye would hug and kiss until they finished, no matter what I'd say.

I yelled a hello to Bettye and trudged into my office to look around. Coffee dripped through the maker, and several extra cups had been set out waiting for any of the network people who cared to participate. I didn't want to start something new for the hour before Rachel and company arrived, so I spent time reading through the new published changes to the Tennessee Code, our version of criminal law.

Fifty minutes later, I heard Bitsey's nails clicking on the tile floor. I stuck my head out the door to see The WNXX TV crew standing by while the dog did her version of a Highland fling, turning in circles at Rachel Williamson's feet.

Rachel knelt down, and Bitsey rolled over to get her tummy tickled. Obviously, that pair had become buddies, too. I smiled. Maybe I was only responding to my dog's affection to Bettye and Rachel. Maybe I was just a sucker for good-looking women.

Rachel stood up, smoothed her skirt and straightened her jacket. She wore a charcoal-green wool suit. The color looked similar to our Prospect PD uniforms. Her skirt was straight and snug, ending two inches above her knees. Beneath the open jacket, she wore a fitted pale-yellow T-shirt.

When I first met Rachel and looked for words to describe her, I thought of the expression 'a brick outhouse'. Throw in a delightful little dimple in the center of her chin, perfectly styled brown hair and you have a good description of the woman voted best-looking TV personality in Knoxville.

"Morning," I said.

"Hi." She touched my arm and kissed my cheek.

I lowered my head to accommodate her.

"How's it goin', John?" I asked cameraman, John Leckmanski.

"Doin' okay, Sam. How are you?" He extended his hand.

"Sam," Rachel said, "This is Cindy Rommel and Cathy Brewer," introducing her two companions. "They're going to be working the sting for us today."

"I love it when she uses cop talk," I said, looking at Cindy and Cathy.

Rachel smiled. John grinned and tilted his Green Bay Packers ball cap back an inch.

"Hi, ladies, you look like two tough customers. Going in wired?" I asked.

"We sure are," Cindy said. "Got hooked up before we left the station."

"I've got a video camera in my purse," Cathy, a cute blonde, said, and showed me a miniature camcorder in her handbag. A tiny lens opening barely showed on the outside.

"Ain't technology great?" I suggested.

Cindy, a short brunette in her late-twenties, had brought her not-so-cool-looking Chevy Cavalier for Earl and Logan to play around with. John grabbed a cup of coffee and took the two girls and his camera across the parking lot to meet the mechanics. He had worn something from his combat photographer's collection—blue Jeans, a gray flannel shirt and a camouflage vest with a hundred little pockets.

Rachel and I went into my office. I sat down in one of my guest chairs; she took the other and crossed her legs. Her skirt rode up, showing lots of thigh. I think the woman tries to make me crazier than I already am.

"Easy job today?" she asked.

"Yep."

"See any problems?"

"Nope."

"Is there a good place for John to park and get some footage?"

"Yep."

"Is this your Gary Cooper imitation?"

"Yep, but I can also do Jimmie Stewart and Clint Eastwood."

"I know. I've heard Clint before."

"I like your outfit. If Prospect PD ever gets an aviation division, I'll ask you to be our flight attendant."

"Oh, that was sexist. I'd want to be a detective."

"We don't have detectives."

She wrinkled her nose. "Why do I like you?"

"I'm nice and cute as hell."

"Oh, brother! But I guess this *is* like your uniform color."

"It is, and it looks good on you. I should say you make it look good, shouldn't I?"

"Thank you, sir. And you are cute, even with your gray hair." She tempered her snide remark with a big smile.

"Thanks. I'll buy a Color Comb."

"Why don't you wear a uniform more often? I've only seen you wear it once. You look handsome in uniform, all your medals and all."

"Thanks, but once is enough. I like the anonymity of plain clothes."

"I doubt you could remain anonymous in any crowd."

I tried to sound like James Mason when I said, "You flatter me, madam."

"And you love every minute of it."

"How'd you get so smart for a little girl?"

"I'm a college graduate."

I thought about the difference in our ages.

"How old did you say your father was?" I asked.

"I don't remember mentioning it, but he's sixty-eight."

"Oh, good."

"Good, he's sixty-eight?"

"I mean, is he in good health?"

Her smile turned into a genuine laugh.

"Yes, he is. Quite good, thanks for asking." She shook her head. "You're a piece of work, Jenkins."

"I do better on the witness stand."

"I'm sure you do. Mind if I make an observation?"

"Please do."

"You could be a hundred, and no girl would believe you're old."

"You sure know how to make a middle-aged guy feel good."

"You usually do a good job of making me feel good, too."

I was running out of clever things to say—and courage all at the same time. But Bettye looked into the office and provided me with a little time to think.

"Sam, Earl just called. He wants to talk to you about the car he's working on. He asked for you to go over and see him."

"Thanks, Betts."

Saved by the bell.

I needed a refresher course in keeping out of trouble.

"You want to see what's going on?" I asked Rachel.

"You bet, boss. I'm on the case."

Earl wanted to get creative. He suggested closing up the gap on a spark plug or two to cause the car to misfire and run rough. He suggested that Cindy explain the problem, making it sound like transmission troubles. Cathy, who'd be along for the ride, would claim that she experienced similar troubles once with her car...a problem solved by a transmission shop.

This all sounded fine with me, Earl being the expert on automotive subterfuge. In ten minutes, the crew was good to go.

I called Junior Huskey off the road to ride along as security in the van that John drove, the one he marked with removable magnetic signs, making it look like an electrician's vehicle.

Rachel and I sat in my unmarked Ford down the road apiece. She used my binoculars to watch the girls and Elrod transact their business.

The operation worked as slick as grease on a hot griddle. The girls drove in, explained their dilemma to Elrod who stalled and asked them to return another time to hear the bad news.

John had parked the van across the road from Elrod's den of illegalities, zoomed in with his camera and photographed what he could of the transaction.

Cindy and Cathy later played the tapes from the spy camera and the back-up audio recorder. I watched Elrod um, ooh, and aah at the car. He drove back and forth over the length of his lot several times, said maybe the bands were slipping or the converter wasn't converting or who knows what, but he wanted a few hours to run more tests and be sure. Cindy told him she'd call that afternoon. They left in Cathy's Miata. A few minutes later John drove the van back to the PD parking lot. Then we all sat around in my office.

"Ms. Williamson, I believe you called this one a piece of cake?"

"Mr. Jenkins, I believe I did."

"Good job, guys. Your little spy camera makes this one foolproof. Another like this and I'll get a warrant. Then we can all revel in Elrod's legal demise."

"Okay, Chief, when do we do it again?" Rachel asked.

"Really getting into this undercover stuff, aren't you?"

"Well, yeah."

"What do you think, guys? Is she a good street boss?"

"The best," Cathy said.

Cindy nodded enthusiastically. John, the wiry little guy, just smiled.

I looked at Rachel. "How's tomorrow? Bring a new face—just one this time. We'll have her call for a ride after Elrod does his thing."

"Friday's fine. How's ten-ish again?"

"Ten-ish would be simply smashing, my dear," James Mason said.

Rachel and I smiled at our inside joke.

I thanked the two young ladies again, gave John a light 'buddy to buddy' slap on the shoulder and resisted the temptation of planting a kiss on Rachel that would have made Clarke Gable beg for pointers.

* * * *

The final fieldwork in our sting operation started at ten-ish Friday, December 22nd. It went off as smoothly as the others did. An assistant producer named Angie Valle dropped off her car, recorded and taped her dealings at Smoky Mountain Transmissions and agreed to retrieve her 'repaired' Ford Escort early the following week. That left us with a quiet, uneventful weekend before the holiday, or so I thought.

The Elrod Swaggerty case certainly seemed like the piece of cake we'd all been calling it. A few days after Christmas, Elrod would be arrested, arraigned, released on bail and perhaps persuaded by his attorney to enter into a quick plea bargain agreement with the district attorney.

The adverse publicity stemming from Rachel's expose would no doubt put Swaggerty out of business in Prospect, but considering his propensity for the dishonest dollar and his non-existent scruples, I knew old Elrod would certainly ride again. Just where and in what capacity was a question I couldn't answer.

Elrod Swaggerty represented the sort of miscreant cops love to put away or, if nothing else, have fun giving him grief and costing him money.

But we'd come to the holiday weekend, and Elrod would have to wait. Thinking back, that Saturday could have gotten me into more trouble than any criminal case I've ever investigated.

Chapter Four

After years of retirement, my body knew no weekends. On Saturday morning, I woke at six as I always do. Bitsey remained asleep on her plaid doggie mattress about ten feet from the bed where Katherine and I slept.

For a week, the weather had been damper than usual. That dampness coupled with the cool mornings caused my sixty-year-old skeleton to feel like I'd just gone over Niagara Falls in a fifty-five gallon-drum. From all the years spent as a cop and soldier, I'd been banged, bruised and injured so many times, a chiropractor once told me she thought my X-rays looked like I'd been thrown from the top floor of a six-story building. I stretched a little, but still felt like only a full body rub with Bio-Freeze would make me feel any better.

I rolled over on my left side and put my arm over Kate. She felt a lot warmer than I did. I put my hand under the nightgown that had ridden up over her hips and rubbed her tummy. She made some sound half way between a moan and an exclamation of pleasure. Being the randy bugger I am, I let my hands wander. The murmurs she made in response didn't sound like objections.

At 7:30, Katherine agreed to get out of bed. Bitsey still lay snoring on her cushion under an old Scottish wool car rug.

We made the bed, assumed the dog might eventually wake up and wandered into the bathroom. Kate brushed her hair and would go downstairs and get ready for breakfast, while I'd go through the morning ritual of shaving and so forth. I looked in the mirror, blinked and hoped I didn't really appear that bad. How could a guy who grew up looking pretty good wake up looking so bad?

"Hey, Katzy, do I look this terrible every morning?" I asked.

"You don't look terrible, sweetie. You're just a little rumpled," she replied.

"Rumpled? I look like I'm half man and half Shar-pei. I've got bags under my eyes, puffy cheeks and…is my hairline receding?"

"Your hair looks just fine, Sammy. You just need to comb it."

"You gonna love me when I'm old and ugly?"

"You'll never be ugly, Sam-a-la, and of course I'll always love you. What do you want for breakfast, hot or cold cereal?"

I assumed she meant that to be reassuring. Anyway, it made me feel a little better. "Hot," I said.

"Okay, see you downstairs."

By eight, I'd completed everything necessary to make me presentable to the rest of the free world. I woke my pampered dog and carried her downstairs because her fourteen-year-old legs didn't function perfectly until she became fully awake. Once in the kitchen, I spotted the local news on a little television hanging beneath the cabinets.

Kate stood at the range cooking a pot full of steel cut oats. I cut a couple of slices of raisin-walnut bread.

"Kate, m' love," I said. "As the Presbyterians I knew as a wee lad used ta say, 'We've been put on earth ta suffer.' M' left leg feels so bad I must be a born-again Presbyterian this mornin'."

"Your Scottish accent is good enough to fool the mayor of Pitlochary," she said.

"Thanks, sweetie. Tell my talent agent."

"Are you going to do anything about that leg? Can't you go to the doctor or the VA or someone?"

"It's been almost forty years now. The pain comes and goes. What can anyone do? It makes for good war stories, and pretty girls like you feel sorry for a genuine war hero."

She came close and touched my cheek. "Oh, my poor hero. On these damp, cold mornings you walk around looking like Walter Brennan."

No doubt that too was meant to be reassuring.

While we ate our Scottish porridge, Kate said she intended to use the day to prepare her program for the Friends of the Tennessee Libraries board meeting she'd be attending after the first of the year, a job that would take her most of the day.

I intended to drive to Knoxville and pick up a package of Lebanese zatar spices, a few cans of fava beans to make ful mudammas and a gallon of good Turkish olive oil from a Middle Eastern grocery store. Afterwards, I'd check out a couple of used bookshops and finally, buy new wiper blades for the Healey.

The relatively warm temperature dictated my uniform of the day: a pair of freshly washed and pressed blue jeans, a checked flannel shirt and a polar fleece vest. I slid a Smith and Wesson Chief's Special into its hi-ride holster and attached that to my belt, sitting just over my right hip pocket. No one would ever see the bulge.

Ready to travel, I kissed Kate and Bitsey good-bye and fired up the Austin-Healey. After thirty minutes, I left US-129 at the Kingston Pike exit, turned left and headed toward central Knoxville.

The stately brick homes on that stretch of Kingston Pike were all professionally landscaped. Mother Nature and her unseasonably moderate weather had fooled the pampered vegetation that year. The normally dormant plants bloomed like it was late March or April. Rows of forsythia made bright yellow barriers between yards and the street. Quince bushes bloomed in full flower. Deciduous magnolia trees showed off their white and pink blooms. Crocuses poked through beds of mulch looking fresh and colorful, while daffodils and jonquils stood at attention, six to eight inches tall, some also in bloom.

I ran all my errands, found a couple of used books at bargain prices and at noon, decided to treat myself to a sandwich. Heading back east on Kingston Pike, I turned into the Western Plaza and pulled the Healey a dozen spaces away from any other vehicles in one of the rows near the Fresh Market, one of a small chain of upscale grocery stores.

After strolling through the double automatic doors, I saw no appreciable lines of customers at the cash registers, so I hurried along to the deli island, grabbed a Greek salad wrap-sandwich, spooned a couple dozen Kalamata olives into a plastic dish and made a quick march back toward the front. Finding them out of Dr. Brown's cream soda, I opted for a container of Green Mountain dark roast coffee next door at Ben & Jerry's. I paid for my goodies, left the market and turned right to fetch the coffee.

Finished with Ben & Jerry's, I walked toward my car under the covered sidewalk. Just after passing a display of apples, pears and assorted citrus outside the Fresh Market, I started counting my handful of change. Not looking where I was going, I almost bumped into an attractive woman wearing a pair of bootleg jeans and a double-breasted red jacket over a navy blue turtleneck.

"Sam! Hi!" Rachel Williamson said. She looked as surprised as I felt when we didn't collide.

"Rachel, hey. I'm sorry. I wasn't paying attention."

"That's okay. No harm done." She smiled, standing there holding two bags of groceries.

"What are you doing here today?" I asked foolishly. "Silly question—you live here. I guess you're getting in touch with your domestic side?" I pointed to her groceries.

"Sure. My domestic side is assisted by Mrs. Stouffer."

"Let me help you with your bags. Where's your car?"

She led me to a gold SUV parked four spaces away from the Healey and opened the hatchback. I deposited her bags and covered them with a cargo net. We looked at each other for a long moment.

"You're here alone today?" she asked.

"Yeah, ah…I wanted to run some errands. How about you?"

"I am, too. Boyd took the boys to the ice rink."

Jerk, I thought, taking your sons skating is a nice fatherly thing to do, but if she were my wife, I'd get her on skates and do some serious ice dancing. We'd look great doing a one-armed Detroiter.

"Is that your sports car?" She pointed at the Healey.

"Huh? Oh, yeah, that's mine."

"Well, can I see it? Or is it a 'her' like a boat?"

"It's an 'it,' like a car. Sure you can see it."

We walked over. I still held the coffee and my lunch in a bag.

"Is this a Jaguar?"

"Right country, wrong factory. It's an Austin-Healey."

"Oh sure, you told me that once," she said. "I thought Austin-Healeys were small and funny-looking. This is really cool. Very sexy."

"They used to make something called a bug-eyed Sprite," I said.

"They were small and sort of funny-looking. This is their big car."

"Remember telling me you'd take me for a ride?"

"I remember that."

"Well, since we're on our own today, how about it?"

"Won't be as much fun as driving through the mountains, but we can try to tear up some blacktop."

"Sounds exciting," she said. "Hey, since we're going for a ride, how about that holiday lunch today?" Then, looking at the coffee cup in my hand, she added, "Oh, you already have coffee. Is that your lunch?"

I shook my head and opened the trunk of the Healey to drop the sandwich and olives inside.

"No. Just something I picked up. I'd rather have lunch—now that I have someone to eat with. Hang on a minute." I stepped over to a trash basket at the end of the aisle and tossed in my coffee cup.

"That's a pretty small trunk," she said.

I slammed the boot cover and switched into my Scottish accent. "Aye, lass, the car makes me look cool, but it's no very practical." I opened the passenger door for her. "Hop in, and watch me do my impression o' Jackie Stewart."

She sat down and swung her legs in.

"I don't know who Jackie Stewart is, but you make me want to read Brigadoon."

I walked around to the left side, dropped into my seat and tapped the gearshift lever into neutral. When I turned the key and pressed the starter, the big Phase Two engine growled to life.

"It sure sounds fast," she said.

I didn't want to ruin my image by saying her soccer mom Lexus could mop me up in a quarter mile—better to perpetuate my newly acquired mystique.

"Are you ready, girl?"

She nodded and gave me a smile that could have melted a glacier.

Then my evil Scottish twin said, "Aye, off we go then."

After pulling out of the parking lot, I rolled up to the traffic light at Kingston Pike and waited. From inside my head, a little voice begged my attention. Tap, tap, tap. I blinked.

"Hey, asshole," it said, "Are you nuts or what? You're taking this girl for a ride and then lunch. What's next, dip-shit? Remember, you're both married, and the last time I looked, not to each other."

He made a valid point. After this, would I feel like a philandering turd? Kind of late to say no. We're just going for a ride and then to lunch...in a public place. Next time I'll think before I speak.

"You still with me, Sam?" Rachel asked.

"Yeah, sorry. Just thinking about where to drive."

Snappy answer, Jenkins. But she looked happy with it.

I turned right onto Kingston Pike then, at the next light, swung into the turning lane and made a left onto Lyon's View. We ascended a small hill and found ourselves flanked by large and expensive Tudor-style homes. Actually, they were bona-fide mansions. Each sat on large landscaped lots, fronting on a portion of the Tennessee River called Fort Loudoun Lake. It's not really a lake, but rather a wide swell in the river that gave beautiful views toward sections of the UT campus on the opposite shore.

We passed the Cherokee Country Club on the left, a low sprawling series of attached whitewashed stucco buildings of an old English, half-timbered style, complete with real slate roofs. The golf course sat on our right, the Zoysia fairways now the color of dry wheat. The golden fields contrasted sharply with the cloudless, royal blue sky. We soon passed a huge red-roofed Spanish hacienda rivaling the Hearst mansion at San Simeon.

Then I found myself on the bumper of an old car going twenty-five miles an hour. You can't show off a sports car behind one of the driving dead, so I switched down to second gear, twitched the wheel to the left and started to pass the old-timer. The twin Abarth exhausts growled as I accelerated in the left lane. Some girls might have frowned at my antics or gotten scared. Rachel looked at me and smiled bigger than before. I thought she was having fun.

From a driveway on my left, a woman in a white Cadillac Deville turned onto the road and drove straight at us. I nailed the gas and made a hard right in front of the old man and his decrepit car. Quickly, I turned the wheel back to the left to straighten out. That maneuver tossed Rachel to her left. She let out a little squeak and wrapped her hand around my bicep. The little boy showing off for his new girlfriend flexed his muscle.

31

Finally, back zigzagging over the winding country road with everything safe again, Rachel squeezed my arm a second time.

"You're much bigger than I thought," she said.

Evil woman. I needed a cavalry saber to cut the sexual tension.

"My mother used fertilizer when I was young," I said.

She laughed. "How do you keep coming up with these things? I can't count the times you've made me laugh."

I'll bet I could.

"Humor started coming to me naturally. Right after the lobotomy, that is."

Another laugh. "You are such a liar."

Yeah, I haven't even started.

The road began veering away from the lakeshore. The Tennessee Veteran's Cemetery sat on a gentle slope to our right. Row upon row of identical tombstones stood on a manicured lawn that even in January showed a vivid green. I couldn't begin to count the graves in that necropolis of ex-military men and women of all ranks, lying together—some heroes, some cowards and some who 'also served'. I always get a little melancholy around military graveyards.

At the bottom of a hill, I turned right onto Northshore Drive, heading back toward Kingston Pike. We passed a beautiful old Episcopal church on the right.

"Would you like some really good Italian food?" I asked.

"I thought you'd never ask."

"You know where I'm going?"

"I think so."

"Pizza Hut, right?"

"I doubt it!"

Aha! She wasn't a cheap date.

Once again, I heard a tapping inside my head.

"Hey moron," my little voice said, "you just said *date*. What's with you? You're sixty years old, and you said *date*. Wake up, Jenkins! Reality check! Hello!"

We stopped at the light on Kingston Pike, turned left when it changed and began ascending Bearden Hill. With the car still in second gear, the exhaust pipes roared like a male tiger in heat.

"This thing sounds pretty sexy, mister," Rachel said.

I hesitated before responding. "I have nothing clever to say that won't get me into a lot of trouble."

Her smile accentuated the dimple in her chin. Her dark eyes took on an almond shape.

After shifting up to third gear, the tiger calmed down a little. The driver had gotten hot under the collar, but at least the tiger started to behave himself.

Near the top of the hill, I turned into a driveway leading further up to *Bravo*, an outstanding 'Cucina Italiana'. Not exactly a term you hear often in East Tennessee. It means that ain't a pizza joint.

I opened the passenger door and helped Rachel out of the low-to-the-ground roadster. She kept her large sunglasses on when we entered the restaurant. Maybe she felt a little guilty and liked being *incognito*. The Latin word sounded appropriate to use in an Italian restaurant.

Three attractive hostesses, all in their twenties, and all wearing different style black dresses, greeted us. One of the girls picked up two menus and started heading toward the main dining room, a large open space with lots of windows and lots of light. I asked if we could sit in a cozier and less trafficked area behind the hostess station. She didn't object, and I felt even more like someone cheating on his wife and trying to hide while doing so.

It seemed like Rachel was used to business lunches with guys who didn't consider her a date. She took off her coat and hung it on the back of her chair before I could help. She also pulled her chair out and seated herself. Katherine would have waited for me. But maybe I just encountered a generational thing.

"This is a nice spot," Rachel said. She took off the shades and put them into her purse.

Our server, a pretty blonde in her early twenties, looked like a UT graduate student with a real girl-next-door face. The five silver stud earrings running up the edge of her left ear looked out of character and surprised me. I wondered if she wore silver jewelry in her belly button but didn't ask. The waitress introduced herself as Emily and promised to take care of us.

Rachel wanted white wine, so I ordered a bottle of Torre DiLuna pinot grigio. Smooth—that came right off the top of my head. I'd been there before.

Our wine came in a silver plated ice bucket. To make Emily happy, I sipped the sample of wine she poured for me.

"Wow, it's not vinegar," I said.

Emily giggled. Rachel rolled her eyes. With a smile designed to boost her tip, our server poured a full glass for Rachel and then one for me.

After Emily retreated toward the kitchen, I sat back and listened to Jackie Stewart go into action. "Cheers, lass. Here's to pretty girls and auld sports cars."

"Thank you, sir. That was a nice ride, but I'd still like to do it in the mountains."

Did she hear what she just said?

"Sounds like another reason for lunch—a picnic maybe?"

Apparently, I'd become unable to control my mouth. Perhaps there's an over-the-counter medication to control that problem.

Rachel nodded and smiled and took a tiny sip of her wine. I swallowed almost half of mine.

She looked at her menu for all of sixty seconds, closed it and pushed it to the edge of the table. I took much longer. I'm usually hungry at lunchtime, and it's difficult for me make a decision when everything sounds good.

"Sam," she said, as I glossed over the Sicilian selections and moved toward Tuscany. "I know you were a detective in New York for twenty years."

I nodded and looked at her over the tops of my glasses. "Uh-huh. Detective lieutenant, actually."

"Of course." She smiled at my vanity and continued. "And you were a soldier for a long time, and you taught criminal law at a community college. But I really don't know much about your non-professional life. How about it, mister? Talk, or I'll have to get out my rubber hose."

"How do you know all this?" I asked.

"I Googled you."

"Oh God, I feel violated."

"Don't be stupid. I also learned a lot from the press release your mayor put out when he hired you."

"Oh, well. I didn't think you'd find anything on Samuel Jenkins-dot-com except my exploits in front of a web cam."

"I'll check that one, too, but before I pant and drool all over my computer, tell me something about you. What do you like to do? Do you have hobbies? Do you play golf?"

I usually hate to talk about myself, and that imaginary bell saved me again. Emily stopped by to take our orders. Rachel wanted the insalata mista, which I learned was mixed greens, tomatoes and gorgonzola in balsamic vinaigrette. Chick food. I chose something more substantial, something called Pasta Woozie—described as wood-grilled chicken, sautéed spinach and sun dried tomatoes over penne in a slightly spicy Alfredo sauce. 'Fantastico!' Or so the menu said.

I finished my glass of wine. Rachel still had eighty percent of hers left. I poured myself another and offered to top hers off. She declined, but reminded me of her question.

"Ah, me…yes. I haven't played golf since '71 when I left Korea. I read a lot—some fiction—historical novels, a few hard-boiled private eyes and cops, lots of history books, colonial America—pre-Revolution mostly." I paused and took another gulp of vino. No sense overwhelming the girl.

"That's it?' She sounded disappointed.

"No, not exactly."

I drank more wine. In the background, Dean Martin sang *An Evening in Roma.* It sounded dreadfully appropriate.

"When I retired, I learned how to make old-fashioned guns. I use all hand tools as they did in the 18th century. It takes a lot of time. Making them teaches me patience."

"Do you use these guns as a policeman?"

"No, they're things people used 250 years ago, big flintlock long rifles—Daniel Boone stuff. Sometimes I carve the stocks and engrave the brass. It's a creative outlet."

"Do you make them from scratch?"

"Wood and metal, mostly."

She laughed and shook her head. "I should have known that was coming."

"You're gettin' there," I said.

"Can I see one?"

"Yeah, but I'd feel a little funny walking into your station with a five-foot longrifle at right-shoulder-arms. But I've been thinking about hanging one on my office wall—to give the place a touch of historic class. As soon as I do, come and see it."

"I will. Now what else do you do?"

"You're relentless."

"I have a nose for news." She wrinkled her nose to emphasize the point.

"As a young cop, I used to shoot in competition, combat pistol matches. And you've seen my old sports car. It takes a lot of time and effort to keep it looking spiffy."

"It sure is…spiffy." She laughed at my choice of words. "Tell me about shooting. Were you good? Not long ago you had to shoot someone. I remember that, and I hope you don't mind if I bring it up. You must be pretty good to do what you had to do."

An easy incident to remember, but I would rather not and brushed it aside, determined not to let it ruin our lunch.

"Since you're asking in such a forceful way, Mizz TV reporter, I guess this is no time for modesty, is it?"

"It's not. Go ahead, I'm all ears."

"Okay, unless you're on intimate terms with a genuine gunslinger, you've probably never met a better shot than me," I said.

"Wow, I guess that tells me. That good, huh?"

"Pretty damn good as a kid. Not bad at all as an old man."

"I'm impressed."

"I'm glad."

She smiled and took an imperceptible sip of wine. "Now, keep going. Tell me what else you do."

I sought reinforcement from Senor Torre Di Luna.

"Back on Long Island I owned an old-fashioned sailboat, something called a Cape Dory sloop. We took it out on Peconic Bay a lot."

"I love sailing. It's so romantic."

Why did she have to say that?

"Yeah, it can be. Have you been on a sail boat often?"

36

"Only once. On vacation with my parents. I was young then."

We spent almost two hours talking. I told her more about me—about Long Island, about my first car, a '58 Volkswagen, about Jones Beach and surfing, a little about the Army and a little about my former PD.

She told me about Pennsylvania, about county fairs, the 4-H Club, the Girl Scouts and high school. The bottle of wine sat empty, and she hadn't finished her first glass.

"Sam, I have two more questions for you. You ready?"

"This sounds serious. Should I excuse myself and disappear out the men's room window?"

"If you do, I'll hunt you down and…beat you up," she said.

"I believe you. Ask your questions."

"I'm having a great time today and can't remember when someone's made me feel this good."

Uh-oh!

"But I have to be honest. I feel guilty—like I'm cheating on Boyd."

Trust a woman to bring up that kind of thing.

"I guess if I thought about it more, I'd feel awful." She hesitated, looked at the table and spun her wine glass in little circles. "How do you feel about what we're doing?"

"You're not alone, kiddo. I started feeling guilty the other day, flirting with you on the telephone. When you asked to go for a ride and go to lunch today—I knew better, but couldn't say no. Are you going to tell your husband we had lunch today?"

"Oh God, I don't know. Are you going to tell Katherine?"

"I asked you first."

She frowned. I gave in.

"Just kidding," I said. "I guess I should tell her, but how do I tell a complete story, answer questions and not make her feel badly? Ostensibly, we're just having lunch. But it's not hard for someone to read into this."

She looked at me again and started to laugh.

"We're in the middle of a serious conversation, and you make me laugh again."

I must have looked puzzled.

She continued, "Ostensibly? No one says ostensibly."

"What? That's an acceptable word. Probably in the Scrabble Dictionary."

"I know it is. You just don't hear it used in many conversations, that's all."

"You're the one with the degree in journalism. I finished college on the GI Bill. You're the one who should be using all these erudite words."

"You know what I got my degrees in?"

"I'm a cop. I know everything."

"Ha!"

"What?"

She didn't answer, but lost her smile again.

"Sam, from the very beginning, don't you think we've been more than just professional associates?"

I lowered my eyes and let out a puff of air. "Yes, ma'am, I confess. You're the only reporter I've ever clicked with. And you are more than just a professional associate. From that first time we met, something happened—call it an involuntary action. To say I'm attracted to you because you're beautiful would be unnecessary. So is everyone who turns on the television. But there's more. You're smart, charming and professional. You smile at all the right times, and when you laugh, I... Well, what all-American boy could resist? But on top of all that, you don't let getting a story interfere with doing the right thing."

She closed her eyes for a second and looked pleased with my compliment.

"Hey," I said, "you're the only girl I'd ever leave home for. If things were different and you didn't mind hanging out with an old guy—who knows? But things are different, aren't they?"

She nodded slightly and again looked at her wine glass. I wish I knew a graceful way to tell a woman what needed to be said.

"No matter what, we're friends, right?"

I tried to catch her eye, but she began twirling her glass again. Then she looked back at me with an almost nervous smile. Then she shook her head and said, "Oh, Jenkins, I hate you!"

"No, you don't. I'm irresistible to women. And I'm modest, too. What's your second question?"

That got the desired effect. Her smile came back.

38

"How the hell can you eat so much and not get fat?"

I never answered her question. Emily walked by and gave me a look that said, 'What's an old guy like you doing with a TV star?' *That* would influence her tip. And then Jimmy Roselli began singing *Inamorata*. The beautiful song interrupted our conversation. Rachel looked like a schoolgirl at the Friday night dance. She smiled at me. I returned the smile and should have ordered another bottle of wine.

* * * *

A half hour later, we pulled back into the parking lot at Western Plaza. I chose a spot next to her Lexus. Rachel rummaged around in her oversized purse, pulled out a ring with enough keys to open all the cells at Rikers Island and pressed her thumb on the black remote entry device. The lights blinked, the locks opened.

"Thank you, Sam. Today was really special. I loved everything."

"You're welcome. And I enjoyed myself, too. It's nice having a buddy as pretty as you."

She closed her eyes tightly for a little too long, opened them and looked up at me. Then she went up on her toes, kissed my cheek and punched me on the shoulder.

"You rat! You miserable rat! I'll call you next week. Oh, God, I hate you!" She opened the car door, jumped in and drove away.

One of the nicest things a girl can say to a guy. If that was a movie and we weren't two married people, I would have planted a passionate lip-lock on her. But we weren't in a film, and as my little voice said, I needed a reality check.

Chapter Five

Thanks to the modern marvel of the compact disc and Netflix, Kate and I sat on our love seat and watched an episode from the first season of *NYPD Blue*. Detective Andy Sipowitz just finished calling one of his witnesses a moron when our phone rang.

"Stanley," I said, "is there a good reason you're calling me at 8:45 on the night before Christmas Eve?"

"Depends on your definition of good. Billy Puckett just grabbed a guy about to torch your boy Swaggerty's transmission shop." y

Twenty minutes later, I walked through the doorway to the squad room and looked at our would-be arsonist.

"For chrissake, Alvin, what in hell were you going to do?" I asked.

Alvin Bunker sat in an armless chair, his right wrist shackled to a three-inch steel ring attached to a battered metal desk. He raised his head and looked at me.

"Ya shouldn't oughta be takin' the Lord's name in vain, sir. I'll answer yer questions, but swearin' ain't good fer ya soul."

I closed my eyes and shook my head.

"Oh balls, Alvin! Screw my soul. What in hell were you thinking?"

"Uh, boss?" Stanley interrupted. "Maybe Billy should tell you exactly what he saw and what happened."

"By all means," I said.

Officer Billy Puckett was in his late-twenties. Next to Stanley, he looked short and stocky. Billy joined Prospect PD in 2004 after his discharge from the Marine Corps and a tour in Afghanistan. During the summer when he wore short-sleeved shirts, I noticed two USMC tattoos

40

on his forearms: An eagle, anchor, and globe on one and the famous bulldog wearing an outdated steel pot on the other.

"Boss," Billy said, "I seen this Dodge pickup sittin' on the street next ta that tranny shop y'all are lookin' at while I was headin' fer this first aid case futher up the road. That was about ten ta eight or so. Seen two people sittin' there not doin' nuthin'."k for first aid case.

Billy Puckett unscrewed the cap on a sixteen-ounce bottle of Dr. Pepper, took a long drink and recapped the bottle. I waited.

"Well," he continued, "after the ambalance took my victim ta BMH, I passed by the tranny shop again and seen the same truck. So, I did a flip and pulled up behind them figgerin' I'd check'em out. Soon as I put on my blue lights, this ol' boy bails outta the passenger side and beats feet on me."

When Billy finished his statement, Alvin Bunker hung his head and began picking at a hangnail with his free hand.

"So," Billy said, "I cuffed this gennelman," he pointed to Alvin, "ta the steerin' wheel, took the keys for the truck, and started runnin' after the other guy."

Billy did the Dr. Pepper routine again before continuing.

"He had too much head start on me. Lost him."

Stanley said, "Jamey Hawkins and I cruised the area looking for the runner. No luck."

I nodded at Stan and then looked at Puckett.

"What makes you think they were going to set fire to the building?"

"Three five-gallon cans of gas in the bed of his pickup."

"Alvin," I said, "I shouldn't ask—I know the answer. But what in hell were you thinking?"

"I figgered that man needed ta pay fer what he done ta Lorene."

"You couldn't wait for me to arrest him?"

He didn't answer.

"Who was the other person with you?"

"Nobody."

"So Officer Puckett saw a phantom run away from the truck?"

No answer.

"I saw you driving a Chevy pickup the other day. Who owns the Dodge?"

More silence. Puckett enlightened me.

"Truck's got a sign on the door. *Foothills Lawn Maintenance and Bush Hawgging.*

If it grows, we mow it and a phone number. Tag comes back ta one Leroy Bunker, Prospect address."

"Leroy's your son," I said, looking at Alvin, "the one who took auto shop in high school."

"Yessir," Alvin said.

"Where did he go?"

No answer.

"Look, Alvin," I said." Officer Puckett did you a big favor tonight. He kept you from setting fire to Elrod's fix-it shop."

Bunker's head went back down, and he checked the condition of his thumbnail.

"You know what kind of penalty an arson conviction brings?"

Bunker looked at me and shook his head.

"It's a felony, Alvin. For doing something stupid, you and your son would end up in state prison for a few years. Shit, you could still be charged with attempted arson."

"We ain't attempted nuthin'," he said.

"You're a lawyer now?" I asked.

He hung his head.

"You took fifteen gallons of gasoline and parked outside a place you wanted to damage. You did more than just think about it. It's called committing an overt act."

"The man needed to pay." His voice had a touch of defiance in it.

"The man will pay, you schmuck. Have patience. Do it your way and you end up the bad guy."

Alvin went back to hanging his head.

"What do you want to do about his son?" Stanley asked.

"You check his house?"

"Hawkins did. Locked up and dark."

"Where's Leroy?' I asked Bunker.

He set his jaw and remained silent.

"Look, Alvin, I might be able to let you slide on this, but I want Leroy. Both of you get to hear me read you the Riot Act. No Leroy and I let Officer Puckett arrest you. Understand?"

He nodded.

"Where would he go?"

"Ta see Dunkey."

"Leroy has a friend named Donkey?"

"Not Donkey, Dunkey. Name's Duncan McNeil."

"Duncan McNeil. Nice Scottish boy."

"Naw, he's from Tennessee."

I looked at Stanley. He's good with a poker face. Puckett smiled.

Fifteen minutes later, Stan and I met Jamey Hawkins outside a small frame house on Wildwood Road in an old section of Prospect. The place sat almost two miles from Smoky Mountain Transmissions where Leroy Bunker bailed out on his old man.

"You're the youngest," I said to Hawkins. "Cover the back in case Leroy is still in a running mood."

He nodded and grinned. "Gotcha covered, boss. You old timers leave everything to me."

Like Billy Puckett, Jamey Hawkins was in his late-twenties and an ex-Marine. Originally from Michigan, the tall blond kid migrated to Tennessee for a job at Prospect PD arranged by his friend, Puckett, with whom he served in Afghanistan.

We gave Jamey two minutes to get into position before I knocked on the door.

A redheaded man with a short beard answered holding a longneck bottle of Coors. I showed him my badge.

"He'p ya?" he said.

"Duncan McNeil?"

"That's me."

"We're looking for Leroy Bunker."

"He don't live here."

"I know that. We were told he came here a little while ago. His father's in trouble. We need Leroy now."

"Ain't seen him."

Stanley tapped my shoulder and pointed past McNeil. "Who just closed that door?" he asked.

"Ain't nobody here 'cept me," McNeil said.

I noticed another open bottle of Coors sitting on a coffee table in the living room.

"Really?" I said. "Pardon us." I pushed him aside.

Stanley took hold of his arm and ushered him along. McNeil didn't object. Stan is six-foot-four. Few people object to what he does.

The door Stan pointed at opened to a dark basement.

"Is there an outside door to the basement?" I asked.

McNeil shook his head. I flipped the light switch.

"Leroy Bunker?" I called out. "Prospect Police. Come on up. We need to talk."

Ten seconds and no answer.

"Don't break my balls, Leroy. Come up now, and we'll treat you like a gentleman. Ignore me again and I'll toss a tear gas canister downstairs and ruin your evening."

Five seconds later: "Okay, I'm comin' up. Don't throw no tear gas."

Stanley snickered.

Who carries tear gas?

A young version of Alvin Bunker stepped to the base of the stairs and clasped his hands on top of his head.

"Are you armed?" I asked.

"Got a pocket knife," Leroy said, looking like a prisoner of war.

"Walk up. Let's talk."

Two minutes later, McNeil and Leroy sat on a sofa in the living room. Jamey Hawkins went back on the road, and Stan and I began to question our subjects.

I handed Leroy his bottle of Coors. He looked surprised, but took a long drink.

"Stupid thing you almost did," I said.

"I guess."

"A cement block building doesn't burn very well, but you'd still get charged with arson. It carries a hefty penalty."

"Yeah?"

I nodded. "You left your father to take the heat."

"He told me to go."

"And you just abandoned him?"

He shrugged.

"And you, Mr. McNeil. For your smart-ass act of stupidity, you could be charged as an accessory."

"Me?"

A smart lawyer might controvert my claim that a material act of criminal conspiracy had been completed. But Dunkey McNeil wasn't a smart lawyer.

"The cop who's sitting with Mr. Bunker right now did you guys a big favor tonight."

They both frowned questioningly.

"I would have waited for you to pour out the fifteen gallons of gasoline and nabbed you just as you struck the first match. But he did the right thing."

"Why's that?" Leroy asked.

"Because we're after someone more important than you. You're just an impatient dumb-ass acting like a vigilante."

Leroy hung his head. McNeil continued looking at me.

"I told your father I'd take care of Lorene's problem... And I will."

Leroy rolled the beer bottle between his palms and finally looked at me.

"I don't have to arrest you tonight." I let that idea sink in. "But I can, at any time, if you act like an idiot again. I'll arrest all three of you if I have to. Clear?"

They both nodded. A hint of a smile broke on McNeil's face.

"Look up class E felony, Mr. McNeil, before you feel relieved."

The smile disappeared.

"Okay, finish your beer, Leroy, and then take your father home."

Leroy Bunker took another pull on the bottle and set it on the table in front of him.

"Yessir. Thank ya."

"Sergeant Rose will take you back to the police station."

He nodded.

"And you, Donkey, behave yourself."

"It's Dunkey."

"Whatever."

With that cleaned up, I headed back home to join my wife, dog and Andy Sipowitz. Along the way, I wondered if the Bunkers could keep it in their pants for a couple more days. An interesting choice of words since my next thought was about lunch at Bravo.

Chapter Six

At 2 p.m. on Christmas Eve, the outside thermometer showed sixty degrees—a great temperature for Labor Day, but for December 24th, too warm for my taste.

Having no ambition at all, I decided to sit around guarded by Bitsey, the fearsome attack terrier, and read one of my new used books. My choices were *Wolfe at Quebec* by Christopher Hibbert or *A Soldier of Manhattan* by Joseph A. Altscheller. I chose the non-fiction by Hibbert—it would be a start on my reality check. After only half an hour, I climbed my way up the cliffs to the Heights of Abraham with Rogers' Rangers and Frazier's Highlanders.

Around 3:30, I deemed it cocktail time and mixed myself a vodka gimlet with a dash of Rose's lime juice and a dose of Kettle One—very smooth stuff. I heard about it from a private detective from Boston I met on a case twenty years ago. He looked about ten years older than me, about my height, but had me by twenty-five or thirty pounds. Solid weight—a real moose. He wasn't a bad looking guy, but his nose had been broken, and scars marked the territory over his eyebrows—I guessed an ex-pug. He drove a ratty MG-B, didn't look like someone rolling in money, but man, did he know how to spend it in a restaurant. He seemed like a good man and ate as much as I did.

While I sipped my gimlet, Kate came down to fetch the glass of sauvignon blanc I had poured for her.

"We haven't spoken about it, but are we going out for our Christmas Eve dinner?" she asked between sips.

"It's traditional. Can't see why not."

"Good. Before we go, how'd you like an early Christmas present?"

"I'd love one. What did you get me?"

"Do you remember my little black dress? The one I wore years ago?"

"Yeah, one of my all-time favorite things."

"Well, I bought another one. Not an exact duplicate, but pretty close. And because you liked the other so much, this one is all for you."

"And you've kept it a secret?"

She smiled.

"Gonna show me before you put it on?"

"Sure, follow me upstairs."

She went into her walk-in closet, unzipped a cloth dress bag and extracted the new little black dress. Holding it up against her, she asked, "What do you think?"

"So far very nice, but I think it needs you inside."

"I can do that."

"It's almost four o'clock. Try it on, give me a minute to get excited, a few more minutes to help you take it off and then some time for me to ravage you. That leaves ten or fifteen minutes to get dressed again and head somewhere for dinner."

"Sorry, Sambo, no ravaging before dinner. Save it for later and I might be convinced to let you have your way with me."

"Who can ravage on a full stomach?"

"Leave some room!"

"If I must. Okay, where are we going?"

"I don't know. Do you have someplace in mind?"

"Anywhere you'd like, love. The meal is immaterial when I'm sitting there looking at you."

"Aren't you sweet? Okay, let's go to Bravo. I love that place."

Yikes! Taking the criminal back to the scene of the crime. I'd done it often as a cop. Sometimes the suspect cracks. It would test my mettle.

"Sounds like a great evening," I said. "Bravo, you and the little black dress."

"Don't forget the push-up bra."

"Wow. A Christmas to remember."

At 5:50, Katherine walked downstairs to meet me in the living room.

It may be the only time in recent history the woman came close to being on time, much less ten minutes early.

She made a sexy pirouette and asked, "Well, what do you think?"

"Soc mao, momma-san! You look terrific!"

The little black dress was a sleeveless affair with narrow straps, and a plunging neckline. Kate provided her own stunning cleavage—gads, I just love push-up bras. The skirt's hem ended an inch above two of the cutest knees in the free world.

"If you weren't married to such a tough-guy, I'd steal you away."

"Buy me dinner, mister, and I'm all yours," she said.

"Best offer I've had all year."

* * * *

At 6:35, we pulled into the lot at Bravo—too early to need a reservation. A group of three young women met us at the hostess station. Two of the three were the same ladies I met the day before. Just my luck the same girl who took Rachel and me to our table picked up two menus, gave me a 'look' and asked if we wanted a table in the main room or somewhere more private, pointing to the tables behind the dark wood-paneled hostess station. Someone so young shouldn't try being a smartass.

Don't play chicken with me, young lady, I thought. I've faced off against some really bad dudes and never blinked.

I smiled diplomatically. "Pick a spot, Kate. It's your evening."

And so, we walked to the main dining room.

Eating at Bravo is like visiting a restaurant made from the old ruined Temple of Bacchus. Full and partial Tuscan columns were randomly placed around the room. Huge leaded glass, bowl-like chandeliers hung from the high ceiling, but they offered only a soft romantic light.

We had a different server that night. Emily was off duty. Good, I might have had to use the same spontaneous clever jokes again.

Kate and I shared an appetizer of fresh mussels steamed in white wine and herbs. We each drank a glass of Stival pinot grigio. For a salad, I picked Insalata Della Casa. Kate chose the Caesar. Later, we ordered Mama's Lasagna Bolognese accompanied by a bottle of Nero D'Avola that cost the earth. I ate all my lasagna while Kate took half of hers home for Bitsey. Like the dog would have a chance against me tomorrow at lunchtime.

We arrived home before nine o'clock.

In the bedroom, I watched her step out from her closet, something just slightly smaller than Rhode Island. She closed the door and shut off the light.

Still in her new dress, but with bare feet, she walked toward me and somehow used her arms to create an even more incredible cleavage than I'd been staring at all night.

She asked, "So, after seeing this dress for a few hours, do you think you like it?"

"I think it creates the greatest mixed emotions of my life."

"How so?"

"Well, I can't seem to take my eyes off you with it on. But the animal lust it generates makes me want to rip it off. Tough decision for a simple guy like me."

She moved closer and pressed up against me.

Smiling, she said, "Feels like you're happy to see me, soldier. Maybe I can help you decide. I'll need help with the zipper if you can manage."

"I have an expert's badge in zippers," I said.

With my arms behind her, I maneuvered the zipper down below her waist, and she turned around. I took a step backward for a better view. First the left and then the right strap came down. Then she wiggled out of the dress, tossed it onto the bed and turned again to face me. She stood there showing me a new black bra that created so many gorgeous curves, I considered it an engineering masterpiece. The matching panties weren't half bad either. I made a mental note to buy stock in Victoria's Secret.

"Wow, you're full of surprises," I said. "Two more presents for me?"

"No one else sees them, Sammy."

"If I ever hear about Hugh Heffner doing an issue devoted to girls your age, I'm sending a picture in."

She stepped close to me again. At times like that, being farsighted has its disadvantages. Damn frustrating if you're into visual stimulation.

"You want to take one of those little blue pills?' she asked.

"Sweetie, I don't need a little blue pill as long as you've got those skimpy black undies."

Chapter Seven

On Tuesday morning, December 26th, Boxing Day in Canada and the UK, but just the day after Christmas to us Yanks, I planned to continue working on my case against Elrod Swaggerty.

As I drove east toward Prospect on US 321, the intense winter sun shone directly in my eyes. But everything turned to shade once inside the Walland Gap. Then without notice, something, obviously a bird since Pterodactyls are mighty hard to find nowadays, flew overhead and in front of the Crown Vic. A big tom turkey, just a shade smaller than the last C-119 I saw, left the trees on the north side of the road and flew in a strange head-up attitude across the four lanes and landed on the steep slope bordering the south side of the highway.

He looked awkward and troubled as he flew and landed like a paratrooper dropped into rough terrain. He stumbled, rolled and finally righted himself and shook off the leaves and debris he collected, doing his best to regain some dignity. He reminded me of someone with experience who should have known what they were doing, having a hard time of it. I wondered if what I saw held some psychological symbolism, but decided I really should knock off that self-analysis crap.

After spending almost fifteen years in East Tennessee, I knew the holiday was officially over. By afternoon, all traces of Christmas would disappear. Things were different back in the northeast where holiday decorations stayed around until Little Christmas on January 6th.

I really couldn't blame the locals. Since the first weekend in November, radio stations played Christmas music all day, every day. Even before Thanksgiving, stores and malls decorated for the holiday, and merchants made a full court press to get the residents into a buying mood. After two months of having "the season to be jolly" shoved down our throats, it seemed like a good idea to put Santa and his minions to rest for another year.

At 8:15, the thermometer outside the municipal building already read fifty degrees. The weatherman said the unseasonable temperatures would continue for several more days.

That morning I entered the building through the rear public entrance, not the private back door to the PD. I try to vary my behavior patterns in case assassins are waiting for me. In addition to those counter-terrorist measures, I wanted to see if Mr. Files and Spurgie started dismantling the decorations in the lobby and hallways.

They had already pulled the garland off the banisters and down from the walls over the doorways. And the fake Christmas presents from under the twelve-foot artificial balsam were packed away for another year. Long before noon, the tree itself would be packed and hidden in the basement.

This was the week when civil servants all over the country took the opportunity to slow down and muster up the energy to ring in the New Year.

After having coffee with Bettye and hearing about her family Christmas, I got down to business.

I took all my documentation, copies of video and audio tapes, statements, court information, prosecution worksheets and arrest and search warrant applications to Moira Menzies at the DA's office.

I found Moira at her desk with the window at her back offering a romantic view of the new jail.

Being chief assistant to the district attorney general for Blount County buys you the ability to slough off minor cases to junior prosecutors. I wondered if she would deem the Swaggerty caper worthy of her personal attention.

In her early fifties, Moira was an attractive, well-dressed blonde who was a hundred and ten percent all business. In addition to those good features, she didn't seem to like me very much. She didn't think I acted like a team player.

I once explained to her that in school I received poor marks in 'works well and plays well with others'—a futile effort. She'd never feel sorry for me even if I claimed to be a failed product of a substandard suburban school system. The truth is, I really am a team player—as long as I'm captain of the team, and I make the rules.

I sat there mentally twiddling my thumbs, while she looked over the paperwork and read the statements.

"I'll say one thing for you," she began. "You cross all your Ts and dot your Is. This is a well-prepared case."

"Yeah, not bad for my first effort," I said.

She scowled at the glib remark. I had hoped for at least a tiny smile.

"You used your wife and several TV station people to sting this guy?" Her question held a hint of exasperation. "Why the hell didn't you coordinate with county CID?

"I thought they might be too busy?"

"Yeah, right. Are these people going to be credible witnesses?"

"I don't see why not. The TV girls wore camcorders and filmed everything. A county crime scene investigator did all the before and after photography. The Prospect mechanic did all the set-ups and examined each vehicle before and after the alleged repairs, and my wife has been a great witness each time she had me convicted of something."

"You know, Sam, I wish you'd knock off the feeble attempts at humor."

"Did you know, Moira, in Scotland your family name is pronounced Mingees?" I asked.

She scowled again. "Now just what the hell does that have to do with anything?"

"Nothing, actually. I just thought a little extended family trivia would be interesting."

"You're a piece of work, Jenkins."

That time I got a decent smile. She looks so much nicer when she does.

"As much as I hate to admit it," she said, "you've got your ducks in a row, and you seem to know what you're doing."

"You flatter me, Counselor."

"Yeah, right."

We ended with that thought and adjourned to a judge's chambers where I stood in front of his desk grinning like the village idiot, acting like the shortstop on *his* team. Shortly thereafter, I left with an arrest warrant for Elrod Swaggerty and a search warrant for the entire property occupied by Smoky Mountain Transmissions.

I thanked Moira in the hallway outside chambers and dutifully pulled my forelock.

I saw Elrod's arrest and prosecution as a clear headshot. Moira would be crazy not to handle it herself. Easy points in her win column.

But I did have one concern. The itemized invoices Elrod gave each customer were a little sketchy. They stated nothing more than "rebuild transmission." Elrod's attorney might argue the term was ambiguous and need not actually mean the work is necessarily extensive, just expensive. Thankfully, Elrod, in an effort to be dishonest and look professional all at once, broke the total down into parts and labor.

With Earl Biggins' testimony, no jury with a modicum of empathy for the victims would countenance the cost he charged. After rolling the possibilities around in my mind, I thought Elrod could hire F. Lee Bailey and still be dead meat.

Later, back at the PD, I called Rachel and found her at work. She seemed to be spending a lot of time at the station lately. I asked if she wanted to film us taking Elrod from the shop in cuffs. Of course she did. She wouldn't miss it for the world. She said she and John would be in Prospect around two o'clock.

Good, I thought, I could have lunch—alone—in peace, before messing with Elrod. But before I could relax over a scrumptious repast, I wanted to tidy up a few logistical matters.

First, because Elrod's shop was in his sector and he loved the times I showed him how to be a world-class detective, I asked Bettye to call Junior Huskey and let him know he'd be making the arrest. Next, I called Sergeant Stanley Rose, my four-to-twelve shift supervisor and an ex-LAPD street crime cop. I assumed he'd like to work a two-to-ten and be there for the rip-off. And last, I told Mayor Ronnie Shields what would happen in case he received calls inquiring about the massed police presence in beautiful downtown Prospect.

After all that, I prepared for lunch.

* * * *

At ten minutes to two, Rachel and John showed up. John wore a typical "war zone" outfit, and Rachel looked like she consulted Kate on how an unofficial female detective should dress when dealing with hoodlums. She wore snug blue jeans, a black turtleneck under a Virginia Tech sweatshirt, and a dreadfully expensive-looking leather jacket.

"You two look like you're auditioning for parts in a remake of *The Year of Living Dangerously*," I said.

"Hey, be nice to me," she said. "I provided you with some key personnel for this operation." She sounded like a section commander from an associated police agency.

"Yes, you did, and I'm grateful, and I'm always nice to you. Don't I give my favorite TV newsgirl exclusive stories on all the big deals here in metro Prospect?"

"Investigative journalist and news anchorperson if you please."

After making her point, she punched me in the arm.

"Touchy, touchy," I said. "You know you're beautiful when you're faking anger."

My comment generated a big smile.

"Hey, John, does she smack you around, too?"

"No, she's afraid I'll drop the camera."

When Junior and Stan Rose came in, we discussed the game plan. Bettye called two other sector car operators and instructed them to meet us near the transmission shop at 2:30.

The sixty-degree temperatures of several days earlier had cooled slightly. The cloudless Wedgwood blue skies we'd been enjoying had turned to a muddy, hazy gray hanging over Prospect. The pollution of Knoxville and Oak Ridge had been blown southeast by the prevailing winter winds.

When we pulled up at the repair shop, it took me less than a minute to spot Elrod sitting in his office reading a magazine. Another young man worked on a pick-up truck in the garage bay, and two others sat on folding chairs nearby talking with him, drinking soda from cans. We sat twenty yards from the open garage door and heard a radio playing. Someone lamented the loss of his girlfriend and contemplated his exodus to San Antone. The song didn't sound like one of the icons of country and western to me.

Len Alcock, Bobby John Crockett and Stan Rose pulled their marked police cars curbside, blocking the driveways after Junior and I drove up to the office door. The two soda drinkers were about to run when Alcock and Crockett put the arm on them.

Stanley rousted the mechanic, a guy who looked like he ate pit bulls for breakfast, before he could hide in the supply room off the work area.

Junior followed me into the office. I walked up to a scarred and dented gray metal desk. An open bag of pork rinds lay on top, next to a two-liter bottle of Mello Yello. A half-eaten corn dog hid in a wrinkled wrapper.

"Hi there," I said. "I'll bet you're Elrod Swaggerty, aren't you?"

He was a thin, shady-looking character with short hair and sideburns ending below his earlobes. His dark blue mechanic's outfit hadn't seen soap in a long time.

Elrod eyed me for a few seconds and then shifted his look to Junior and back again to me. If he didn't assume I was a cop, he was more mentally bereft than I anticipated.

"That's me." His voice cracked a little as he tried a nervous smile.

"*The* Elrod Swaggerty?" I started to enjoy myself.

"Uh-huh. Whot's up?"

I held up a copy of the arrest warrant for him to see. "I know you were hoping Officer Huskey and I came from Publisher's Clearing House and we were about to give you a check for a million bucks, but I'm sorry to disappoint you."

I heard Junior try to stifle a laugh, which came out like a combination snicker and snort from a clogged sinus passage. I should have remembered to smack him when we finished, but didn't.

Someone in the garage turned off the radio, stopping the Nashville sound.

"Elrod, my friend, you're under arrest," I said.

"Whot fer? I didn't do nuthin'."

"You just committed a double negative in public. If you didn't do nothing, you must have done something. Might I take that as an admission of guilt?"

"Huh? Do whot?" He was almost gasping.

"Elrod, son, you have the right to remain silent. I suggest you avail

57

yourself of that right before I feel compelled to flatten your head with a brick."

"Hey now, don't go gettin' mean an' hateful on me, I really didn't do nothin'."

"Pal, you haven't seen hateful yet," I said. "We're only having a spirited conversation here. If you see me call in a helicopter or break out a field phone with little alligator clips attached to wires, you might infer I'm going to get nasty."

I heard Junior giggling behind me. I should tranquilize him the next time we go on an arrest.

"Let's go, guy. On your feet. Time to put the cuffs on," I said.

"Cuffs? Are you crazy? I said, I ain't done nothin'."

When he stood, I gave him a push and moved him up against the wall behind his desk. Just to the left hung a two-foot-tall calendar showing a girl in a bikini, holding a gallon can of anti-freeze, standing next to a shiny black Mustang with the hood raised.

"Assume position one, Elrod. Hands on the wall and walk your feet back some."

Elrod seemed familiar with the steps to that dance. I took hold of his belt and backed him up even more, and then I used my right foot to spread his legs wider.

"I'm going to search you now," I said. "Is there anything in your pockets or on your person that is a weapon or might cut me, stick me or in any other way piss me off?"

"Do whot?" he croaked again.

"Now listen carefully, Mr. Swaggerty. These are not multiple-choice questions, just a simple true or false. Do you have a weapon or something sharp on your body?"

"I got me a folder on my belt—that's it. It ain't concealed."

I removed a cheap knock-off of a Buck lock-back knife from a beaten-up leather pouch on his belt and handed it to Junior. I finished patting him down, put cuffs on him, double locked them and brought him back to the position of attention.

"Whot am I charged with? I got a right ta know!" he whined.

"Larceny by inveiglement—four times and scheme to defraud."

"Do whot?"

Obviously, vocabulary wasn't one of Elrod's favorite subjects.

When Junior and I walked our prisoner out to the car, I saw John Leckmanski filming the festivities from a discrete distance, far off Elrod's property.

I looked toward the garage area and thought Stan and the boys also hit the jackpot. Elrod's three minions were in cuffs, too. Stan found the mechanic with a shirt pocket filled by a baggie brimming over with the evil weed. The guy drinking Dr. Pepper was wanted on a Blount County traffic warrant for failure to pay fines, and the lad with the Mountain Dew was named on a bench warrant from the Rockford Justice Court for failure to appear. The two cops would transport the prisoners. Stan Rose would stay to secure the scene and inventory any cash found in the office.

The time involved in messing with Elrod's mind and processing his arrest would take us well beyond the 3:30 deadline for arraignments. Swaggerty would spend the night as a guest of Prospect PD and be transported to the county Justice Center in the morning. I timed the arrest that way for two reasons. I thought of Elrod as a first-class scumbag who needed to remember you don't screw around in Prospect. And second: I wanted to give my favorite TV newsgirl time to catch him tomorrow after he made bail and see if she could get an interview during the morning light.

When Rachel and I spoke, I suggested she attend the arraignment. She and John could watch the judge set bail, but because the county deputies and court officers may be less enamored with good-looking female reporters than I am, they wouldn't let her get close to the defendant. I thought they should wait in the Justice Center parking lot until Elrod's release and follow him back to Prospect, when he'd undoubtedly go to his shop and check on the status of the working capital he left behind. There he'd find a copy of the search warrant with an inventory of the confiscated or secured property.

I've lived to regret that suggestion ever since.

* * * *

I overestimated Elrod Swaggerty. Rather than calling the attorney he used on previous occasions and waiting for his arrival, he requested and received the services of a public defender sitting in the courtroom.

Even a legal aid lawyer didn't need to be a judicial acrobat to get a local businessman, charged with a non-violent crime, freed on reasonable bail. In fact, Elrod, with assistance from an ever-ready local bail bondsman, got sprung for five thousand cash.

Elrod's first order of business was to make a phone call. In a short time, he met with a woman, his sometime live-in girlfriend—an overweight bleached-blonde who wore enough cheap perfume to overshadow the industrial stink of Elizabeth, New Jersey.

While I stood in the courtroom speaking with the duty ADA, Rachel and John watched the duo leave via the prisoner's exit and find Blondie's car. The girlfriend drove an old black Trans-Am while Elrod rode shotgun, heading east on US 321 bound for Prospect. Several car lengths from their rear bumper Rachel and John followed. Unknown to any of them, a white Ford van followed John and Rachel, making a third vehicle in the procession heading toward the transmission shop.

Chapter Eight

The events subsequent to Elrod Swaggerty's release from custody by the Blount County Sheriff on Wednesday, December 27th unfolded very quickly.

The 'perfumed lady' drove directly to Smoky Mountain Transmissions. When she dropped off Elrod, they appeared to be deep into a serious domestic dispute. Elrod slammed the door of her Pontiac hard enough to rattle the windows. John and Rachel heard him say, "I swear I don't know why I bother, Merlene!" Then he walked to the door of the shop.

Not to be outdone, Merlene yelled, "Go fuck yerse'f, Elrod, you selfish sum-bich!" She rolled up her window and, as best she could with an out-of-tune engine in the Trans Am, laid rubber exiting the parking lot.

John followed Rachel toward the office of the repair shop, his camera already running. Rachel held a cordless microphone and prepared to speak with a less than cooperative subject. From the shop window, Elrod apparently saw them coming. Before Rachel could open the shop door, Elrod pushed his way out, slammed and locked the door and briskly strode to his old Chevy El Camino parked alongside the building wall.

"Mr. Swaggerty," she said. "You were arrested by Prospect Police for allegedly charging customers large sums of money for repairs you never completed. Would you care to comment?"

"I done tole ever' body, I ain't never done nuthin' illegal. Now y'all leave me alone!"

Elrod spoke for the record as he brushed by and locked himself in his car. A night in the slammer had done nothing to improve his grammar.

John jumped out of the way as Elrod gunned the El Camino in reverse, did a classic 'bootlegger' turn and blasted off down the street.

Rachel stood there disappointed. But perhaps in saying nothing, Elrod made a statement not to be overlooked by the jury pool who watched the six o'clock news.

Not wanting to waste his trip to the transmission shop, John Leckmanski stepped back and panned the outside of the building. Rachel waited a few yards away.

A white van bounced into the lot and pushed its way between John and Rachel. The driver, a man in his early thirties, stood a little over six feet tall with more than two hundred pounds of solid weight behind him. He took a large stainless steel, semi-automatic pistol from a shoulder holster, exited the vehicle and looked around, but pointed his gun at no one.

He circled in front of the van, took two more steps toward Rachel and said, "Miss Rachel, get in the van, I don't mean ta hurt ya."

Rachel looked at the big man with surprise. She saw the gun he held at his right side and a wave of panic spread through her. "John!" she screamed to her partner. "John, help!" Then she tried to use her microphone to hit the man confronting her.

The big man stepped closer, crowding her. As Rachel swung at him, with what looked like a practiced move, he trapped her arm under his. As she struggled, he tucked the pistol into his waistband and reached into his jacket pocket for a plastic bag, pulled out a cloth soaked with sevoflurane, and pressed it tightly against her mouth and nose.

John Leckmanski rounded the back of the van and raised his camera to hit the attacker. But before connecting, he received a single blow on the left side of his head. The strong man had allowed an unconscious Rachel to slide to the ground and wielding the heavy gun, cracked John's skin, leaving a nasty gash diagonally over his eye, through the brow and onto his cheek. The force of the blow was enough to knock him unconscious and leave Leckmanski bleeding and suffering a major concussion.

The man pushed open the side door of the van, scooped Rachel up in his right arm and easily swung her body into the empty cargo area. He bent over, picked up the drug-soaked cloth, stuffed it back into the plastic bag, sealed it and replaced it in his pocket.

It took only moments for him to drive out of the lot. The whole incident took about ninety seconds.

* * * *

We're not quite sure how long John lay there. At 10:55, Bettye dispatched Junior Huskey to investigate the report of a man lying in the parking lot of Smoky Mountain Transmissions. A few minutes later, my cell phone rang.

Junior said, "Sam, you need to get over to the tranny shop right away. Your friend, John, from the TV station, got himself assaulted. He's alive, but hurt real bad and unconscious."

"You call Rural Metro yet?"

"Yes, sir, Bettye's got the ambulance comin', but you need to get here anyways."

"Where's Rachel? She okay?"

"She ain't here, boss. The microphone thing she uses is on the ground, but I cain't find her nowheres."

"Shit!"

I told Junior I'd get there as soon as possible. After leaving the Justice Center, I had stopped at the city garage to tell Earl and Logan what their help had gotten us in court. As soon as I finished speaking with Junior, I trotted across the parking lot to the back door and entered the PD. I walked up to Bettye's desk trying to look as calm and under control as I could manage. Over the years, I'd taught myself to fake a look of cool composure for the rest of the world while near boiling on the inside.

"Bettye, from what Junior described, I can only assume Rachel was with John, and someone's abducted her."

She spun her desk chair around to look straight at me.

"I'm going to find Junior," I said. "Call the county duty officer. Ask for a crime scene unit to meet us. Ask specifically for Jackie Shuman if he's working. Then call in everybody, and call all the other surrounding departments. See who's available to meet us at the scene. I want every inch of the area combed for possible witnesses or anything else they can find. If you need help with the phone work, ask someone in the building. I'll call as soon as I get to the shop. When I give you more information, call county dispatch and have them put out an alarm on a possible kidnapping. Call Ronnie and bring him up to speed. Apologize for me not calling personally. As I get additional information I'll keep calling in so you can update everyone concerned. Keep your fingers crossed. Okay? Got all that?"

"Yes, sir, I do." She looked at me intensely and nodded. "I'll get it all done for you, Sam. Don't worry."

"Thanks, Betts. I know you will." I turned to go.

"Sam?" she said. "Be careful."

I smiled and nodded back.

When I arrived at the shop, I watched Junior helping the ambulance crew get the still unconscious John Leckmanski ready for his trip to Blount Memorial Hospital. I saw his camera on the blacktop. It looked unbroken and I hoped to find a usable tape inside. Rachel's mic lay there too, maybe fifteen feet away.

Two other Prospect sector cars were parked on the roadway, their blue lights flashing. The two cops had already begun knocking on doors in the mixed commercial and residential neighborhood, looking for potential witnesses. Junior knew nothing more than I did at the moment. We both stood there. He waited for instructions, and I felt clueless about what really happened.

"Junior, run Elrod Swaggerty through motor vehicles and get an official description and plate number for his vehicle. Put out an alarm to pick him up for questioning. He lives just outside the district in the county's area. Drive to his house and see if he's there. If he is, grab his ass, and call me. If he's MIA, go to the court and see if they have an ID on a chubby blonde woman who wore too much perfume. She picked him up after arraignment. Merlene something, I think. Then go, and see that shithead, Alfie Hornbeck at Triple-A Quick-Bail and find out what he knows about Elrod. He paid the bond. Okay? Got all that?"

"Yes sir, I'm on it," he said.

"Good boy, Junior."

As Junior Huskey left, a white and green county sheriff's car pulled up. A uniformed Lieutenant named Ollie McClurg got out of the car. I'd only met him once before, knew little about him, but was happy to get any help I could.

"Hello, Chief," he said. "Dispatcher tole me y'all might need a li'l he'p." Ollie was about five-foot-nine, in pretty good shape and looked to be in his mid-forties. His dark blue uniform was spotless and he looked generally squared away.

"Lieutenant, thanks for driving out here." He shook my extended hand. "So far I've got one TV cameraman knocked unconscious and a reporter, Rachel Williamson, most likely abducted."

"The TV newsgirl? I know who ya mean. Pretty woman, real pretty."

"That's the one. I hope to hell she's okay."

"We all need ta pray we find her."

No, Lieutenant. I think we need to find someone and beat his ass until he tells us where she is!

"I've got my whole group on the way in and asked for mutual aid from everyone in the area," I said. "Sergeant Lambert called for one of your crime scene units. Would you help me by seeing he gets whatever he needs here?"

McClurg nodded.

"She had to have been abducted in a vehicle. Maybe your CSI can find something about that. The news van is right here." I pointed to the van parked near us.

"I'll do anythin' I can," he said. "Jest let me know whatcha need."

"Thanks, I appreciate that. Sergeant Stan Rose should be here any minute. I'm going to notify Mr. Williamson. Stan will take over here."

"I'll be here, too," he said.

"Keep your fingers crossed."

"I'll pray for her."

"Can't hurt."

It took me five minutes to get back to the PD and learn that Bettye had already taken care of all I asked.

I'd known Rachel for six months, but didn't know where her husband worked. That was only one of the important things I wanted to find out. I stopped my forward motion for a moment and began thinking how I should proceed. I hadn't planned on any more than questioning Elrod Swaggerty, who I assumed was one of the last people to see Rachel and John before the incident. But Elrod was nothing but a simple crook, a conman with no evidence in his background to suggest he'd be prone toward violence or kidnapping.

So far, none of the officers conducting the neighborhood canvas had called in any news. The cops patrolling the roads around the crime scene hadn't learned anything about the vehicle used in the abduction, and the people I sent to search the vacant land near the shop reported no progress.

For me to work an extremely time-sensitive investigation, I needed at least six full-time people to keep things going around the clock. That would deplete half my patrol force, leaving only a few cops to handle routine patrol and the calls for assistance coming in daily. With no reason to believe any of the county detectives had experience with a complicated missing person's case, much less a flat-out kidnapping, I'd be the only supervisor with a past history of dealing with an abduction. To get any results, I'd first have to train the other cops who'd work on the case and still have them know only the basics. I needed competent, experienced help. And if I were Boyd Williamson, I'd want more than a small town policeman with limited resources looking for my kidnapped wife.

So, before Boyd made a call, bruised my ego in the process and took everything away from me, I decided to look for help on my own—on my own terms.

I called Ralph Oliveri.

"FBI Knoxville, Oliveri," I heard as he answered his office phone.

"Ralph, Sam Jenkins."

"Hey, buddy, what kind of favor can I do for you today? You want a bunch of agents to help you chase some cattle rustlers up into Kentucky?"

"I need help with a serious problem, no kidding here."

"You sound serious. What's up?"

"Partner, the shit just hit the fan, and I'm up to my armpits in excrement. I've got a TV cameraman assaulted and unconscious in the hospital, and the best I can tell is Rachel Williamson has been abducted off the street in Prospect. I doubt I could do an adequate job alone."

"You want to turn the case over to us?" He spoke with more than a little skepticism.

"Don't sound so surprised. I need you to cut me some slack here, Ralph. My stress battery is running on fumes."

"Okay, okay. Sure I can get you help."

"My call is not exactly all altruistic. I figure as soon as I tell the husband, he'll want to call you anyway. I want to pre-empt that so you and I can come to terms."

"I can't promise you any terms. You know when we work a kidnapping *we* work the case."

"I know that. First, listen to what I have to say. I'd like you to ask your boss if you can be primary agent on this. That should be easy. And I want to continue to investigate on my own. I won't step on any toes, I promise. I'll assist you. If I learn anything, I'll call...immediately. Ralph, this one is personal. I'm putting my ego aside here. I need as much help as possible to find her quickly. Please, Ralph."

There was a silence on the line, then...

"Okay," he said. "That's reasonable. But, Sam, I've got to ask you. And I've asked this before, kidding around, but now I'm serious. Are you and Rachel, ah...more than friends? Oh, hell, are you having an affair? Are you two intimate? I need to know before I go to Carl and get this the way you want it. You know how the truth can come out at an embarrassing moment. We'd both look stupid if you tried to hide anything."

"Same answer as before, buddy. No. No affair. I am not having sex with that woman. Jesus, I sound like Bill Clinton! No, Ralph, no affair. More than friends, maybe, but nothing has gone anywhere. Honest injun. Some time, not on the phone, I'll pour my heart out if you want to hear something, but for now, take my word on this."

"I do. And I think Carl will probably say okay to all you want, but I've got to say, I think he has sort of a love-hate feeling about you."

That was the last thing I needed to hear.

"Really? I got him a front row seat for the press conference and gave him fifty percent of the credit on that IRA thing. That should account for the love. Why does he hate me? Jeez, I'm pretty goddamn lovable."

"Hate may be a little strong. I think he looks at you with great apprehension."

"Huh?"

"Why? Because you did as good a job on the IRA thing as he could have done. A better job, maybe. You got the results. Any more questions?"

"I'll take all that under advisement. Meantime, let me tell you what I know…"

When I rang off, we agreed that I'd contact Boyd Williamson. I'd also take charge of collaring Elrod Swaggerty and seeing what, if any, involvement he had in this. Ralph or another agent would go to the TV station and see if they could learn anything about threats, enemies, stalkers or any of the myriad imbeciles who might become obsessed with a celebrity.

I called the station's general manager to get a work address for Boyd and alerted them to hang loose, say nothing and wait for imminent FBI intervention. Meanwhile, I'd find the husband.

Chapter Nine

As a successful investment broker, Boyd Williamson worked long hours to make money for his clients and commissions for his family. The station manager at WNXX told me I could find his office on Executive Park Drive in West Knoxville. I called first to see if he'd be in the office, but only told his secretary I needed to speak with him urgently, and he should under no circumstances leave before I arrived.

The building's lobby looked spic and span, but the decorating reeked of the early-nineties when the entire commercial world of East Tennessee turned mauve and gray. Soft Musak played from small recessed speakers in the hallways. All of the furniture was black and chrome. A seven-foot silver Christmas tree stood in a corner of the lobby with multi-colored lights twinkling, reflecting off the shiny branches and silver-colored furniture. A real psychedelic light show.

A member of the small platoon of receptionists walked with me to the secretary's area outside Boyd's personal office. I showed an attractive thirty-something redhead my badge and identified myself. A twelve-inch version of the LSD Christmas tree sat on the corner of her desk. She wore a Kelly green dress and hoop earrings as round as navel oranges. Her nameplate said Trisha Brumby. I explained what I wanted.

"Oh, I'm sorry," she said. "Mr. Williamson is presently on the phone and has several international calls stacked up. It might be a long while before he can see you."

Sometimes I handle frustration well—sometimes not.

"You don't seem to understand. I have urgent police business to discuss with him. I can't wait—his calls can."

"What is this in reference to? Perhaps I can help you." She tried again, using her sweetest voice and winning smile.

"I don't know how else to put this, Ms. Brumby. My business can't wait. I need to see him—no, he needs to see me—immediately. If he's on the phone, walk in and tell him to hang up. Then delegate the responsibility for those stacked calls to someone else. I need him now."

Her smile disappeared, and the voice now sounded a little sharp. "Sir, this is a business office. You cannot…"

"Stop!" I held up a hand. "No more excuses. You're a lovely young woman, but unless you'd like to find yourself handcuffed to your chair and charged with obstructing police business, you'll get him to hang up and see me now."

I heard my voice rise. She rested her hand on the phone, probably preparing to call security or just the biggest guy in the building to remove me.

I bent forward, getting my face a little closer to hers. "Are you familiar with the term pronto?"

She made a face, but walked over and opened his door and disappeared for only a moment. Then, out she came with Boyd Williamson on her heels.

He frowned and asked, "Is there a problem here?"

I showed *him* my badge. It was getting a workout.

"Mr. Williamson, my name is Jenkins. I'm chief at the Prospect Police Department. I must speak with you privately."

"Mr. Jenkins, I have several very important phone calls to make, and they're all quite time sensitive."

"No!" I snapped at him. "There is nothing more important than what we have to discuss—now, in private." I pointed toward his office.

"Where did you say you were from?"

"Prospect."

"Prospect? My God!"

It looked like he finally started thinking.

"Did something happen to Rachel? She said she was going to Prospect today."

I jabbed a finger toward his open door. He turned and moved.

I looked at his secretary. "Hold any calls, unless they're important

70

and non-business related." She wrinkled her forehead and looked at me with confusion written all over her face. "You'll understand if one comes in."

I followed him into the office and closed the door. Boyd Williamson generated in me a first impression of mild dislike. I've always been judgmental where yuppies are concerned. I guess *yuppie* is already an archaic term, but it seemed to fit him adequately. He was only about five-seven and looked in reasonably good shape. I figured he might play squash with the boys after work. He wore a crisp blue shirt with a spotless white collar and white French cuffs. I hate shirts like that. Finely braided leather suspenders held up the light grey, pleated trousers to his two-thousand-dollar suit. A yellow polka-dot 'power tie' completed his ensemble. His short curly hair looked very dark and shiny from some kind of hair gel or mousse. Scrub him up a bit and he'd have been good-looking.

"Mr. Williamson, there is no easy way for me to say this."

His face looked awful; he expected the worst.

"Rachel is missing," I said. "I believe earlier today she was abducted from a parking lot in Prospect."

"What? Abducted? Like kidnapped?"

"Yes."

I told him about the assault on John Leckmanski and the basics of what I knew.

"The last I heard, he's still unconscious," I said. "And so far, we have little other information."

That stopped him in his tracks. His mouth hung open. I continued.

"My department isn't large enough nor do we have the logistical resources to co-ordinate an investigation like this. I've asked the FBI to help us. I'm going to call them and let them know where you are. They'll need to speak with you—right now."

I didn't want to hear any more noise about international calls or other professional obligations. He didn't interrupt.

"They'll want to get your home set up with communications equipment in case the kidnapper calls with a ransom demand for either you or the station."

He kept staring at me, probably half in shock. The barely audible elevator Musak played from hidden speakers.

"Do you have someone to stay with your sons when they finish school?"

He shook off the thousand-yard-stare. "You know we have two sons?"

"Might I call you Boyd?"

He nodded.

"My name is Sam, Sam Jenkins. I know your wife. She's ah...she's interviewed me a couple of times. You and your sons came up in conversation."

He nodded again. "I can have someone pick them up. Do you think that's wise?"

"I do. It would be good if you can have someone they know at the school before their last class. I think the FBI should have an agent there as well."

I wanted to protect the kids in case Rachel had been targeted, not because someone wanted her personally, but because the abduction was a statement made to Boyd. Perhaps he pissed someone off or owed someone something—and wasn't paying off in a timely fashion. But that was an area the FBI could explore.

We paused for me to call Ralph Oliveri who said Special Agent in Charge Carl Harmon agreed with me investigating as long as I utilized Ralph, who would lead the team, as a clearinghouse for my developed information. Ralph planned to personally visit Boyd's office and drive him home while another agent drove Boyd's car there. A third agent would accompany Boyd's designee to pick up the two sons.

And still another agent would go to the TV station to see the manager about problems, stalkers or weirdo mail.

It only took Ralph twenty minutes to drive from downtown to West Knoxville, just north of the Cedar Bluff exit off I-40. During those twenty minutes, Boyd and I talked. He seemed to know little of Rachel's business. He confessed to long hours and a propensity toward focusing on his work and sounded apologetic when he spoke about himself. Even I couldn't dislike him then. He looked genuinely shattered over what happened to his wife.

Unless Boyd could pull off an Academy Award performance, which

I doubted, I believed his sincerity. Anyone that visibly upset would certainly be in love with the person who just fell victim to the serious crime I described.

When Ralph and his partner arrived, I left. On my way out, I apologized to Trisha Brumby and offered a brief explanation, cautioning her to keep everything confidential. I spoke nicely and smiled. Maybe she wouldn't hold a grudge. If she did, I'd get over it.

* * * *

I decided to take the less direct route back to Prospect. Rather than leave Executive Park Drive and travel a couple exits west on I-40 and then take the Pellissippi 'Speedway' back to Blount County, I drove east on 40 and exited at Route 129, the Alcoa Highway.

The sun was fading and I didn't want to keep plodding ahead without a game plan. My leg ached from the dampness, I had a nasty tension headache, and I had missed lunch. Top that off with having no leads or even ideas to help me find Rachel and I was not a happy gumshoe.

I called Kate, told her what happened and that I couldn't estimate when I'd be coming home.

Then I called Bettye. She promised to tell Ronnie Shields that the FBI would be in and around the building for the next few days and didn't exactly cheer me up by saying Elrod Swaggerty couldn't be found at home.

While we spoke on the phone, Junior radioed in saying he found a Wildwood address for Merlene Purdy, Elrod's floozy girlfriend. Her house would be a good place to start looking for our fugitive mechanic.

Bettye would have Junior meet me there when I reached the area. She and everyone else volunteered to hang around for the duration. Just like in all the old war movies, *all leaves were cancelled.*

Her last job was to call Carl Harmon at the FBI office and get a laundry list of phone numbers so we could call them with any new developments.

I was starving, and my stomach wouldn't stop growling, so half a mile down the road, I pulled into the convenience store at a Pilot gas station. At the counter, I asked an overweight black woman for a large coffee. While she filled the red, yellow and black cup nearly to the top, I grabbed an Otis Spunkmeyer orange-cranberry bran muffin and read the nutritional information on the wrapper: 13 grams of fat. *Yikes!* However, desperate times called for desperate measures. The woman turned around to put a plastic top on the coffee cup, and I read her nametag. Arletta looked at me as I dangled the cellophane clad muffin in the air for her to see.

"Honey, y'all look frazzled. Hard day t'day?"

"Yes, ma'am, the hardest."

I handed her a five-dollar bill.

"Dat's okay, honey. My man Otis will fix y'all rot up. I loooves dem muffins."

"Thanks, Arletta. You just made my day. Take care of yourself,"

She smiled, showing me a big gold-capped tooth and handed me the change. I hit the road with a little renewed vigor.

I drove another half mile south on 129 and pulled into the blacktop parking lot of Marine Park to drink my coffee and gobble up the greasy Spunkmeyer.

The facility, a Knox County owned boat-launching site on the Tennessee River adjacent to the Naval and Marine Corps Reserve Center, sat across the water from a heavily wooded island.

As the winter sun set in the west, the sky took on a gray-pink cast. I sipped the scalding coffee, set the cup on the dashboard and watched the steam fog up my windshield. I unwrapped the muffin and took a bite. Arletta had excellent taste in bakery goods.

As I blew across the rim of my coffee cup, I heard Canada geese honking and watched them skim the water's surface, landing smoothly on the river bend. Several moments later, a half dozen blue herons flew above the island's trees and roosted in basket-like nests.

If the one heron I saw represented good luck, this crew offered even more.

I ate the rest of Spunkmeyer's finest, washed it down with more coffee and started driving back to my territory with a vision of Elrod Swaggerty in my sights.

Chapter Ten

At 6:00, I drove into the Wildwood area. The Ford's GPS helped me find Merlene Purdy's place. Darkness kept me from seeing a lot of detail, but I could tell the area where she lived didn't qualify as the high rent district. Woodlands bordered the road on both sides, with several vacant lots between some of the homes. I saw older houses, newer mobile homes, and on a curve, a mailbox with 'Purdy' painted on the side in uneven letters marked the driveway where a doublewide sat sixty feet from the blacktop. A five-hundred-dollar aluminum-framed carport sat next to the home, and behind that, I saw a prefab utility shed. Protruding from behind the shed, barely visible from the road, I spotted the ass end of an old El Camino.

Only a quarter mile up the road, I found an intersection with a street sign. I was lucky. In Tennessee, not all roads are marked. They probably think if you don't know where you are, you don't need to be there. I called Bettye from my cell phone, giving her a location, and she dispatched Junior Huskey to meet me. Ten minutes after I hung up, he pulled alongside my car.

"Howdy, boss. You locate that ol' boy?"

"I guess, kid. The El Camino's behind the shed at his fat girlfriend's house. We'll sneak up a bit—you take the back, and I'll knock on the front door. You being younger than me, if there's any chasing to do, you can handle that, okay?"

"You got it, boss, I'll relive my days as a linebacker," he said.

Although I felt like trash, I pulled off a smile. With my window rolled down, I heard the distinctive sounds of two barred owls off in the distance speaking to each other. Wood smoke from a fireplace tainted the air.

"Hey," I said, "thanks a bunch for hanging around and helping out. I know you're on your own time now."

"Shoot, Sam, we gotta find Miss Rachel. No reason fer any of us ta go home till we do."

"Yeah, Junior, we'll find her. I know we will."

I felt a lump in my throat, and my eyes started getting a little wet. I was proud of Junior and all the other cops and grateful for their selflessness. And I really wanted to get a grip on my sixty-year-old emotions.

Junior and I finalized our plan. We took the short drive back to Merlene's place, and I gave him time to walk around to the back of the doublewide. Luckily, there were no dogs nearby to hear Junior and betray his presence. He covered the ground silently and moved into position.

An illuminated Christmas wreath hung on the front door. Seven of the twelve lights had burned out. After I knocked hard on the metal door, Merlene answered wearing a pink and white parachute-cloth jogging suit and a black turtleneck. Her double chin hung over the rolled collar like rising dough drooping over the edge of a bowl. She resembled an English bulldog wearing bright red lipstick and blue eye shadow.

"Yeah?" Merlene spoke with all the class of a warthog.

I held up my badge. "Prospect Police. I'm looking for Elrod Swaggerty."

"This ain't Prospect. You got no right bein' here." She took a drag from the cigarette in her hand and blew smoke upward from the corner of her mouth. I wanted to smack her with a fourteen-ounce blackjack.

As she started to close the door, I jammed my foot against the frame and stopped its motion.

"Lady, I'm a cop in the whole goddamned state. Unless you want to find your fat ass in jail, drag Elrod out here."

She didn't controvert that, but Elrod probably recognized my voice and wanted no part of me. I heard the shuffle of feet and the back door open as the rubber seal was sucked away from the jamb. Then Elrod bailed out. I looked Merlene in the eye.

"Get outta my way!" I growled.

She didn't controvert that either.

I jogged through the house, amazed at the amount of square footage in a doublewide. A straggly live Christmas tree stood between a couch and recliner. The improvised decorations looked like they were made by retarded gnomes. I pushed the swinging back door aside, descended the iron steps and found Elrod squirming on the ground like a panic-stricken cockroach. Junior Huskey pressed his left knee between Elrod's shoulder blades and bent his right arm back in a hammerlock.

"You ready to take a ride, Elrod, and have a talk like two gentlemen," I asked. "Or do I have to beat the shit out of you first?"

"I keep tellin' ya, I ain't done nuthin'. I ain't got no damn reason to hide nuthin'," he squealed. "Jesus have mercy, why cain't y'all leave me be?"

"Elrod, when this is all over, come see me about speech therapy and grammar lessons. Meantime, let the nice policeman put the cuffs on you."

From behind me, I heard the lovely Merlene offer an opinion. "Fuckin' po-leece brutality is what it is."

Back in the squad room, Elrod gave me a chronological account of his day from the time of his release on Alfie Hornbeck's five-thousand-dollar bail until the time Junior damn near broke his neck.

It all seemed to jive. My only problem came after telling him about the assault and kidnapping. He kept squawking out the same old story about 'doin' nuthin'', having no accomplice and having no reason to hurt 'nobody'. He claimed he, 'Damn sure didn't want to kidnap no re-porter.'

Junior sat with me, listening to Elrod's answers. I expressed mild displeasure with our prisoner.

"Elrod, you are pissing me off like I can't believe. You say, 'I ain't done nuthin'' one more time and I will not be responsible for what I do to your scrawny ass."

"Man, please. I done tol' ya, I never did nuthin' to that re-porter."

I stood up, rubbed my eyes and shook my head.

"What are you gonna do now, boss?" Junior asked.

"Now, I am genuinely annoyed. After I get some water, Elrod and I will have a *serious* conversation."

* * * *

I didn't believe a word Elrod said. His track record branded him a conman and a liar.

After getting a cool drink, I wanted to start another round of going over the same material, waiting for him to contradict himself, but he asked, "Kin I take a leak?"

"Hold your water for a while. I'm not finished with you." I wanted him to feel some discomfort.

"Damn, but I got ta pee like a race horse."

"Cross your legs."

Junior snickered.

"Please, or I swear I'll wet my pants," Swaggerty said.

A light went on inside my head. Okay, Elrod, old boy, I thought, you can use our men's room. And when you're finished, I'll save some time and skip the good cop/bad cop act and go directly to bad cop/psycho cop...all by myself.

I unhooked the handcuff that bound him to a steel ring bolted to the desk in the squad room. Keeping a tight hold on the free cuff, I fastened it to his other wrist behind his back.

"I'll take him to the commode, boss," Junior offered.

"That's okay, kid. The downstairs john is broken. I'll take him to the second floor."

"Sam, I jest..."

"It's broken, Junior," I insisted. "I'll take him upstairs."

Officer Huskey looked confused.

I walked Elrod down the hall and past Bettye's desk. As I approached, she spoke to a patrolman on the radio. I kept my hand on Elrod's shoulder as we walked to the double glass doors that separated the reception area from the hall of the municipal building.

Bettye finished her radio transmission and asked, "Where you goin', Sam?"

"The men's room's broken, Sarge. I'm taking this guy upstairs to use the john."

Bettye Lambert's no street cop, but she's far from being gullible.

"Sam!" She sounded much louder than I've ever heard her speak.

I looked into her eyes for a few seconds. Neither of us spoke. I looked away and pushed Elrod out into the hall. We went up the rear staircase, turned right and found the door to the men's room roughly above our 'D' cells.

All the day workers had left the building hours earlier. The halls were dark; only dim security lights partially illuminated the halls.

I pushed open the door, flipped the light switch and ushered Elrod in. Before moving away from the door, I used my foot to jam a rubber wedge, one the cleaners used to keep the door open, between the floor and the door bottom. I wanted the room closed off to the outside world.

I removed the cuffs from Elrod's wrists and pointed to the row of urinals.

"Okay, partner. The facility is all yours."

When I heard Elrod's water passing into the porcelain fixture, I stepped over to the window, turned the lock and pushed open the sash.

"Elrod, you know the trouble with public restrooms today?"

"Do what?" he asked.

"They all smell funny. We need some fresh air in here."

"Huh?"

I watched him finish, jiggle and zip up his trousers.

"We've been speaking for a while now, and perhaps you've sensed that I don't want to hear any more bullshit from you. Right, Elrod?"

"I cain't unnerstand why yer sayin' that," he said. "I been tellin' ya the God's honest trouff."

That was the wrong answer for Sam's Quiz Show.

I grabbed him by the throat, swung him away from the urinals and slammed him into the wall next to the window.

"Jesus, man, you're choakin' me," he croaked.

"One more time, sport. Who clocked the guy at your shop, and where's the woman?"

I spoke from between clenched teeth. Elrod gurgled. His eyes bulged, and he looked scared. Then I choked him a little harder. He sputtered and tried to shake off my grip.

"Elrod, you can't imagine how much you're pissin' me off."

I pulled him a foot away from the wall and slammed him against the concrete again.

"I got no fuckin' idee what you're talkin' about. You're fuckin' crazy, man."

I could hear traffic on Main Street and car doors slamming in the Hardee's parking lot across the road. The smell of stale cooking oil from the deep fryers floated in the night air.

"Elrod, listen carefully, goddamnit," I said through gritted teeth. "If you don't tell me where your buddy's holding that woman, I'm going to rip off your head and shit in the hole."

My face was only inches from his. I could smell his smoker's breath and body odor. He reminded me of most of the inmates from any correctional facility I'd ever visited.

"Last chance, asshole," I said. "Tell me where you've got that woman stashed, or you won't believe what comes next."

I squeezed his throat harder. His face turned crimson. He must have gotten so scared he forgot to breathe through his nose and sputtered for a breath. My nose almost touched his. I clenched my teeth and assumed my eyes looked a bit wild.

"Talk!" I bounced his head against the concrete block.

But he still said nothing. He tried to shake his head. His eyes looked like those of a frightened animal.

I assumed that inside Elrod's head, thoughts profound to him and to which I'd not be privy, rolled around like gerbils on a wire Ferris wheel. He looked into my eyes and what he saw must have frightened him. He wasn't looking at the benevolent policeman who delivered babies and helped old ladies cross the street. The eyes he looked into were influenced by circumstances beyond their owner's control. They represented a second personality, one activated by a perceived need to solve unsolvable equations with violence and cruelty, because reason and diplomacy had failed.

Elrod must have felt bile rising in his throat because he made choking noises. And his fright was great enough to loosen his bowels.

Then I hit him. I stood flatfooted, leaning forward. My fist came from next to my ribs, driven hard into his abdomen. I used my shoulder and torso and the weight of my entire upper body to hurt him. A professional punch, not something you see in the average street scuffle.

A great whoosh of air and a spray of spittle came from his mouth and sailed past my left shoulder. He began to double over. I pushed him back against the wall and then spun him around.

My left hand pressed his face against the concrete block. With my right hand, I latched on to his belt and with my left, I took a big handful of shirt collar. I slammed him against the wall again, pulled him back, stepped to our left and doubled him over the windowsill. I heaved up, and with him more than half way out the window, only my hold on his belt kept him from falling two floors down onto the Dumpster and the blacktop below.

"You've given me a case of the ass like a Russian bear, Elrod. You're way out of your league here. Why are you holding out on me? Is this worth dying for?"

"Jesus, man, I ain't lyin'. I got nuthin' ta say. I swear ta God, I don't know nuthin' 'bout no woman. I done tole ya. I swear!"

Then he began to cry. He mumbled, whimpered and again said, "I swear ta God. I don't know nuthin'. Go ahead an' kill me, but I swear, I don't know nuthin', and there ain't nuthin' I could tell you."

Elrod had annoyed me so much, I just wanted to drop him and let him die. But at that point, with his life literally hanging in the balance, I doubted he was some kind of hero who would clam up and refuse to rat out his accomplice. His words rang true.

I yanked up on his collar and belt simultaneously. When he landed back on firm ground, I released him. He turned, slid down the wall and slumped on the floor with his back against the cinder blocks. I slammed the window and locked it and then bent down, grabbed his shirt and pulled him to his feet.

"Jesus Christ, man, don't hit me again. Please, I'm wore out," he sighed.

"You just bought back your life, young feller," I said. "You're such a gutless bastard I truly doubt you had anything to do with the kidnapping."

"I done tole ya a hunnert times, I walked away from that woman and drove off. I swear to Jesus."

I looked down at Elrod. His light blue, washed-off jeans were now dark all around his crotch and down his legs.

"You just drained your bladder. How could you pee in your pants?"

"Oh, man, don't get no closer. That ain't all I done."

I shook my head in disgust. "Remember what I said about you being an asshole? Come on, let's get you downstairs, and you can clean yourself up."

We turned and started toward the door. As we stood only a few feet from the men's room entrance, it sounded like all hell started breaking loose. It startled me, and I assumed Elrod might have deposited some additional bodily waste into his shorts.

"Sam, you alright? Open the door!"

Stanley Rose slammed on the woodwork and bellowed in the corridor. He hit the door with his shoulder, with all the force his 235 pounds could generate.

"Christ almighty, Stan! Knock it off, and I'll open the door."

It took me several tries to pry the rubber wedge from under the door. Stanley had pushed with such force the doorstop almost became permanently jammed. I finally opened the door and looked at Stanley.

"Bettye called me. She said she thought you were going to kill this guy. I..." He looked at me and stopped.

"It's okay, Stan. He's still alive." I spoke in a calm, soothing voice. "He needs a little cleaning up, but he's fine. I don't think he had anything to do with abducting Rachel."

Stan tilted his head, as if unsure what he just heard.

"Let's get him downstairs, and then you can take him home," I said.

Stanley took hold of Elwood, sniffed and made a face. "What's that smell?"

"Sorry," Elrod said, "but he done tore me up. I ain't kiddin', sir. He scared the shit out o' me."

I laughed.

Downstairs, Junior found a pair of orange prisoner pants and took Elrod to our shower room to clean up the mess he made when he fouled himself. I walked back into the reception area. When I came within a few feet from her desk, Bettye stood up.

"Sam, I..." She started to speak, but then stopped.

"It's okay, Betts. Give me a few minutes, and we'll talk," I said.

She looked upset.

"Sam, I wanted to…"

I stopped her by putting my hand gently on her arm.

"It's okay. Nothing much happened. But…thanks for being concerned," I said.

I walked toward my office and called Ralph Oliveri's cell phone number.

"You find anything interesting yet?" I asked.

"Maybe. The station manager said a few years back Rachel did some investigative work that led to Knox County dicks locking up a guy. He just finished doing two years. Got out a couple of months ago. His PO says he's seen him twice, but not since. We're working on him."

"Maybe something. He have any ties in Prospect or anywhere else in Blount County?"

"Haven't seen any yet, but I just sent out an alarm. You and all the rest of the local PDs should have it by now."

"I spoke with Elrod Swaggerty—the guy who last saw her at the transmission shop. It's not him. I'm sure of that."

"You're sure?" Ralph sounded surprised. "He have a good alibi?"

"No alibi—he last saw Rachel standing in the lot as he drove away from her and the cameraman. I guess she was taken right after that. Elrod doesn't have the balls to assault John. And I seriously doubt he has an accomplice who would help with this."

"Yeah, how can you be sure? Maybe we should take a run at him."

"Ralph, trust me on this one. Elrod and I just finished a serious and meaningful conversation. He was scared of me. He didn't give anyone up. He shit in his pants…literally. Are we okay here?"

"I really didn't think you'd slack up on someone who may be good for this."

"No, I wouldn't."

"I'm up at Rachel's home now," he said. "We'll leave an agent here all night to monitor the phones. Can you meet me here tomorrow morning? Her husband will be here, and her parents are flying in tonight from PA. I'll have them picked up. Nine o'clock okay?"

He gave me the address.

"Was the ex-con the only idea those people at the station came up with?" I asked.

"So far," he said.

"Who'd you speak with?"

"I didn't. Bonnie Rowatt spoke with the station's general manager."

"I don't know her. She speak with anyone else?"

"I would think so, but didn't ask specifically, why?"

"Three guesses, Ralph, and the last two don't count."

"Okay, okay, things have been hectic. I haven't had a chance to snoopervise yet."

"I know some of the people at WNXX. I'll stop by tomorrow when I leave the Williamson house. You have anything you need done tonight before I cut all my OT volunteers loose?"

"Unfortunately, no."

"Okay, see you tomorrow morning." I hung up.

Junior and Stan insured that Elrod had cleaned himself up adequately. The three stood in the hall near the doorway to my office, Elrod wearing his wrinkled shirt and a pair of shapeless drawstring pants. He held his blue mechanic's jacket under his arm and clutched a plastic trash bag holding his dirty jeans. I approached.

"These officers are going to take you home or back to Merlene's—your choice. Don't plan on leaving the area, capiche?"

I confused him again.

"Understand?"

He nodded.

"After that, we'll see you in court," I said.

He looked anything but defiant, sheepish almost. I couldn't imagine the feeling someone would have after fouling their knickers in front of several cops. But I had to hand it to Elrod; he mustered up the gumption to try and get in the last word.

"Ya know I could sue y'all for what ya done ta me t'night," he said.

I said nothing for a long moment. Instead, I reactivated my psycho-cop stare, trying to bore my look through his eyes and into his puny brain.

"Give us a moment, would you gentlemen?" I looked at the two cops. "In there!" I said to Elrod, pointing to my office.

Once inside, I closed the door and the blinds to my picture window facing the lobby. Time for another serious talk.

Chapter Eleven

I looked at him with a demented grin. "Sure, you miserable little shit bag, you could sue. You might even get a few bucks because the city attorney might want to shut you up and save his court time."

I stepped to within inches of him. We stood nose to nose again.

"But then I'd really be pissed off. And you know what would happen next?" He didn't answer. "Well?"

"No, sir," he said, with as much bravado as he could manage.

"Upstairs was easy, Elrod, I wasn't really mad at you. It was just business. You remember I never used my gun?"

He nodded, and I watched his Adam's apple jiggle up and down.

"You piss me off by getting personal and there's no more talking. No more Mr. Nice Guy. I'll just kill your ass. Comprende', amigo?"

"Do what?" His eyes bugged out like a choking frog. Elrod made me think he might pee in his new orange pants.

"You heard me, you little shit stain! I'll kill you. Dead! I'll cut you up into little fuckin' pieces and scatter you all over the Smoky Mountains. You think anyone will ever find your bones after the wild dogs get finished with your remains? You think anyone could arrest me for killin' you? I'm smart and know all the tricks. And if someone typed *asshole* into a computer, your picture would jump up."

"Jesus Christ, man, you're crazy." He sounded scared again, and his eyes bulged even larger.

"You better believe it, sport. And I'd advise you to let that public defender take a plea on your court case, and you better not say anything about our conversations tonight. If you break my balls about anything, I might kill you for that, too! Do we understand each other?"

85

"Yessir, I hear ya."

I completely changed my demeanor. "Good. Very good. Nice to see you again, son. You enjoy the rest of your evening." I gave him a friendly, fatherly smile, put my hand on his shoulder and walked him out to where Stan and Junior waited.

As Elrod and his escorts left through the back door, I heard him say, "That fuckin' guy's nuts, man. Who the fuck is he?"

It's nice to leave a lasting impression on your customers.

But then it was time for me to face the music. I walked over to Bettye's desk, stood next to her and did my repentant little boy act.

"Hi there," I said.

She'd been reading the newspaper. After I spoke, she took off her glasses and tossed them onto the desktop.

"Oh, Sam, what did you do?"

She's really quite lovely when she's concerned about me. Her blonde ponytail swayed from left to right as she shook her head.

"I only tried a few unconventional interviewing techniques. Nothing too radical."

"Sam, you scare the livin' daylights outta me. Why do you do things that can get you inta such trouble?"

"Gee, Betts, I remember Nietzsche saying, 'All things are permissible.' I haven't even scratched the surface yet."

"I don't know much about this Nee-chee, but I *do not* want to see you get fired, Sam Jenkins. We couldn't take another Buck Webbster around here."

Bettye wasn't fond of the former chief.

"I won't get fired, love. For twenty years, I kept me, the police department and all the cops who worked for me out of trouble. Experience counts."

"Just please don't do something like that again. I don't want to lose you as a boss or a friend."

"Well, shucks, little darlin', a man's gotta do what a man's gotta do."

Damn, but that sounded like John Wayne speaking. On the other hand, maybe I just imagined that.

"Sometimes, Sam, you are more than I can handle."

"Well, sure, but I'm so derned cute, it shouldn't matter."

The woman actually growled at me.

* * * *

I looked at my watch. At 8:30, adrenaline was pushing me along. I probably couldn't stop if I wanted to. However, I thought we'd come up against a stone wall. None of the people interviewed claimed to have seen anything. None of the cops developed any usable information. The kidnapper or kidnappers had yet to communicate with anyone.

Perhaps the ex-con Ralph learned about could be found. Sometimes your first leads, the easy ones, are the best. The vagabonds and miscreants of the world are rarely members of MENSA. I hated to admit it, but I stood at an impasse. It seemed like time to pack up for the night.

"Bettye, my love, I think we need to get out of here. Let's send all the volunteers home, too. Tomorrow's a new day. I'm going to give all the guys in the cars a shout,"

She spun her chair around and gave me room at the radio.

I keyed the microphone sitting on her desk. "Prospect headquarters to all units. Any officers on overtime may go 10-28 for the night with my thanks. Regular units continue to patrol and when possible check the area around Smoky Mountain Transmissions for anything of value. Sergeant Rose will coordinate. Any new information of importance, 10-13 Prospect one at his 10-50.

Units 504, 508 and Stan Rose in 535 all gave me their 10-4s.

"Prospect headquarters to all units, thanks again guys. Thanks very much. Prospect headquarters is 10-28 until 0800 hours tomorrow morning. County 911 and dispatch will handle communications until then. Prospect headquarters, out."

Bettye and I closed up shop. I walked with her to the marked PD Explorer she drove and made sure it started up okay. I fired up my Crown Victoria and headed toward Walland.

Then came the hard part. I allowed personal feelings to creep into my head. They can only hamper an investigation. I started thinking how Rachel might feel and could only guess. Few of us will ever know the fear she must have experienced that day. My concern about her, my disappointment at not knowing more and my feeling of impotence meant nothing compared to the problems facing our kidnap victim. I felt shitty and reasonably sure I wouldn't sleep peacefully that night. But I needed food, a couple of drinks and I needed Kate to give me a pep talk. On the drive home, I thought about how to handle one of the most difficult things a cop ever does—tell the family of a victim you don't have good news for them.

* * * *

I parked the Ford nose out in the turnaround, stumbled out and tried to stretch away some of the day's tension. Having no luck, I sniffed the damp air. It felt considerably colder. My left leg was killing me, and the right shoulder I dislocated in 1975 hurt like hell. My traps had tightened up as hard as the steel cables on the Brooklyn Bridge. My body told me, among other things, it would probably rain soon, while my nose said snow wasn't too far off. I felt miserable.

I had failed to generate either a good idea or an innovative thought all day and qualified as a mental mess. Once my mind came down to earth, the cold settled into my body. The sport jacket and sleeveless sweater I wore didn't feel adequate for the weather. A winter coat would have been more appropriate.

Kate had left the outdoor light on for me. As I walked along the porch to the front door, past the twinkling white lights wrapped into garlands of evergreens and between the pair of three-foot candles glowing in the night, thoughts of what might be happening to Rachel jumped back into my head. Those thoughts stayed with me for the remainder of the night and ultimately disturbed my sleep.

When a person is abducted and no ransom demand is forthcoming, it's almost impossible to determine what may be happening to them. Few of us know what goes on in the minds of those psychotic or sociopathic individuals who perpetrate kidnappings. Only *their* imaginations limit what might occur. Sometimes the more you know from experience, the less acceptable your thoughts become.

I opened the front door and stepped into the foyer. To my left, Kate sat on the sofa watching a rerun of *Law and Order, Special Victim's Unit*—not exactly a light, upbeat story. Bitsey, who slept next to Kate, jumped off the couch, shook herself to wake up and wiggled over to fall on the carpet at my feet. I gave her a ration of attention and stood up.

"Hey, Sammy," Kate said, "I'm sorry you had such a tough day. They've had little bits about Rachel on the news but not a lot. I guess neither you nor the FBI are saying much."

"Hi ya, cutie." She kissed my cheek. "No, we're not. And, yes, the worst day I can remember, and I'm not even the one in trouble."

"Do you know anything yet?"

"Not much."

I gave her a quick rundown of what I had learned since we'd last spoken.

"The poor woman."

"You bet."

"How about John, the cameraman?"

"Last I heard, he's stable but still unconscious. He took one nasty shot to the head."

"I'll bet you'd like a little drinky-poo."

"A little drinky-poo would be great. A large one would be even better."

I sat down on the sofa. Bitsey joined me. To our left, the grand Christmas tree Kate spent a whole day decorating glowed with holiday cheer. On the television, Detective Elliot Stabler just lost his temper and slammed a suspect against the wall. My violent propensities were being validated by a Hollywood hero.

Kate brought me a glass of Laphroaig with several ice cubes. Like a proper connoisseur, I sniffed first. The fragrant, peaty smell of a Western Isles single-malt whisky seemed appropriate for the cold and damp evening. The alcohol would be a welcome but mild anesthesia. I swished the cubes around and took a long sip. It was a start.

"Think you'll want to eat?" Kate asked.

"I don't feel like it, but I need something."

"I went to Kroger and bought cold cuts. Ham or turkey?"

"Oy, all these hard questions. Ham and mustard go well with whisky. Would you mind?"

"Keep your daughter company, dahling, and I'll make you such a sandwich, you'll enjoy," she said.

"You're a first class shicksah, Kats. Believe me when I tell you that."

"I believe, dahling, I do. In a minute, I'll be back."

Kate disappeared, and I scratched Bitsey's head. On the tube, Captain Cragen started yelling at Stabler, telling him he was out of control.

No shit, Donnie, and how long have you known Elliot?

Kate brought in my ham sandwich. Next to it lay a large spear of *kosher* pickle. An oxymoron? Just strange partners? Who cared? Both tasted great, especially when washed down by single-malt scotch. Man, that was livin'.

After my second drink, we went upstairs, showered and got into bed. Kate got there before me and started reading. When I slid under the duvet, she put her book aside. I let out a long sigh.

"Are your shoulders tight?"

"Quite."

"Turn over. I'll see if I can fix them."

I took off my pajama top and flipped onto my stomach. Kate massaged my neck and trapezius muscles for several minutes. It felt good, but probably didn't remedy much.

I felt her finger tracing the old shrapnel scar on the right side of my back.

"What are you going to do next?" she asked.

"Keep going by myself. Hope the FBI can do something. Hope they get a ransom demand or some communication from the person or people who have her. Bottom line is I feel responsible for her being at the transmission shop. I doubt this would have happened if I hadn't drummed up the case."

"I understand you feel that way, but can you see how someone might question the validity of that idea?"

"Sure, but that doesn't help me any. I love denial—it makes the world go round. But I've got a self-image to deal with, too, and no one does something like this in my sector and walks away from me. I could live with Ralph Oliveri finding the bad guy, but I'd rather do it myself."

"Just like Marshal Dillon?"

"It's not a matter of theatrics, Kats. You've heard my theory before. In my position, it's necessary to be the meanest mother on the block so

I'm effective in my job and, to some extent, for it to get easier as the word gets around."

"You're not God, Sammy. You can't make everything you want happen."

"I've got a better track record than God. I never let Hitler run amuck in my precinct for twelve years."

"Sam!"

Blasphemy, thy name is Jenkins.

Katherine gave me a long goodnight kiss and offered to sit up with me if I had trouble sleeping. Getting to sleep was never difficult. Sometime later, I began to dream—a dream I'd remember when I awoke.

* * * *

Rachel and I sat on a balcony or veranda of an outdoor café. We overlooked a calm bay with beautiful scenery that horseshoed around the dark blue-green water. I drank from a half-empty mug of beer. She sipped an almost full, stemmed glass of white wine.

Rachel wore the same off-white suit I saw when we met six months earlier in the parking lot outside Prospect PD. But I seemed to be much younger. I wore a yellow Hofstra University T-shirt, faded blue jeans and a pair of tan Topsiders with white socks.

Slouching in a chair with my feet resting on the rail in front of me, I told Rachel about the beaches on Long Island, about the best spots for surfing—from the Azores at Long Beach to Tobay, out east along the Ocean Parkway.

I stood and looked over the rail at my old '58 Volkswagen cabriolet parked with the top down and my nine-and-a-half foot Hobie surfboard propped behind the driver's seat, sticking up and out over the folded rag-top.

When I turned around and looked back, Rachel was gone. Her drink sat on the table, and her purse hung over the back of the chair. With a feeling of mild panic, I looked at my feet and realized my shoes and socks were missing, too.

I questioned four people at the next table about where the woman sitting with me had gone. No one seemed to hear or even take notice of me. No one answered. I tried several more tables and got the same reception.

The waiter who served our drinks stood a few feet away with his back to me. I spoke to him. When he didn't respond, I grabbed his shoulders and spun him around. It was a different man. Seeing another waiter—same dark hair, same white shirt, same black pants, I turned him around, too. That wasn't even a man, but a woman with short hair. No one would speak to me. I felt anger and frustration.

At the back of the veranda, I took a staircase leading down to ground level, only to find more stairs at the bottom on which I continued. Everything led to nothing. I wanted to call out, call her name, but I was afraid someone would hear me.

Following the stairs in their downward spiral caused me to get lost. I couldn't go up or down any longer. Nothing made sense, and nothing looked familiar.

I awoke at 12:40 and didn't want to return to the dream. I blinked and tried to clear my head, certain I couldn't find an ending if I tried.

Pushing the dream aside solved nothing. It only made room for non-stop thoughts of what to do next. I wondered what I'd say to Rachel's family and worst of all, what might be happening to her as I tried to sleep. Generally speaking, I think dreams suck.

I flipped, turned, got up, lied down and felt totally flummoxed for hours. I last remembered hearing the clock strike 4:30. Then I slept again, but also dreamt again.

At 5:25, I awoke and lay there for half an hour before getting up to shave.

A new day to face.

Chapter Twelve

I put on a tan wool suit, light blue shirt and a tartan plaid tie. It was only thirty-six degrees and raining gently. The weatherman at WNXX told us it wouldn't get any warmer during the day. He expected the rain to continue and turn to snow in the higher elevations. I took out my genuine Burberry trench coat, something I paid the earth for and hadn't worn in years. They introduced the style for British Army officers in the First World War. A little dated perhaps, but I thought it made me look continental and rather sinister. *James Bond, eat your heart out.*

I drove through what Knoxville considers morning rush-hour traffic. A New Yorker would call it a few cars. I pulled up to the Williamson home, a large pre-war house in a stately old neighborhood near the Tennessee River, at 8:50, a few minutes prior to Ralph's arrival.

The duty agent let me in and walked with me to the living room. I hoped Boyd wasn't wearing suspenders. He wasn't. A small favor, but I appreciated it. He and I shook hands, and he introduced me to Joe and Pauline Kiel, Rachel's parents.

Rachel once told me her father had retired from the power company back in Pennsylvania several years earlier. He stood about five-six, a solid little guy with a strong handshake and an honest, good-looking face. He and Boyd tried their best to hold on to a manly demeanor in spite of the worst possible occurrence of their lives.

Pauline was short like Rachel. She too shook my hand and looked me straight in the eye, appearing tougher than either Joe or Boyd. Where Rachel was dark, Pauline had gray hair—nicely cut in a short classy style. She needed and wore little make-up. I thought the old girl possessed a truckload of character and looked as attractive as her daughter.

I couldn't think of something to say and fumbled around for a few words of assurance, made a little small talk and felt a welcome relief when Ralph walked in with his new partner, Bonnie Rowatt.

Westminster chimes from an old tall-case clock begged our attention and rang nine times. Most of us looked in that direction.

After the interruption, the two agents began covering all the bases on abduction protocol, with Oliveri doing most of the talking. Ralph was a pro; Rachel's family could expect the best possible service.

At first, I didn't like Bonnie. She was a good-looking redhead in her late twenties and obviously a newbie to the Bureau. But she tried too hard to act and sound like a tough old-timer. Her gray business suit with a knee-length skirt looked too Hollywood FBI. I don't think she liked me either. I've never been able to mask my emotions very well.

Before we left the day crew of two agents to monitor the phones, Pauline Kiel walked over to me.

"Do you think you'll find my daughter?" she asked.

She looked at me, not the others; I'm not sure why. Her expression demanded an honest answer, and I found myself unable to lie to those eyes.

"Yes, ma'am. I do. I promise you. I'll find her."

The few seconds it took her to reply seemed as interminable as a sweltering thirty-one days in August.

"Thank you," she said. "I believe you will."

An eight-foot, live Christmas tree stood in a corner of the living room. The fragrance of Scotch pine gently scented the room. Some of the boys' gifts were still under the tree next to a small village scene around an oval mirror lying on the floor meant to represent an iced-over pond.

We each said our good-byes, mumbling words of reassurance. Then Ralph, Bonnie and I walked outside and stood under the covered front porch, protected from the rain. Bonnie wrinkled up her nose and frowned, silently indicating she disliked the wet weather.

"Sam, I don't doubt you know your onions," Ralph said. "But was it wise to promise the mother you'd find her daughter?"

"Probably not. I just needed to give her some hope. Probably needed some myself."

"You know the longer this drags out," he said, "the less chance there is for a good ending."

Bonnie stood quietly holding a gray umbrella that matched her top coat, her frown still present.

"Yeah, I know that, and I know you're doing all you can. I'm going to start up again today and do what I've always tried to do—the impossible." I shrugged. "I'll call you if I get anything."

As I walked toward my car, I heard Bonnie. "Who the hell does he think he is?"

Bitch.

"You might shut up and learn something from him," Ralph said.

Good man!

Someday Bonnie might learn the old guy's hearing is better than she thought.

* * * *

On the first day of the investigation, nothing came from the neighborhood canvas my cops did in Prospect. However, I just didn't buy the idea that no one saw anything. Someone did. Someone called 911 and hung up quickly. But who? Over the years, I've learned that viable witnesses often don't come forward unless you pry them out of the woodwork. Some believe others will offer up the needed details, and they can avoid becoming involved. Others just don't like cops. And some have their heads up their asses in ways unimaginable to the average person.

I've always said, 'When in doubt, re-visit the crime scene.' Preferably at the same time the original incident occurred. People are creatures of habit. Many people do the same thing, at the same time, every day. I hoped I could find such a person that morning.

I hadn't stayed long at the Williamson house and could drive back to Prospect and be in position before the estimated time of occurrence of between 10:30 and 10:50. I picked up a coffee from Arletta at the Pilot station and drove south. When I parked the Ford adjacent to Elrod's shop, I called Bettye.

"The Mayor's been looking for you," she said. "I told him what we did last night. Well, most of what we did anyway."

I sensed disapproval in her voice. Once we began working together, Bettye grasped the concept of upward discipline quickly.

"Thank you, madam. I appreciate how you look after my welfare."

"H'mpf. He wants to see you," she said. "Asked me if the FBI was on the case, why you needed to be out of town."

I swallowed the first nasty thing that came to mind and took a second to muster up an appropriate dose of diplomacy.

"Please tell his majesty the FBI is not making any great headway on this, and there are several things I need to do, none of which he would have the faintest clue why. Forget the last part. I should be back this afternoon. Tell him the department is functioning quite well. Calls are being handled, and you are every bit as competent as I am and much less prone to be insubordinate when you don't get your way. Reassure the shaky young bugger you'll do just fine handling things for the amount of time I need to be away from the office playing gumshoe."

A spark of mischief crept into her voice." What's a gumshoe?"

"Are you really that young?"

She giggled.

"Tell our fearless leader he should keep it in his knickers, and as soon as I know something worth talking about, he'll be the first to hear."

"You sure you want me to tell him all that?" she asked.

"What I want you to tell *him* would embarrass me to tell *you*. You are a lady. I am not always a gentleman. Tell him what you think he wants to hear. Use your intelligence guided by experience. I'll be back later. I'll call you once in a while just to check in. Okay?"

"Okey dokey, boss. Good luck."

* * * *

I sat for almost forty minutes in a steady, gentle rain that my ancestors would have called a 'wee Scotch mist'. My coffee was gone, and my sixty-year-old bladder wished I hadn't drunk it. I looked down the street through the windshield and occasionally into the rear view mirror.

About ten minutes later, I saw an old man, barely walking upright, coming down the road toward me. He wore a dark blue raincoat, an orange UT baseball cap and on the end of a leash, a little brown poodle toddled along trying to keep dry under his umbrella. The dog wore a pink knitted sweater. When he was a few yards from my car, I got out and stopped him.

"Morning, sir," I said. "My name is Sam Jenkins. I'm the police chief here in Prospect. Can we talk for a minute?"

"Was wonderin', young fella, when ya'd git around ta me."

"Sir?" I said.

"Said, I's wonderin' when ya'd come an' ask me if'n I knew somethin' could he'p ya."

He reached down and picked up the poodle to keep her dry. The old dog had as much gray in her beard as me.

"What is it you need to tell me, sir? What did you say your name was?"

"I didn't tell ya, and ya damn well know that, son. I'm Ermun Tillman. Live jest up the road some, well a good walk up yonder, anyways—mor'en a half mile or so. Have done fer sixty-five year ever since I married Josie."

"And none of the police officers canvassing the neighborhood spoke to you?"

"Nosir. Stopped a'fore they got ta my house."

I sighed, and the poodle wiggled into a more comfortable position.

I smiled. "Who's this, Mr. Tillman?" I scratched the dog under her chin.

"This here's Coco. She don't like the rain. Me neither."

"Well then, how about we all sit in my car and keep dry?" I opened the door for him.

He nodded and set Coco on the front seat. The dog shook violently. Water spattered all over the upholstery. Mr. Tillman folded his umbrella and got into the front seat. I walked to the other side of the car and got in. His coat smelled damp and musty.

"Alright, sir," I said. "I have a feeling you're going to tell me something helpful."

"I believe I am, son. T'other day, Coco an' me's a'walkin' on this here road when I seen a big fella in a white van park over yonder."

He pointed to a spot near Elrod's lot.

"This here fella waited till that young lady and the fella with the big movie camera done finished with that re-pair man. Then he drove up betwixt 'em."

"Where were you standing?" I asked.

"Right here, across from the shop."

"What happened next?"

"I seen the fella with the camera run at the big fella, and he—the big fella, that is—he hits the cameraman ta de-fend hisse'f. Then the big fella, he picks up the little girl and puts her inta the van—then he drives off."

"Mr. Tillman, that information is very useful. Can you tell me more about the big man who drove the white van?"

"Bigger'n you by mebbe two inches—heavier, too. Had him short dark hair, wore a tan Army jacket with a pattern to hit. Dark pants, mebbe dungarees."

"Anything special about the van? Any signs? Ladders on the roof? Anything?"

"No, jest a van. Not a mini-van, mind ya. M' granddaughter's got her one o' them. Cain't see why she bought it. Mebbe fer her kids. Anyways, the white one, hit was bigger. Got two letters off'n the tag, too."

"Really?"

"Course really. Somethin' HV, somethin', somethin', somethin'."

"A Tennessee plate?"

"This ain't North Carolina, son. A Blount County plate it was."

"Did you happen to notice what make of vehicle it was?"

"Make o' ve-hickle? Well, I seen one of them li'l blue ovals, so I s'spect t'was a Ford. Course I never much liked Fords m'se'f. Always was a Chevy man. M' daddy, he was, too. Genner'l Motors all the way, he was. My granddaughter's mini-van now, that's one o' them things from Ja-pan. Cain't unnerstand why she won't buy Amurican. She's borned rot here."

"Mr. Tillman, I don't know how to thank you. The woman who was abducted is a personal friend. I think this might help me find her."

"Well then, young fella, ya shoulda talked ta me sooner."

"I don't want to sound ungrateful for the information, but I have to

98

ask, why didn't you call sooner. Why didn't you report the assault when it happened?"

"'Cuse me, but I shore did report it. How'd ya think y'all got here in the first place?"

"You called, but you didn't leave your name."

"Called from the pay phone up by Gerald's weldin' shop next block up. Figgered you'd take it from there. Then I set home a'waitin' fer somebody to stop by, but ya didn't, did ya?"

"No, sir, someone should have. Tell me where you live, in case I have to speak with you again?"

"I done tole ya, rot down the road here—number 4103—li'l white house right there, yonder, sixty-five year now."

"Thank you again, sir. Can I drive you home?"

"Course you cain't. Coco needs ta do her bidness. Cain't do that inside no ve-hickle."

"Okay, Mr. Tillman, I'll see you again."

The old man took his time getting out of the car. Once he had his umbrella open and the little dog under his arm, he ducked his head and said, "Anytime, young fella, but best not come 'tween noon an' three o'clock. That's when I eat m' lunch and watch m' stories."

How much luck would I have filling in the blanks on a license plate with something, HV, dash, something, something, something?

Chapter Thirteen

When you're a world-class sleuth, you need to be suave and clever. It's not cool to uncover a major clue and behave like a little kid who just found Willie Mays' rookie-year card in his package of Topps bubble gum.

I did my best to keep from burning rubber out of Elrod's parking lot, but I did drive back to Prospect PD as quickly as possible.

"Betts, my love, fire up your computer and see what you can get on a white, full size van with a Tennessee plate, blank, HV, blank, blank, blank. Maybe a Ford."

Her face lit up. "Sam, where'd you get this from?"

"I found me a gen-u-ine witness."

"Well, they!" she said.

Tennessee women all say that. But I've never been able to figure out who 'they' are.

"Run that any way you can think of and make a list for me. Sorry, I don't have to tell you how to do it."

She smiled.

"I've got to go back to Knoxville and talk to some people at the TV station. I'll be back as quick as I can."

"I'll be here," she said. "And, Sammy," I looked back at her, "You look real nice all dressed up like that. You ought'a do it more often."

"Thanks, Betts. You're quite beautiful yourself."

* * * *

On the trip north, I stopped for a quick sandwich at Buddy's

Barbeque on 129 and should have taken longer to enjoy the food, but I was hot in the pants to get to Knoxville. Back in the car, I fumbled with my cell phone and finally got a number to ring.

"Hello, this is Tess Haley from 5 O'clock Magazine. I'm not at my desk right now, but please leave a message at the tone, and I'll be sure to call you back."

"Hello, Tess. This is Sam Jenkins from Prospect Police. I hope you remember me. If you're there, please pick up. I need to speak with you about Rachel..." I didn't finish my entire message.

"Hello, this is Tess."

"Hi, Sam Jenkins from Prospect PD. We met a couple of months ago."

"Sure, I remember. You had that cute little police dog in your office," she said.

I chuckled at her calling Bitsey a police dog.

"Tess, I need your help. I've been trying to find Rachel and want to talk to you and anyone else at the station who might know something important. Can I stop by in about twenty minutes?"

"This is awful about Rachel. God, when I think about it, it could happen to any of us. Of course, I'll help. I'll be right here. What can I do for you?"

"We need to look back and think of anything that maybe connected to the person who did this. You know, stalkers, obsessed fans, hate mail, assorted weirdos, anything."

"I'll do anything you want."

"I know an FBI agent spoke to the station manager, but probably no one else," I said. "Can you check around and ask all the other people there if they remember Rachel getting mail or calls from someone who might fit the bill? I'm grasping at straws here."

"Of course I can. I'll see you in a few minutes."

The earlier rain had turned to what forecasters call a wintry mix, and the temperature began dropping. Luckily, the temperatures in the valley stayed above freezing. The higher elevations, with a four-degree lower temperature for every thousand feet of altitude, would start getting either ice or snow with some accumulation expected.

As I pulled from Buddy's parking lot, an eighteen-wheeler passed me and quickly switched back into the right lane, spraying slush and brine all over my Ford. I thought I had left all that winter ambience back in New York.

It took me the predicted twenty minutes to reach the station. In the lobby, a huge plasma screen TV showed the current on-air program. Jed Clampet, Ellie Mae and Granny conversed out by their ce-ment pond. Jed looked amazed at something Granny said and replied, "Weeell doggies!" On the other walls, plaques and framed photos showed highlights of the station's past fifty years. I saw Ronald Reagan cutting a ribbon, opening the 1982 World's Fair in Knoxville. Howard Baker and a former mayor stood side by side. Dolly Parton and Kenny Rogers posed for a picture.

The receptionist buzzed me in from the lobby and escorted me past rooms with all sorts of technical equipment. She ushered me into a glassed-in conference room with a long oval table and eight padded armchairs. Tess Haley and her co-host Russ Gibbons sat there waiting for me. Tess introduced me to Russell.

"Haven't we met before?" he asked.

"We have. My wife was on your show about a year ago. You have a good memory."

"Oh, really. What did she talk about?"

"She was pitching a program for the county library. She does publicity for them. I stood around acting like her chauffeur and hired muscle."

They both smiled at my classic humor.

"Actually, I tagged along to meet all the pretty girls," I said.

Tess smiled again for me. She was very pretty—short, with almost black hair down below her shoulders, big brown eyes and built like a swimsuit model. But since I'm interested in looking at a complete package, I'll mention her great personality, too. We met formally a few months earlier when she televised the ceremony where Bettye and Stan were promoted to sergeants.

Russell was about my height, but heavier. He acted friendly, smiled a lot and had the kind of face that would make women think he'd be a good husband and father.

"How can we help?" Tess asked.

"As I said before, an FBI agent spoke with your station manager. She asked him if there was anyone known to have a grudge against Rachel or if he knew about an obsessed fan who wrote to her, stalked her or…who knows? He told her about a guy who ended up in prison partly because of an investigative piece Rachel did three years ago. The agent apparently didn't speak with anyone other than the manager. I thought by speaking with you and some others, someone might remember something helpful."

"We went around and spoke to everyone here today," Tess said, "and called anyone not working. No one seems to know much more than we do, but we'll take you around and introduce you—you may be able to jog someone's memory."

"Okay, good," I said.

Tess continued. "While Russ and I were kicking this around, we remembered someone—he wasn't really a stalker, but more like a pest."

Pests can fit nicely into the weirdo category.

"Rachel did a segment on an ex-cop," she said. "A guy fired for using excessive force or something like that. She interviewed him briefly and asked to hear his side of the story. He must have thought she sympathized with him. After the story aired, he kept calling and asking her to have lunch with him. He wanted to 'tell his whole story'." Tess made imaginary quotation marks in the air.

"Do you remember his name or any more about him?"

Tess and Russell looked at each other. She shook her head. He shrugged.

"Not much," Russ said. "I remember he'd been in the Army and served in Iraq or Afghanistan, I think. Sorry, I can't remember what department he worked for. Blount County Sheriff maybe."

"Yes," Tess said. "It was Blount County. Rachel interviewed him in Maryville at the Justice Center. You know what? Tommy would know."

"Tommy?" I said.

"Tom McCall, Rachel's former co-anchor, the one before Jack Larson."

"Oh sure," I said, "the guy who wore more makeup than Rachel."

"That's Tommy," she said with a big smile.

Russ laughed.

"Where is he now?" I asked.

"He went to an affiliate in Denver," she said. "I'll get you his number."

The three of us made the rounds of the station personnel. I learned nothing. Jack Larson, the new co-anchor, wasn't in yet. I'd let Bonnie Rowatt call him. Tess gave me Tom McCall's phone number in Denver.

"Is there a quiet place I can use to call Tommy?"

"Sure," Russ said. "My office is this way." He extended an arm pointing me in the right direction. "You can spread out on my desk—make yourself at home."

It was still early in the Mountain Time zone. I hoped Tommy did the morning news, and I'd find him at work rather than at home. I called the Denver station, spoke to an operator and got switched to an assistant executive producer. She told me Tommy was in, but at an important meeting.

"Miss, I understand how some meetings can be important, but I'm from the Police Department in the city of Prospect, Tennessee. I need to speak with Mr. McCall immediately. It's extremely important. I'm not sure if you folks have gotten the news yet, but Tom's former partner has been kidnapped. We need his help badly."

"Kidnapped? Oh my God."

"Yeah."

"Where did you say you were from?" She sounded a little dubious.

"Prospect, Tennessee."

"I've never heard of that," she said.

"I'm not surprised. Until this morning, I'd never heard of Denver either."

There was silence for a few seconds, and then she laughed a little.

"Hold on, please. I'll get Tommy, Mr...? Ah...?"

"Jenkins, Sam. Police chief. One each, tall, dark, and handsome."

She laughed again. I'll bet she liked me. Two minutes later, McCall picked up.

"This is Tom McCall. What did you say happened?"

I told him.

"Good Lord!" I assumed no one out west had received the news.

"Mr. McCall, I received information that some time ago Rachel interviewed a policeman or ex-policeman who persisted in calling and asking her to lunch. Do you know anything about that?"

"Yes, I sure do remember. A Blount County deputy. He got fired for something. I'm not sure what. He told Rachel he'd been in the war, came back to his job and then got fired."

"What was his name?" I asked.

"Oh, damn. I should remember, but it was long ago. Daniel, Darrell, Darnell? Darrell maybe. An unusual last name. Can't remember it though."

"Did this guy really make a pest of himself?"

"Yes, he was constantly calling her and leaving messages. I think he's the reason why she never answers her phone before she hears a message."

"Did he ever come to the studio to see her? Ever stalk her, wait in the parking lot, anything like that?"

"Yes, he did try to see her. She made the mistake, if you can call it a mistake, of being nice to him. When he got fired, she asked him to tell his story. But once wasn't enough for him. He wanted to keep talking to her."

"Were the police ever called?"

"No, not that I know of. I don't think it was ever necessary. The time he came to the station, Rachel asked George Clarke, the former advertising sales manager, to tell this guy to bug off. George was a pretty big guy himself. He took care of it, and the ex-cop sort of faded away after that."

"Okay, so we've got an ex-Blount County cop—Darrell or something close to that—who was fired. He also did recent time in a war zone. Correct?"

"Yes."

"Do you know if he was a former active duty soldier or an activated guardsman or reservist?"

"I can't remember from which component, but yes, he had been called up. He worked as a deputy, then went away for some time and came back."

"Ever see the man?"

"Sure. He was tall, beefy—well built, with short, dark hair. Other than that, an average face. I might recognize a photo."

"Great. Anything else I should know?" I asked.

"If I think of anything I'll call you. Give me your number."

I did.

"Will you find her?" he asked.

"Yeah, I'm going to find her. I'm not supposed to say that, but yes, I'm going to find her and bring her home. I just wish I did it two days ago. Hey, thanks for all your help. It gives me something to go on."

"You bet. Call me and... Just please call me when you get her back."

"I will. Thanks again."

Then I dialed the Blount County Criminal Investigation Division and asked for Jackie Shuman.

Chapter Fourteen

"You remember a deputy named something like Darrell, Darnell, or Daniel who got fired not too long ago, possibly for excessive force?" I asked Jackie.

"How 'bout Darrell Korner? Got fired for punchin' out a county commissioner."

"Sounds promising. Tell me about him."

I spun Russ's high-back swivel chair to the side and crossed my legs. Several framed family photos sat on his desk—two boys, a younger girl and a pretty, blonde wife.

"Darrell locked up the man's son for DUI," Jackie said. "The ol' man tried to git it squashed. Darrell took offense and tagged 'em. Sheriff fired him."

"You make it sound so simple. What's this Darrell look like?"

"'Bout six-one or two. Solid, mebbe two-ten or so, dark hair. Nice guy."

"Sounds like my man. He get activated or federalized with a unit that went to the Middle East?"

"Yep, part o' the 278th. Did eighteen months or so active duty when they had went to I-raq."

"Can you go to your personnel people and get me his home of record, DOB, local and out-of-town relatives…anything you can think of that would be important?"

"Sure. Take me a few minutes or so. I'll have ta call ya back."

"Okay. Call Bettye and give her all the info. I'll ring you later. And thanks, Jackie. I owe you for this."

"No sweat. You like Darrell fer this kidnappin'?"

"Startin' to look that way, partner."

"Sam, you listen close now." Jackie lowered his voice and sounded serious. "If it comes ta y'all goin' toe ta toe with Darrell, you be careful. He is one tough boy. Good with a gun, too."

Once again, the thought, why me? came to mind.

* * * *

I left Knoxville and headed south on slick roads. The rain continued, and the temperature hung there, just above freezing. When I reached the spot where Route 129 intersects with the Pellissippi Parkway, I got an unobstructed view of the mountains. Snow covered the peaks, giving them the look of a Bundt cake heavily dusted with powdered sugar. Compared to the slop I'd just driven through, it offered a little cheerful beauty to an otherwise lousy morning.

As I continued driving past the airport on the 'Motor Mile', a stretch of road littered with auto dealers, fast food restaurants and a mobile home manufacturer who used an inflatable twenty-foot gorilla to draw one's attention, my cell phone sounded off. Bettye told me the hospital called saying John Leckmanski had just regained consciousness and was fit to receive an official visitor. I saw no reason my smiling face shouldn't be the first to welcome him back among the living.

After driving through Alcoa and into Maryville, past more burger joints, gas stations and super markets, I stopped at Blount Memorial Hospital.

It took me a few minutes to locate Leckmanski; he'd been moved from the ICU to a private room. I found him awake but still groggy. Bandages covered almost half his head.

"Man, I hope you feel better than you look," I said.

"Hey, Sam, good to see you." His voice sounded weak. "I feel like shit since I woke up, but I'm alive. How's Rachel?"

I let out a little air before answering and almost felt ashamed to tell him. "The guy who clocked you took her, John. I'm still looking for them. The FBI is on this, too."

"Ah, shit, man. I should have stopped him. But he pulled a gun and hit me before I could connect with the camera."

"I figured that. Listen, you did what you could. Don't beat yourself up over this. He's already done enough."

John closed his eyes and gently shook his head. "I shoulda played it differently. I feel responsible."

"Join the club."

He blinked and squinted and then looked ready to ask another question. But I wasn't there to give answers.

"You were unconscious for a long time. Feel good enough to answer a question or two?"

"Sure. I'd like to help."

I grabbed John's chart from the Plexiglas cradle at the foot of his bed. Between his injuries and the Percodan the attending physician prescribed for pain, John looked like he might nod off at any time.

"Tell me what he looked like," I said.

A man in a hospital gown walked past the doorway dragging a rolling IV rack. Two tubes connected him to the bags hanging from the chrome-plated device.

"Couple inches taller than you," John said. "Six-two, maybe. Over two-hundred, dark hair, like a grown-out crew cut. Had on a desert camo jacket and blue jeans."

"Was he alone?"

"I think so. Didn't see anyone else in the van."

"Tell me about the van."

"A big one, a stretch van—white Ford—not new, but clean. Some kind of roof rack, too. Not many windows, just up front and in the back—like a workman's van."

"The tape in your camera didn't show him or the van. You didn't notice a plate number, did you?"

"No such luck."

"Damn good description though. I'm pretty sure I can ID him. Maybe an ex-cop Rachel interviewed once."

"An ex-cop? You gotta be kiddin'."

"Maybe not. I'll try and scare up several photos of the suspect for you to check out. If I can't get back to show you, I'll send someone else."

"Sure. Whenever you're ready."

"Good," I said. "With the amount of info I'm getting on this guy, I've got enough to call Oliveri at the FBI and talk about search warrants. Then we'll go from there."

John nodded and winced as he moved his head. "Sam, you've got to find her."

"Yeah, partner, I sure do."

* * * *

I arrived back at the PD twenty minutes later. Bettye had prepared a list with possibilities of a van having HV in the plate number and a bigger list with all plates containing an HV in the sequence. Jackie Shuman had already called Bettye with the information from Darrell Korner's personnel file and some non-recorded things, too. He also emailed ID photos to Bettye's computer. I called him back.

"Does your man Darrell drive a white Ford van?" I asked.

"Nope, got him a black Monte Carlo Super Sport more'n twenty years old, but super clean—real nice. I mean be-utiful. He loved that car."

"Him or you?" Sitting at my desk, I tried to shrug off my jacket and encountered trouble with the second sleeve.

"Him or me what?"

"Hang on a second," I said. "I'm trying to shed my suit jacket." After getting squared away, I picked up my phone again. "Who loved the car most, him or you? It sounded like you got all misty when you mentioned the black Super Sport."

"I'd love ta own somethin' like that, but he wouldn't never sell that car for a van."

"Darrell drove a white Ford stretch-van with a roof rack when he grabbed Rachel. The plate had an HV in the sequence. Bettye pulled some possible numbers and got a list of recorded owners. I'll read a few names. Tell me if you know anyone."

"I'm listenin'."

I rattled off several names. When I mentioned a Glenn Copeland, Jackie stopped me.

"I believe Glenn Copeland is Darrell's uncle. Man's got a plumbin' business in Murrvull. When Darrell got canned, the uncle gave him some

110

work now and ag'in."

"Jackie, I think we've got our man. Now I need to find out where he is. As far as you know, is the address you gave current?"

"Fer as I know. He ain't got him no wife. Parents live out to the Asbury area off Sevierville Road. If he ain't worked much, he might'a give up his apartment—maybe livin' with his momma and daddy."

"I appreciate your help, kid. You want in on this if we need a crime scene tech?"

"Sure, why not? FBI gonna like that?"

"We'll see. Thanks. I'll talk to you."

I walked out to Bettye's desk.

"Sergeant Lambert, you are fantastic with that computer and an absolute princess. One of the names you found is the uncle of my best suspect."

"Sam, that's great. What are we doing next?"

"Either Ralph or I will get warrants and hit his apartment and the parents' house—uncle's, too. I'll call Ralphie now. For this much work, we'll need FBI manpower."

She nodded.

"See, the Feds are good for something after all."

"You're so bad," she said.

I called Oliveri on his cell phone, gave him the information I'd gathered and asked a few questions.

"What do you know about that missing ex-con?" I said. "You have a physical description from the parole officer?"

"Your description of the doer sort of eliminates him. I got five-nine, one-fifty to one-sixty, dirty-blond hair, last seen with a short beard. Not exactly what the old man or Leckmanski saw."

"Can I find important witnesses or what? You getting the warrants, or shall I?" The good feeling of finding a witness and the victim confirming his information lingered on. I did a three-sixty in my swivel chair while Ralph spoke.

"I'll get them. It'll give Bonnie something to do. She's a lawyer, I'll have you know."

"Oy! Young lawyer becomes a federal cop. And she's such a nice Scottish girl."

"Sometimes I wonder about our hiring practices," Ralph said.

"I've wondered about you guys for years. Now that we know all the dirt about J. Edgar."

"Yeah, what can I tell you? Bonnie's new. She'll learn. Hoover…past history."

"Okay, paisan, call me with the whens and wheres of the warrants," I said. "I'd like to speak with Korner's parents. Put me with that team."

"You got it. I'll talk to you. Now go put on your fightin' clothes."

Chapter Fifteen

From the PD, I went home to change out of my suit and trench coat into something more appropriate for executing search warrants—'fighting clothes' as Ralph called them. I also took Jackie Shuman seriously and assumed Darrell Korner maybe a desperate character and a tough man to take into custody.

After changing, I went into the basement and exchanged my six-shot Smith and Wesson for a seventeen-shot Glock 9mm. I used a whole box of fifty rounds loading up the gun and two spare magazines. I slid the Glock and its holster onto my belt and clipped a double magazine pouch over my left hip.

As an afterthought, I loaded my small Chief's Special and strapped it on in an ankle holster. Next, I began putting together my kit bag in case the affair stretched out beyond that evening and we had to start a big search for Darrell.

I took my old Army duffle bag, which I'd modified by adding a full-length zipper. It made finding small items easier. I dropped in a pair of binoculars and enough warm clothing to keep me comfortable during a cold mountain evening.

Then I loaded up four thirty-round magazines for my CAR-15, a cut-down version of the Vietnam era assault rifle. Three of them went into a pouch I could sling over my shoulder and the fourth I seated into the magazine well of the gun. All that went into the big bag, too.

Rather than walk through the house with enough gear to look like I planned on going to war and give Kate reason to get upset, I used the basement exit into the garage and then walked outside to the trunk of the

Ford. Someone might think all my logistics looked like overkill. Perhaps, but if you have any sense, you don't bring a knife to a gunfight.

Back inside, I ate a couple sandwiches and chatted with Kate about my day and what I learned.

"You're a good man, Sambo. You haven't rested much during this one, even with the FBI helping."

"I'm not sure those people at the Bureau see themselves as my helpers. But it makes no difference. With luck, we'll wrap this up tonight. I hope so."

"Me, too. That poor girl. I hope she's okay."

"I intend to bring her home, Kats, as soon as possible."

"I know you do. And I know you will."

"I wish everyone was as confident as you."

"They haven't lived with you as long as me."

"Wanna be cheerleader for my search team?"

"Probably not."

"Then I'd better go."

"Can I get you anything before you leave?"

"I guess a double scotch is out of the question."

"Wouldn't be professional smelling like a Highland distillery."

"Appearances are important."

"That jacket doesn't appear too warm. Are you taking something more wintery?"

"I've got a bag full of necessities in the car."

"Like what?"

"Things."

"Samuel?"

"An extra gun, gloves, a field jacket. Things."

"What gun will I find missing from the cabinet downstairs?"

"Trust me. I know what I'm doing."

"I know that, but I still worry. Good luck, and be careful."

* * * *

Three teams executed the search warrants simultaneously. During operations like that, the FBI generally utilizes a cast of thousands. Well, maybe a couple dozen agents. The unofficial FBI motto must be, if three will do, use eight or nine.

I've enforced many search and arrest warrants during my time in law enforcement. Usually, the basic job can be handled by two detectives and a couple of uniformed cops as backup. Cover the front door and cover the back. Most FBI supervisors liked to operate under the shock and awe theory. That, of course, can't hurt. You just need the time and manpower. But for all the man-hours expended that evening, we came up with bupkis, zilch, nuthin'.

A good man I knew from the Knoxville field office, Marty Saunders, ran the team at Darrell's apartment. Darrell wasn't home, but we all figured that before anyone got there, and they didn't need an invitation from the homeowner to enter and search.

They found his Black Chevy Super Sport in the parking lot under a protective canvas cover.

Five agents tossed a neat and clean, but unimaginatively decorated, one-bedroom flat in a strip of eight units, making up a single-story dwelling on a side street in a residential neighborhood.

Darrell kept a limited library consisting of old issues of *The Army Times*, *The American Rifleman* and *Guns and Ammo* magazines. That said something about our suspect.

He also owned a computer. Marty told me it took one of the more computer literate agents all of about sixty seconds to get past his password of DJK349—his initials and old three-digit badge number. The only interesting thing found was a folder in his documents section that held four photos of Rachel Williamson, downloaded from either the station's website or Google Images.

Ralph checked the uncle's place and found both Glenn Copeland and his wife cooperative. Glenn admitted Darrell might have borrowed one of his vans. He hadn't formally lent it to his nephew, but when it went missing, he believed Darrell, who had a key, probably took it. He assumed for some money-making enterprise like hauling firewood. He hadn't seen Darrell in a week, could think of no place where he might be and never reported his van stolen.

I hit the parents' home. Bonnie Rowatt and four other agents assisted. Or did I assist them? I wasn't sure.

Mr. and Mrs. Korner and I chatted for a long time. Bonnie suffered my schmoozing the old folks, who were a couple of years younger than me. The father seemed like a nice enough guy, but the mother helped most.

"Mr. Jenkins," she said, "you told us you'd been a soldier. So I guess ya know how our Darrell mighta felt through all that's happened this last year."

"I didn't see what happened, Mrs. Korner, but I might have a better idea of what's going on inside his head than someone else."

She had her son's best interests at heart and thought by telling us about Darrell's difficult times, I'd feel sorry for her boy and remember his pain when we met.

The Korners' home was neatly kept, but hadn't been redecorated since the 1970s. We all sat in the living room on plaid Early American-style upholstered furniture. Bonnie and I declined Mrs. Korner's offer of iced tea.

"Darrel got outta the Army after three years o' active duty," Earlene Korner said. "He didn't find him a job rot away. He looked, but no one was hirin'. Took almost a year 'fore he got called by the Blount County Sheriff."

"That's not uncommon. I collected unemployment for almost a year when I got back from Vietnam."

"While he was lookin' he needed money so, he signed up with the National Guard here in Murrvull."

"You mean the armory out on Highway 321 heading to Friendsville?"

"Yes, sir." Mr. Korner said. "1st battalion, 278th Armored Cavalry Regiment."

"How long did your son work as a deputy before his unit got called up?" Bonnie asked.

"Almost three years, ma'am," she said. "He was a good deputy, too. Got him three commendations from the Sheriff."

"And then he and his unit were sent to Iraq." I said.

"Yes, sir." Mr. Korner took a turn offering specific information. "They was stationed north o' Baghdad. Darrell didn't like it much. 'Cept those Kurdish people, he liked them well enough. Then he got inta that ambush and won him a Silver Star. Our boy's a gen-u-ine war hero, Mr.

Jenkins. Earlene, git Darrell's papers."

Being awarded a Silver Star for conspicuous valor is not a usual occurrence in the military. You've got to earn it through extraordinary effort and heroism.

Mrs. Korner returned to the living room and handed me a black leatherette Army certificate folder. "You kin read what he did fer yerse'f," she said. "It's all rot there on the medal paperwork."

According to the copy of his award, Buck-Sergeant Darrell Korner had been part of a small support services convoy going from point A to point B when several IEDs—improvised explosive devices—also known as roadside bombs, were command detonated, devastating the lead vehicle and damaging the next two in line.

After the diversionary explosion, indigenous combatants—Al Qaeda terrorists or unidentified radical religious zealots or some other anti-American militia group—opened up on the soldiers with automatic small arms fire and rocket propelled grenades.

Initially, several GIs were seriously wounded including a young lieutenant in the lead vehicle. After an RPG flipped the officer's Hum-Vee, Darrell found himself left as ranking member of the detachment, responsible to muster his troops in a resistance and help them survive.

These soldiers were all, in effect, armed truck drivers. They were not Special Forces, not Rangers and not light infantrymen, trained for close encounters of the nastiest kind.

To make a possibly long story shorter, Sergeant Korner, who had infantry training and experience from his active-duty days, established communications with his base camp. He cut through the chaos of that surprise attack and the subsequent firefight and organized the non-wounded, cared for the injured and recovered the bodies of two dead soldiers.

Quickly and efficiently, he secured his people behind the best cover he could find and then repeatedly exposed himself to the hostile fire and brought three newly wounded comrades to a safer location. Much of this occurred after Darrell was wounded himself.

Then he did his best to supervise sustained and disciplined fire on the enemy until tactical air support reached the pinned-down GIs and drove off or killed the belligerents.

Award certificates always make the recipient sound heroic, but I knew enough about soldering to recognize conduct above and beyond the call of duty.

"A Silver Star is nothing to sneeze at," I said, "but had I been Darrell's CO, I would have recommended him for the Distinguished Service Cross and made a giant pain-in-the-ass of myself until he got it."

I handed the folder back to Mrs. Korner. "I've been around the military block enough times to know that what your son accomplished was well worth the higher award. It came damn close to being worth a Medal of Honor. I'm impressed."

My comment brought a tear to Earlene Korner's eye. She hugged the black folder to her breast and said, "Oh, Lord have mercy. What has our boy gone and done?"

After his return to CONUS—Army lingo for the Continental United States, Darrell got back his old job at the Blount County Sheriff's Office.

And he did fine after his return to civilian life until one evening when he decided to do his job to the best of his ability. That big mistake came one night after he observed an intoxicated driver and arrested him. The Korner's version of the incident coincided with Jackie Shuman's official account.

The drunk turned out to be the son of a county commissioner who received the arrestee's one permissible phone call. After the son's invitation to meet him at the sheriff's office, Commissioner X, I'll call him that because I had yet to learn his name, appeared at the Justice Center where the boy's arrest was being processed.

Mr. X believed his status as a local legislator and public servant entitled him and his son to a 'get-out-of-jail-free' card. Darrell didn't agree. So, when Daddy started to bundle up his kid and head for home, Officer Korner protested. And when push came to shove, big Darrell clocked Commissioner X.

Hearing the scuffle, the duty lieutenant intervened and hustled Commissioner X and his son off without further ado. Commissioner X then called the Sheriff who, as with most sheriffs across the nation, was an elected politician first and a cop second. Said fisticuffs immediately cost Darrell his job.

There is no such thing as civil service protection or tenure for a deputy in Blount County, Tennessee. Likewise, there was no judicial machine or due-process guarantee to determine if Darrell Korner acted with justification in his actions. The political monster just ate him alive.

The rest of the saga I surmised. Rachel Williamson might have been the only person interested in this story who was also concerned with listening to Darrell's side. Perhaps Darrell became infatuated with her—I couldn't blame him for that.

All things led me to believe Darrell Korner was the man who went too far with his passion to get closer to Rachel by assaulting John Leckmanski and abducting the object of his affection. I really hoped that he hadn't totally snapped and... I tried to put the other possibilities out of my mind.

So, it came down to finding Darrell as quickly as possible. Unfortunately, Ma and Pa Korner could offer no helpful ideas about where their son might be. They seemed sincere, but I've been fooled before, and they didn't look like stones from which I could draw blood.

I thanked Mr. and Mrs. Korner for their time, gave them my card and asked them to call me if they heard from their son. Bonnie gave them her card, too. I guess it made her feel important. All of the agents involved in the search left the Korners' house and began to wander off toward their vehicles. I stopped on the front walk. Bonnie and another agent named Al Hahn stopped, too.

A foggy mist clogged the air. I watched it swirl in the illumination of an overhead streetlight. Bonnie used an umbrella. Al wore a cap. Like a putz, I stood there getting wet.

I turned to Bonnie and said, "I need to speak with you about something personal."

She looked at me with a questioning expression—a wrinkled brow and a squint.

"Anything you have to say can be said in front of Al."

"No, it can't," I insisted. "Al, would you give us a minute, please?"

Al Hahn had more time in the chow line of an FBI snack bar than Bonnie had on the job. He knew the story. Al nodded and walked toward a gold Crown Victoria parked nearby.

"What?" she said, with obvious aggravation showing.

"When you spoke to the station manager at WNXX did you question other employees?"

"He assured me he had and gave me all the information they knew."

"I spoke with two people I know at the station. They led me to Tom McCall, Rachel's former partner. From those three, I learned about Darrell."

She said nothing, but rolled her eyes and made a face.

"Look, I'm not your supervisor, and I'm not responsible for FBI in-service training. But I needed to tell you this. You were there two days ago. You should have learned about Korner back then."

"Hey, I... What are you implying?"

I held up my hand to stop her noise.

"Bonnie, I'm not jumping in your shit here. I'm just pointing something out. I'm also not going to tell Ralph if you don't. He's the honcho of this operation, and I don't want to put him on the spot of making a decision about some theoretical right thing to do. I thought you needed to know... And I needed to tell you."

She looked at me for a long moment. Her face relaxed, and her expression softened.

"Okay, thank you," she said. "I guess you're right." The attitude seemed to fade away.

"You're welcome... And now you owe me one." I smiled.

Finally, she smiled, too. Even girls who hate me can't resist the old Jenkins' smile. I pointed at her with my index finger and let my thumb fall like the hammer on a gun, a gesture Philip Marlowe called the gunman's salute.

With my attempt at supervision over, Bonnie left with Al Hahn and drove away. I called Ralph to see how all the players made out and learned we suffered three relative strikeouts all around.

I stood in the brisk misty air for a few moments and then dropped my cell phone into my coat pocket.

It was the end of a day, the end of a week and I was at a loss for what to do next. I'd spend the rest of the night twisting my brain for an innovation. We needed to find Darrel Korner.

Chapter Sixteen

"It's Saturday, sweetie. Don't you think taking a day off would be good for you? Take some time to relax? Get a fresh perspective on things?" Kate asked over breakfast.

"I doubt the duty FBI agent at the Williamson house is going to learn anything waiting for a phone call," I said. "This kid doesn't want a ransom. He wants to be with Rachel for whatever reason he's conjured up in his mind."

I scooped a spoonful of maple-flavored oatmeal into my mouth.

"Besides, it's not good for this kind of an ordeal to drag on, and I've got a thing or two I want to do today. If I have any luck, today and tomorrow might just blend into one."

"Running yourself into the ground won't be any good for you or Rachel."

After a bite of sourdough toast, I took a long drink of Sumatran coffee. "Never happen, Kats. As long as I'm eating regularly, I'm able to leap tall buildings at a single bound."

"Be sure you don't misplace your glasses and phone booth, Clark."

Just before 8 a.m., I started out for the hospital, wanting to show John Leckmanski the photos I collected —Darrell's head shots from the driver's license bureau, the Sheriff's office and a recent snapshot from his mother. We needed to know if he had done anything to change his appearance.

After taking the elevator to the third floor, I got lost only once and finally found John's room—just where I left it the day before. I hate big buildings. It would take me thirty days to remember how to find the men's room in that place.

They had removed the bandages from John's head wound. A number of butterfly clips and sutures held the gash closed. I hoped he hadn't looked in the mirror.

"Jesus Christ, John," I said. "Who was your plastic surgeon, Doctor Frankenstein?"

"Nice of you to notice."

"That guy really clocked you a good one."

"Yeah, tell me about it."

In the background, a few bells rang, and a female voice on the PA system asked a certain doctor to call Nurse's Station Three North.

"Still have a headache?" I asked.

"Only when I laugh at amateur comedians."

"Okay, I'll be brief...and serious. Two orderlies confiscated the golumpki and beer I tried to smuggle in for you. So, after you look at these pictures, I'll leave you to get your sponge bath or whatever else the nursing staff has in mind for you."

He smiled and grimaced all in one fluid motion. "I guess the beer could mess up my medication, but why would they deny me stuffed cabbage? Discriminatory to those with a European heritage. I love golumpki."

"Next time I'll bring a partner to create a diversion. No one should be forced to eat hospital food."

As soon as he looked at the photos, he tapped the recent snapshot and confirmed Darrell had done nothing to alter his appearance. Strange, I thought, an ex-cop should be smart and do something to keep from being recognized.

* * * *

Back in my car, I made a call, hoping to find someone who would lead me to know more about one aspect of my suspect's life.

A male voice answered the phone. "Crawford Sports. Kin I he'p ya?"

"Is Randy there?" I asked.

In the background, WIVK played one of the latest country hits.

"Hang on. I'll git 'im."

Two years earlier, when Jackie Shuman brought him to the Fraternal Order of Police range, I met Randy Crawford. In addition to running a ma and pa sporting goods store in Maryville, Randy served as the operations officer at the 1st of the 278th ACR.

"This is Randy," he said.

"Sam Jenkins, Randy. How you doin'?"

"Real fine, Sam. You doin' aw rot today?"

"I need some help, young Major. You got a minute for me?"

"Sure do."

I thought I heard Garth Brooks singing on the radio. Or was it Toby Keith? I knew it wasn't Johnny Cash.

"We're looking for a guy you know from his days in the Guard—Darrell Korner. Remember him?"

"You bet. Had him in my company when I was a captain. Good soldier. I's real sorry he didn't re-up. Whatcha lookin' fer him for?"

"Some pretty bad stuff. He's just a suspect right now, but he looks like my best hope."

"Uh-oh."

"I have a bit of info on him," I said, "but I really want to know everything I can about him. Anything I learn might help me to find this guy."

"I understand. You want me to pull his file for you?"

"I'd really like to speak with some of his close friends. At least one person who served with him overseas, maybe."

"Yeah, okay. As you know, we went over as a unit and stayed that way when we made up the regimental combat team. I was the S-3 then and didn't have much to do with Darrell personally. But I'd say if anyone knows Darrell Korner, it's another sergeant from that company, man named Rory O'Roarke."

The name sounded more Irish than Saint Patrick. "Rory O'Roarke? A Jewish guy?"

"Jewish?"

"Never mind. How do I find Rory?"

"I'll call him. You want to meet him here?"

"Sure. Soon as possible."

"How bad's the stuff y'all want Korner for? Kin you say?"

"Good old-fashioned felony assault to start. He put a personal friend into the hospital. Then add kidnapping of the woman who was with the guy he assaulted."

"Lord have mercy! That the TV newswoman we're talkin' about? They're personal friends o' yours?"

"Yeah, Darrell isn't one of my favorite people right now."

"I guess I wouldn't want to be Darrell Korner when you find him."

"The easy way is always best."

"Sounds like you're leavin' your options open."

"Have to. Always plan for the worst and hope for something better. You know the drill."

"I hear that," he said.

"I need to know why a squared away guy like Korner turned into a head case. I've got to get into his brain to guess where he is and what he's up to."

"Korner always seemed to have his head screwed on tight," Randy said. "Cain't imagine why he'd go and do somethin' like that. Lord have mercy."

"I suppose a screw loosened up somewhere along the line."

"I hear ya. Lemme call O'Roarke and git him here right quick."

"Thanks, Randy."

When Major Randy Crawford said jump, apparently Sergeant Rory O'Roarke asked, "How high, sir?"

In thirty minutes, I found myself driving west on US 321, turning south on Broadway in Maryville, and then merging onto 129 south. Every utility pole featured some illuminated Christmas decoration bolted to it. I could almost hear the kilowatt hours ticking away—our tax dollars at work.

In another five minutes, I parked my Ford in the lot of a shopping center that had seen better days. There was a bank, a private mailbox store, a chain restaurant that sold inedible pizza, a vacant super market, several more empty stores and Crawford's Sports Center.

I parked next to a white heavy-duty Ford pick-up with 'Support Tennessee Fishing' plates and met Randy Crawford and Rory O'Roarke in the back room of the sports shop. I explained my mission to Sergeant O'Roarke, a redheaded guy in his mid-forties who, in the real world, collected his paychecks from the Blount County Highway Department.

"Shoot," O'Roarke said, "Darrell was a good boy—a good soldier. All the guys liked him. He'd done three years active duty. Not ever' one served active time—people looked up to him some. He was airborne, ya know."

"Who'd he serve with on active duty?"

"173rd Brigade, whole time."

"In Italy?"

"Uh-huh. You know where they was?"

I nodded and asked about Darrell's military occupational specialty. "Yeah, I do. You know his MOS back then?"

"Eleven-Bravo," he said, meaning a light weapons infantryman.

"Darrell good with firearms?"

"Yes, sir, he was. Better'n me, Better'n lots 'o others, too."

"He a gun nut or anything extreme?"

"No, sir, I'd not say that. Jest good with his weapon."

"Is he a hunter?"

"Yes, sir. Bear and deer. Went most ever' year."

"Know where he went to hunt? He have a cabin or a special place?"

"He used ta go with some ol' boys he had went to hi-skoo with. I ain't sure jest where. I believe one of 'em did have a place. Mebbe a couple owned it t'gether. Don't know where."

"You a hunter, too, Rory?"

"No, sir, I fish. Bass mostly."

The back room of Randy's shop was full of boxes. Everything from spinning reels to baseball gloves to figure skates were crammed on shelves, against the wall and scattered around the floor in a very unmilitary fashion.

"Darrell seems to have done something very out of character for him," I said. "Did you see a change in him somewhere along the line? Anything like a problem after he fought in that big ambush?"

"He didn't say much ta no one after that. You know, jest continue ta march—do yer job, put in yer time. But he was more quiet, an' much more serious."

"He kill many people in that ambush?"

"Sir, others said he kilt a bunch. If it weren't fer Darrell, they said, they wouldn'ta held out 'til them gunships got there. Darrell's a hero, sir. No lie."

"I know he is, Rory."

A radio announcer in the background spoke of a contest where the tenth caller could win a pair of tickets to the Grand Ol' Opry. I didn't write down the phone number.

"Sir," O'Roarke said, "Major Crawford said you's in the military yerse'f."

"Yeah. Army. Full and part-time. I retired back in '88."

"Do ya drills with the Guard?"

"Reserves."

"Y'all sound like it," he said.

I nodded. "Shows, huh?"

He grinned and nodded.

"Gentlemen, thanks for all your help," I said. "I appreciate your time."

Crawford and O'Roarke were both weekend warriors, people who had lost eighteen months of their lives not long ago and were destined to do the same thing all over again in the not too distant future. I listen to WNXX for the local news, but I knew every newspaper and TV station had been speaking about the next anticipated activation that would put these people back in the Middle East.

Soldiers make little money for the service they render. Sometimes they receive awards to make up for the lack of salary. But medals aren't gifts, and nothing comes for free. I asked myself: What did Darrell Korner have taken away from him? What did he trade to get his Silver Star?

* * * *

On the way back to Prospect, I stopped again at Korner's parents' home. As we sat in their living room, Mrs. Korner poured three glasses of iced tea.

"David cain't use sugar 'cause o' his diabetes," she said, pointed at her husband, and pushed a Mason jar with a long-shanked spoon stuck into a heap of sugar across the coffee table to me.

"No thanks, I'm fine like this," I said.

"Yes, sir. Suit yerse'f."

She smiled as her husband took a sip of tea.

"I understand Darrell is a hunter," I said. "And he had a regular group of friends he went out with. You folks know who these men are?"

They looked at each other but didn't respond.

"You a hunter yourself, Mr. Korner?"

"No, sir, I ain't never been that hungry."

I looked at Darrell's mother. "Mrs. Korner, I need to find your son before this drags on much more. The longer it takes, the worse it's going to be for him."

The pair of them stared at me with blank expressions.

"You understand that if the FBI mobilizes a full-scale ground search," I said, with my eyes locked on Mrs. Korner, "anyone who finds Darrell would be justified under the law to shoot him for kidnapping that woman?"

The shock of the idea affected her. She shot a quick glance at her husband and then looked back at me with fear in her eyes.

"Darrell and his friends from hi-skoo," she said. "They been friends fer years. They had went huntin' jest this past November. Couple o' them boys owns a cabin up somewhere near Happy Valley or Six Mile or somewhere thereabouts. I'm not sure jest where."

Sitting on top of a cupboard, an old clock ticked loudly. On the half hour, a chime struck once.

"If Darrell isn't at his place, isn't with you and isn't with his Uncle Glenn, he's got to be somewhere. It's too cold to live in Glenn's van," I said.

"Yes, sir, we know," she said.

"Will one of you please give me the names of his friends?" I must have sounded desperate.

"Yes, sir, I will," Mr. Korner said. "Will ya promise ta go easy on my boy? Will ya promise not ta kill him?"

David Korner made it sound like he was speaking to an animal control officer about his dog running loose in a populated neighborhood.

I shook my head. "I don't want to hurt your son, Mr. Korner, Mrs. Korner. The more I learn about Darrell, the more I remember my time as a soldier and might have a good idea what he's going through. I just want to find him, and take Mrs. Williamson back to her family."

David gave me the names of three men, and I started back to the PD. On the way, I called Bettye at home and told her what I needed. She said she had taken her young son to the doctor earlier that morning, but volunteered to get her mother to sit with the sick boy and come to work.

We'd start tracking Darrell's friends, with luck find a location for the cabin where he might be holed up, and then mobilize a rescue team. In Vietnam, we called them bright light teams. I hoped we could soon shed a little bright light on Rachel's day.

Chapter Seventeen

Driving east on Highway 321, looking toward the Smokies, I saw the mountaintops white with snow beneath the tall trees. The high contrast and definition on the foothills and the far-off peaks looked spectacular. The clear, cold air smelled of frost.

When I entered the PD through the back door, I heard an unhappy customer in the squad room.

"Well, fuck your own self, mister," a female voice said. "If you think you're putting your hands on me, you can, like, forget it."

I stepped into the room where the cops process those we arrest. Junior Huskey sat at one of the desks, trying to complete an arrest report. Will Sparks stood resting one knee on a chair at another desk across the room, counting a large pile of pills one at a time. The irate voice belonged to a young female handcuffed to a ring bolted to the side of Junior's desk.

"Problem, Officer Huskey?" I asked.

"I'm not tryin' to touch her, Chief," he said defensively. "I jest asked her if she had any scars or tattoos."

"Oh, yeah, I got tattoos. You wanna see 'em?" She started to lift up her tight long-sleeved T-shirt, but the handcuffs restricted her movement.

"We don't need to see them, miss," I said. "Just describe them and when a female officer searches you, she'll verify what you've got. Or you can refuse to speak to us, and she'll just lay you across a Xerox machine and photocopy you."

"Someone's gonna search me? She ain't no lesbian, is she?"

"No, she's not a lesbian. You want me to find one for you?"

"Oh, like, fuck you, too!"

"Sergeant Lambert is on her way in," I told Junior. "I just spoke with her. Let her know when you're ready to lodge the prisoner."

I stepped over near Will.

"Who are you supposed to be, Officer Walgreen, the department pharmacist?" I asked.

He held up a hand to stop me from speaking.

"Two hunnert, forty-six," he said. "No, sir, Junior here stopped this one," he jerked a thumb over his shoulder toward the prisoner, "fer speedin' and found this sack o' pills. She's also got her a suspended license."

"He find them in plain view?"

"'Pears so."

"Not Levittown or Plainedge?"

"Do what?"

"Just a little Long Island cop humor. Plainview is a town there. Forget I said anything. What is this stuff, anyway?"

"The book from your office says Oxycodone." He pointed to an open page from *The Physician's Desk Reference.*

"That would take care of a bunch of bad backs, wouldn't it?"

"Uh-huh."

Will looked like he was thinking. He slapped his forehead and began to count from the pile he had already counted.

"Two forty-six, partner," I said.

"Thanks, boss. Thought I'd have to start all over."

I stepped back over to Junior who looked like he'd finished covering all the pedigree needed for his arrest report and would next start working on the prosecution work sheet. I took one of the forms from his desk while he continued typing and pulled up a chair a few feet from his defendant.

"Pikey Dillard?" I asked.

"Uh-huh." She spoke without looking at me.

"Pikey is your name?"

She looked up. "No, it's somebody else's."

"That's on your birth certificate? It's not just short for something else?"

"Uh-huh."

Pikey was twenty-two years old, her complexion extremely fair, and her chopped hair had been dyed as black as a crow's feather. It made a startling contrast. Her shirt and jeans matched her hair. A row of silver studs ran up the outer rim of each ear, and a large safety pin pierced her left eyebrow. I looked at her for a long moment and thought if you scrubbed her with a push broom and gave her a good haircut, Pikey would probably be a very pretty girl. I read over her sheet a little more.

"When this information goes into the computer we'll find out," I said, "but why don't you tell me now. Before this time, what have you been arrested for?"

"How'd you, like, know I been arrested b'fore?"

"Wild guess?"

She rolled her eyes and sighed, acting bored with the whole process. "Suspended license, DUI on drugs, shop-lifting, bad checks, possession." She thought for a moment, shook her head and seemed satisfied with the answer.

"Ah, so young and yet so busy. Possession of what?"

"Grass."

"Any weight?"

"No, just for my own head."

"Pikey, I'm going to guess that when my friend over there finishes counting, there'll be more than five hundred Oxycodones. You've got a lot of cash tied up in that pile of pills. That's big-time possession—much more than for your own head. We wouldn't have to stretch anyone's imagination if we said it was possession with intent to sell."

She smiled and began shaking her head.

"Based upon your stunning record over the last few years of adulthood," I said, "you're looking at some major jail time. What was that you said about lesbians?"

"I ain't goin' to jail for this. It was, like, a bad search"

"Leapin' lizards! I guess a judge never heard that one before."

"I want a lawyer." She tried to look haughty.

"Good, you need one," I said. "You have the right to remain silent, but I have the right to keep talking. So, keep listening, and you might learn something."

I took a moment to stretch, changed position and crossed my legs.

"We both know you're going away for this—big-time," I said. "Even with an expensive lawyer, you'll be cat meat. This is Tennessee, not some liberal state up north. A nice young thing like you will end up a punk for some big momma. Think about that the next time you've got a smart answer."

She hung her head and made a production of checking out the black nail polish on her free hand.

"While you're exercising your right to remain silent," I continued, "remember the only hope you've got is to open your mouth and tell me about someone bigger and badder than you. Once you go into a cell, *let's make a deal* time is over, and you're getting a one-way ticket to an all-girl gang-bang."

I guess she thought sulking was her best course of action. I continued to read her arrest report.

"You've got a shoulder patch of the 278th Armored Cav tattooed on your ass?" I sounded a bit astonished.

"Uh-huh," she said.

It didn't seem strange to her.

"I'm just curious…why?"

"My ex-boyfriend was in the National Guard."

I nodded and got up to leave.

"Hey, what kind of jail time you think I'll get?" she asked.

Aha! I thought. She's interested in something.

"With your background and attitude, even if you clean yourself up to look like Dorothy Hamill and get a healthy plea bargain—twenty-five years."

"Dorothy who?"

"Doesn't matter. Of course, if you're lucky and behave yourself in the slammer, you might get out in eight and a third with parole."

"I gotta do, like, eight years in jail?"

"And a third. If you're on good behavior the whole time. That means no getting caught with any contraband like grass or pills or found doing something thought to be socially unacceptable."

"Jeez, I'll be over thirty then."

"Yeah, but look on the bright side, you might never need to look for another boyfriend after that. Or you might just feel a little funny each time you get romantic with one."

She looked at me again and picked at a hangnail on her left index finger. Her mouth sagged downward like the sad face on a Greek tragedy mask.

"Gotta run, guys," I said with a smile. "Let me know when you want the evidence closet opened up."

I stepped into the hall and met Bettye walking in. She wore a burgundy pantsuit over a light blue T-shirt, a pair of black high heels and carried a tan raincoat over her arm. Her blonde hair hung loose to her shoulders.

"Wow, did I catch you about to do something special?" I asked.

"No, I just had this on. I figure you're not the only one who can walk around lookin' like a detective."

"Yeah, but what a detective. Hubba hubba, baby."

"Hubba hubba? I think my grandfather used to say that."

"Oh, Jesus!" I said.

"I'm just kiddin'. You are *so* easy, Sam Jenkins."

I shrugged.

"Might I have the names, please?"

"Sure, here." I handed her a slip of paper.

She turned and walked to her desk. I followed and watched her hair sway back and forth, looking shiny and clean.

"Ask them where the hunting cabin is," I said. "See if Darrell has a key. If they know where he is and won't tell, threaten to kill them. I've got to call Ralph Oliveri."

I stepped into my office, went behind my desk and picked up the phone. Ralph answered his cell phone on the third ring.

"You're working a lot of overtime, aren't you?" he asked.

"Yeah, I'm like Dunkin Donuts, I never close. It's been a good day though. My best guess is Darrell's—maybe—in a hunting cabin somewhere in the mountains. We're working on a better location right now."

"No shit? You got all that today?"

"Sort of. No smoking gun, but some pieces are coming together. There's no doubt Korner's our guy. If we locate the cabin, are you available?"

"Sure, I have to be. Call me on this phone. I'll be here and work my end when I hear from you."

"Okay, sport. Keep your fingers crossed. I'll talk to you."

If all my leads fizzled, I'd be back to nothing. We'd check out the cabin, of course, but without luck there, I had no Plan B in mind. Or was I up to Plan C? I asked Bettye how she was making out.

"I have all the numbers and addresses, but so far two voice mails and one no answer. Sorry."

"And I've got two guys in here working on a Gothic pill-head and only one car on the road. I'd like to send cars to check on these people in person. Jeez, with a big department, I could conquer the world, but there are only thirteen of us. Alexander the Great lived an easier life."

"I *am* sorry, darlin'."

"Make a few phone calls, please. See if you can get me two or three people for a little overtime. Then look in the Cole's reverse directory for the phone numbers on either side of these peoples' houses—we need to contact them. See if they have any idea where their neighbors are."

"Okey dokey, boss."

I thought of another question: do good-looking blondes all over the world say okey dokey? Or was I just lucky? I was sure *The Police Chief's Handbook* would not have an answer.

I started walking back to my office to sit down and dream up a new strategy, but Will Sparks met me with a Ziploc bag full of Oxycodone.

"Five hunnert an' eighty!" he said, dangling the bag in front of him.

"I'll have to make a phone call to find out what kind of a street value we're talking about," I said, "but any way you look at this, Junior made a damn good grab."

"Junior asked me to ask you…ah, since you're an ex-detective an' all…an' you're so good at this kinda stuff…an' ah…would you mind fingerprinting her while he finishes the paperwork?"

"Bettye's right, I am too easy." I swung open the door to the evidence closet.

"Naw, you're jest a good guy, boss."

"Yeah, flattery will get you nowhere."

"Sure it does. That's what Miss Bettye tol' me."

"I smell a conspiracy."

Will grinned like a kid just handed his first beer. I shook my head.

I led Pikey into the ID room where we kept the fingerprint board and the tripod-mounted camera. She didn't seem either belligerent or threatening, but when I took her cuffs off, I gave her the same story I've used on countless defendants for as many years as I'd been a cop.

"I've had a *really* bad week, and I am not in a good mood. If you give me a hard time or decide to get tough with me, I promise to beat you so badly you'll spend most of your twenty-five years in the intensive care unit at the prison hospital. Are we clear on that?"

She made yet another face. "And people say I have a serious problem."

I spread ink paste on the glass board with a small roller, turned up my sleeves and got ready to print her.

"Okay, just relax," I said. "Leave your arms loose. Right hand first. Let me do all the work. Follow me when I take a step and don't zig when I zag."

I hadn't fingerprinted anyone in years, but my standard line came out like I processed my last defendant only the day before.

As usual, I rolled a perfect set of prints. Some talents never fade. I'm the Tony Bennett of finger printers. Now, I thought, if I could only figure out how to use a goddamned digital camera.

Pikey stood with her feet on the two footprints painted on the floor of the ID room. I adjusted a board with her name and arrest number under her chin and prepared to snap the mug shots.

"You want to know who I bought the oxy from?" she asked.

"Is that what you want to bargain with?"

"Well, like, he's bigger'n me."

"Where's he from?"

"Knoxville."

"Not my turf. It's something, but it doesn't mean much to me. I'm not a local narc or from the DEA. Personally, I don't give a rat's ass if you young people kill yourselves with these drugs."

"You said give you somebody bigger'n me." Her voice held a hint of frustration.

"Give me someone I care about."

"Like, who's that?"

"I don't know. But now's not the time to hold back. Your first try didn't impress me much, so try again. You know someone who's done any armed robberies? Got any machine guns? Good stuff, for chrissake."

"Machine guns? I'm not, like, in a militia group or somethin'."

"Then I guess you've got a problem."

She closed her eyes for a few seconds and shook her head.

"Yesterday a bunch o' Feds was all over lookin' for Darrell Korner. You interested in him?" she asked.

Damn right I'm interested.

"I've heard about Korner." I tried to sound bored with her question. "I'm more interested in him than some moron pill-pusher from Knoxville. How do you know this guy?"

"He's, like, my boyfriend…the one I told you about."

I pushed my keep-your-cool switch and played her a little more. "All right, hold still a minute." She did. "Say cheese." She didn't.

After she turned for profile shots and I snapped the shutter twice, I capped the lens and turned off the camera.

"I'll call you when the proofs are ready," I said. "You can order eight-by-ten glossies at a discount."

"Yeah, right. You, like, ever get tired of the jokes?"

I ignored the question. "All right, let's talk. I might be interested in Korner, but it depends on what you have to say. We'll take a walk and get comfortable."

I cuffed her again, this time in front. Junior still sat in the squad room working on his arrest package. Will Sparks had already gone back on the road. I called to Bettye.

"Sarge, will you sit in here with us?"

I put Pikey in one of the guest chairs in front of my desk. Bettye sat next to her. I sat in the big chair behind my desk. I hadn't worked out an act with Bettye, but I assumed that if necessary, she'd naturally slip into the role of good cop to my bad one.

"Okay, Pikey, you say Darrell is your boyfriend. How did you meet him?"

"I worked at Blount Hospital when he was a cop. He came in, like, lots, at all hours. I worked shifts and got to see him sometimes. I wasn't

Goth then. He liked me and said I was pretty. He asked me out and I figgered, 'What the hell?'"

"What did you do at the hospital?"

"Duh! Like, I was a brain surgeon. Whaddaya think? I cleaned up…you know, like a janitor. I worked around the clock the whole time."

"Remember what I said about smart answers? I'm treating you like an adult. You want a favor? You want me to talk to the DA about you and get you some slack? Don't crack wise with me. You're wasting my time. Are we clear on *that*?"

"Okay. Like, don't get all crazy on me. If I help you find Darrell, do I get a walk?"

"A walk?" I said softly. I shook my head and smiled. Then I lurched forward and slammed my hand down on the desk. Damn near everything in the room shook. Pikey and Bettye jumped three inches.

"You want a fuckin' walk?" I yelled.

As soon as I said that, I felt uncomfortable swearing in front of Bettye. But I continued my act.

"You've got some nerve, kid. You get caught with a stash of over five-hundred goddamn pills and you want a walk?" I sighed and rolled my eyes.

Then Bettye spoke. "Now Sam, don't go gettin' excited. It's no good for ya. She was just askin'."

Good girl, Betts.

"Asking my ass," I said. "She's trying to play me. Okay, young lady, I might get you some slack for Darrell *and* the dealer in Knoxville. But a walk? If I find Darrell and find him soon, I might be able to get you probation—lots of probation. You lie to me, you screw around with me and you will never—I repeat—*never* see that parole in eight and a third years. I'll do everything in my power to keep you in prison as long as I can. You hear that?"

"Okay, okay. For Darrell and the guy in Knoxville. You promise?"

"Yeah, I promise. Now, no more questions—answers," I said. "Is Darrell the guy from the 278th you got your butt tattooed for?"

"Yeah, but he didn't like it. He said sluts get tattoos. He liked me back then—I was blonde and, like, goodie-goodie. He didn't like tattoos, but he liked me to screw his brains out. I wasn't a slut when we did that."

I shifted my eyes to Bettye, who showed no expression.

"How long were you and Darrell together?" she asked.

"For about a year and a half." Pikey said. "We stopped seein' each other regular—nine, ten months ago, after he got fired."

"So when you and Darrell were banging away to beat the band, where did you go? His place?" I said.

"Sometimes. Sometimes we'd go away for a few days. He had a place in the mountains. Darrell liked to be romantic. He would, like, bring a case of beer, barbeque a couple o' steaks, make like we were married and on vacation."

Controlling my emotions gets difficult at times. I struggled to keep a straight face.

"Yeah, sounds swell. Where's this place in the mountains?"

"Top o' the World," she said.

If I weren't a poker-faced professional, I would have tilted back in my chair and shouted, "Yah-freakin'-hoo!"

"Top O' the World is a big place," I said. "You've got to get me closer than that."

"I can tell you how to get there, but it's, like, easier for me to show you."

"Okay, is it possible Darrell is there now? He's not at home, at his folks' place or with his uncle and aunt. Where do you think he'd go?"

"He's got friends, but he liked the cabin. Said he *loved* to be alone in the woods. He was kinda weird like that."

"You know we're looking for him, and maybe he does, too. Do you think he's there now?"

"Well, I, like, don't *knooow* for sure. He must know y'all want him for somethin' big. He's, like, not stupid. He's got nowhere else to go. It's either there or he'll run, like, somewhere."

"If this is bullshit, Pikey, I'll tell the judge you screwed with me, and we're back to not only maximum hard time, but I'll make sure they send you to the worst place in the Tennessee prison system. Your young ass won't be worth a nickel. You sure this is all true?"

"I swear I'm tellin' the truth. I ain't seen him, but I'll take you to where he, like, used to take me."

"Okay, I'll give you a chance."

I looked over at Bettye and shrugged. She shrugged back.

I asked Pikey, "You want a soda or something?"

"Sure. Dr. Pepper"

I stood up.

After a moment, she asked, "You got anything stronger? I'm, like, a little stressed out."

"Don't push your luck!"

Chapter Eighteen

Reaching a point where I thought my agreement with the FBI should be honored, I called Ralph Oliveri and told him about the new information and my plan to look for the elusive hunting cabin and Darrell Korner.

He claimed to be ready for action and promised to get on the road as soon as I provided a location. However, late on a Saturday afternoon, just before New Year's day, the rest of the FBI wasn't as prepared for a quick response. Ralph thought it might take a couple of hours to mobilize a SWAT team, and only Carl Harmon could authorize that. Then, while the mobilization was in progress, he'd call up several more agents, etcetera, etcetera.

"Ralph, listen to yourself," I said. "This thing can be resolved, and you guys would still be sitting on the tarmac wondering what happened. I can put a half-dozen men who know their way around the woods at this cabin in less than an hour."

A conversation between Bettye and Pikey made it difficult for me to hear Ralph. I stuck a finger in my free ear to tune them out.

"Get your ass on a chopper, Ralphie, and head toward Top o' the World. I don't know exactly where I'm going yet, but when I get there, I'm coming in from downwind. Call me from the chopper. When I hear you, I'll pop green smoke. Then find an LZ and meet me—far enough away so Korner doesn't hear you land. We'll take it from there."

"Downwind? You'll pop green smoke? Where the hell do you think you are? This isn't Vietnam. You carry smoke grenades?"

"Yeah, green smoke. Now, let's get moving. If you can't find a chopper, contact a guy named Randy at Crawford Sports in Maryville. Tell him I said to call the Army Aviation Facility at McGhee-Tyson and get you a ride. Okay?"

"Jesus, Sam, don't you think you're rushing this? And how am I supposed to know where to find a landing zone?"

"Play it by ear. Improvise. The pilot will know where he can land. He who hesitates, partner. Let's do it."

"Okay, okay. I'll call you from the chopper. Keep that cell phone on, and for Christ's sake, learn how to use it."

I snickered. "You got it, kid. See you later, and dress warmly. We're going into the mountains."

Ralph muttered something beyond my understanding of Italian. I turned to Bettye.

"Betts, we've got some organizing to do. Pikey, no offense, but you're going to sit in a cell for a while until we get things ready. Then we'll go find Darrell."

Bettye lodged Pikey in one of our cells, and we started calling the troops. I wanted Stan Rose in on the action. I needed a number two in case I got involved with something before Ralph arrived. I also wanted Junior, Will Sparks, Bobby Crockett, Vern Hobbs, Lenny Alcock and Harley Flatt—all with their hunting rifles. The word around the department was that if it walked in the woods, either Harley or Vern could find it and shoot it.

Bettye and I made our calls. Everyone dropped what they were doing and started on their way in. Two other cops replaced Junior and Sparks on regular patrol.

Over the next twenty minutes, they all walked into the PD in various states of uniform or looking like something from ABC's *American Sportsman*. Everyone looked edgy and raring to go.

I worked out my plan with the guys. I'd be in the front; Stan would be in charge of the rear team. Three riflemen each, front and back. Vern and Harley on opposite corners.

As they waited for the word GO, my troops loitered in or around the squad room. Bobby and Junior joked around. Sparks listened. Lenny Alcock leaned against the rail outside the back door with his pack of cigarettes. Vern Hobbs rested against the wall, constantly moving a toothpick around in his mouth. Harley sat on the edge of a desk, tapping fingers against his leg to the rhythm of music no one else heard. And Stan stood in the middle of the room with an Ithaca riot gun resting on his shoulder, looking like something from a western movie.

I already had my sweater on and carried my field jacket with me. Finally, I took the black carbine out of the duffle bag lying on a desk in the squad room.

"What you got there, boss?" Junior asked.

"Just an old Colt CAR-15 with a little three power scope. Something compact, good in an ankle holster."

A couple of the guys snickered. Junior pressed ahead.

"Looks like yer still in the Army," he said. "Ya reckon we'll do some shootin'?"

"I hope not, but if we have to, I guess our crew can handle it," I said.

Everyone looked at each other. Stan lowered the pump shotgun to port arms. The rest all carried rifles, and we each packed at least one handgun. Darrell Korner might have been a good soldier, but he'd have to be a well-armed Rambo to get past us.

"Junior," I said. "Go get Pikey. Cuff her and bring her. We're ready to go."

He walked off toward the cellblock.

"Okay, guys," I said. "It's show time. Start up the cars."

After the men left the building, Bettye said, "Sam, I'd like to go with you." She looked like a little girl who hadn't gotten an invitation to the junior prom.

I thought about the last time I asked Bettye to back me up. Through no fault of her own, someone almost shot her. Sexist pig or not, I didn't want another incident on my conscience.

"Not this time, Betts. Thanks, but I need you here to run the shop."

"I am a cop, too, you know."

It's difficult to describe how unhappy she looked.

"Yes, you are—a good one. If something happens and I have to call here, you'll know exactly what to do. I can't take the chance with one of the road cops making a mistake on the desk." I smiled and tried to ease her disappointment. "Besides, you'd only get your shoes muddy in the snow."

"Damn it, Sam Jenkins, I want to be with you!"

"Thank you. I mean that. Under other circumstances, I'd want you there. But…you know how it is."

"Damn it, don't you go doin' somethin' stupid, you hear?"

"Me, stupid? Heavens, no."

"You be careful out there, mister!"

"Yeah, kiddo, always." I touched her shoulder and wanted to kiss her good-bye.

Junior held onto Pikey and waited for me at the back door. We were all ready to go. Everyone carried hand-held portable radios in case Darrell, the ex-cop, had a police scanner and could monitor our car-to-car transmissions.

We used no flashing lights or sirens. My convoy of four cars climbed into the Chillhowee Mountains along the Foothills Parkway. Just past Butterfly Gap, we turned off the main road toward Top o' the World, an area developed years ago as a weekend retreat for wealthy Knoxvillians and as a center for rental cabins owned by those who wanted an investment or tax shelter.

That was the original plan of the developers. A large man-made lake had been excavated, roads were paved, and they built a clubhouse overlooking the water. They even provided on-site management for the homeowner's association.

Unfortunately, Top o' the World became famous for being a difficult place to locate potable well water. And the community was so far from the fire protection services that homeowner's insurance required a separate mortgage to pay the premiums—things few buyers think about before signing a contract. And then the lake began drying up.

Today, Top o' the World isn't even close to the Shangri La the developers and buyers planned to emulate. Current inhabitants include former hippies seeking a rustic environment in which to drop out of society, pot users, growers and dealers who took advantage of the remote surroundings and lack of police patrols. Add to that, people who liked the low cost of real estate and thought they could manage living miles away from the nearest gallon of milk and a few original buyers who would hate to pack up and lose so much of their investments.

At one point, it felt like I was leading four cars full of Keystone

Cops when we all turned around and backtracked because Pikey made us take a wrong turn.

Eventually, we found the cabin and parked on a blacktop road in desperate need of repair. A narrow gravel driveway slopped steeply downward from the street into a heavily wooded lot.

I smelled wood smoke drifting our way in the gentle but chilling breeze. It felt at least ten degrees colder up in the mountains than down in town. Birds of all kinds flitted from tree to tree and from bush to bush, trying to peck out a last tidbit of food before the light disappeared. The cloud-ridden sky looked like a dingy garage floor, littered with stains and used oil rags.

Stanley and I made a quick reconnaissance. We walked down the winding driveway to a spot where the trees stopped and a clearing held a small one-story cabin, sided with Texture 111 plywood under a red metal roof.

A narrow covered porch spanned the front of the cabin. The bluestone gravel extended right to the front steps. A few feet from the porch sat a white Ford van with a roof rack.

I looked at Stanley and whispered. "Gotcha, Darrell, you poor bastard."

Stan raised his eyebrows and nodded.

I motioned for us to move to the right within the tree line. Three inches of snow on the ground made walking on the fallen leaves quieter, but it also hid any branches or twigs that might crack and betray our presence. We moved slowly and shuffled our steps carefully.

Directly across from the cabin's front door, I took out my binoculars and checked the windows. There were no curtains—no neighbors, so no need for curtains or shades. Inside, I watched a big man wearing a red plaid shirt and jeans feeding cut wood into a cast-iron stove.

We moved again to get a different angle and another view. Interior decorating did not seem of paramount importance to the owners. A small kitchen with a rude picnic table was to the right. To the left stood a pair of double-decker bunk beds—metal-framed like those the Army issued since the First World War and still used at some bases during Vietnam. I guessed the walled-off area near the bunks held the bathroom. The important thing, though, was a high-back couch facing away from the kitchen. Rachel Williamson sat there with her hands cuffed in front.

The interior of the cabin must have been warm. I huddled outside, bundled up and freezing in the shade of the woods, while inside, Rachel wore a short-sleeved gray turtleneck and a red skirt. The red jacket of her suit lay on a bottom bunk. Her hair needed combing, but she looked okay. Stanley and I crept back to brief the troops.

While Stan and I were away, Ralph had called my cell phone and spoke with Junior. Oliveri had commandeered a ride in a state highway patrol helicopter and called from the air. He said they'd call again when the pilot reached the general vicinity. Junior would find an appropriate spot, pop my smoke grenade, and the chopper could land in a clearing near the lake, almost a half mile away. Once on the ground, Ralph and Bonnie Rowatt, who had tagged along for the ride, would wait for a car and meet us at the cabin.

The layout of the little house didn't change our original plan. Stan and three riflemen would cover the back. They set out to take a position by walking within the woods and approaching from inside the tree line. To keep noise down, they would only break squelch on their radios once, twice and three times when each man reached his position. Once set, my shooters would duplicate their positions in front. No radio noise was necessary. I'd have visual contact.

This all happened quicker than it took to explain.

* * * *

Ralph, Bonnie and I stood roughly a hundred feet from the front door. Junior flanked us and knelt there with his Winchester Model 70 scoped rifle pointed toward a window.

"As much as I'd love to sit here in the woods and sing Cum-Bay-Ah with you guys," I said, "I guess we should see if young Darrell would like to have a chat."

"You have his phone number?" Ralph asked.

"Sure, his ex-girlfriend gave it to me. You think you're dealing with an amateur?"

"Oh, heavens, no."

"I hope you two don't mind," I said, "but I'd like to make the call. I think he and I might have some common ground. You know, old Army buddies and all that. If he found out you were a former Marine, Ralph, he might lose interest."

"By all means," he said. "Pretend we're not here."

Bonnie made a face. I tapped in Darrell's cell phone number. He picked up, but didn't answer immediately. I waited a few seconds.

"Darrell Korner?" I said. "I know you're there. Say hello—it's only good manners."

"Who's this?"

"My name's Sam Jenkins. I'm the Chief at Prospect Police. We need to have a talk."

"Where are you?"

"I have a dozen heavily armed cops and a bunch of FBI agents all sitting outside your cabin. I'd like to come in and have a chat."

"Say that ag'in."

I thought a little exaggeration might grab his attention.

"Listen up, Darrell!" I snapped. "I've got twelve cops and lots of FBI agents all within one hundred feet of your little cabin. I've got ten riflemen, and I can't count the number of shotguns and pistols out here. You understand?"

"Yeah, I hear ya."

"I want to come in and talk with you. I'll leave my rifle out here. You need to hear what I have to say."

Ralph slapped me on the shoulder and whispered, "You're not supposed to do that. It's not part of the deal."

I waved him off, impatiently.

"Darrell, I might be the best guy here to understand what you're thinking. I want to hear your side of the story…I want to come in and talk with you, and I want to see Rachel."

He hesitated with an answer. A pair of noisy blue jays yakked at each other until one flew off the branch of a nearby pine tree.

"You still there, Darrell?" I asked.

"Yeah. Yeah. Okay, but just you. Walk up slow, and knock on the door."

The phone went dead. I handed Bonnie the pistol from my ankle holster and Ralph the CAR.

"You remember how to use one of these?" I asked.

"Hey, I was a supply officer," Ralph said, "but I'll work on it. I sure hope to hell you know what you're doing."

"When do I not?"

Ralph rolled his eyes, and Bonnie shook her head.

"This is not a good thing to do," Bonnie said.

"Gee, I didn't think you cared."

She smiled and looked nice. "I don't. But it's still not good procedure."

"TV is lousy on a Saturday night, and I've got nothing better to do. Y'all hang in there."

I walked along the tree line for ten yards or so and then emerged into the clearing. A chill wiggled up my back when I found myself in the open. It's a feeling I've experienced for almost forty years whenever I look around and see I have nowhere to hide or take cover. But Darrell and I had made an agreement, so I walked past the rear of the van, looked inside and found it empty.

There were three steps to the porch. Automatically, I looked down for a trip wire to a booby trap—nothing there either. I approached the front door, stood off to the side and knocked.

"Open it slow," he said.

I did and peeked inside quickly.

"Step inside," he said.

Darrell took cover by assuming a crouch position behind the arm of the sofa to my left. Rachel sat tentatively on the couch at my far right, her legs tucked up beneath her. She wore no shoes. *Smart*, I thought. Keep your prisoner barefoot. If she got out in this weather, it wouldn't be comfortable, and she wouldn't get far.

I only gave her a quick look and a wink and then re-focused on Darrell. He pointed a big stainless steel Desert Eagle at me, a semiautomatic pistol chambered for .44 magnums—a small cannon.

"Damn, it's hot in here," I said. "You're Darrell?" he nodded. "I'm Sam Jenkins. Mind if I sit down?"

He gestured to the floor in front of the couch. I sat cross-legged, like a visiting Indian chief ready to powwow. I remained silent, wanting to see what he'd do.

He only waited a long moment before asking, "How'd you find us?"

147

"I'm talented. Ask Ms. Williamson. She thinks I'm the real-life Dirty Harry."

He didn't roll over laughing.

"So what's next?" he asked, keeping the handgun pointed in my general direction.

"Look, Darrell, I've got a few guys out there who can put a .308 up a gnat's ass at two hundred meters. One of them could have punched your ticket a couple of minutes ago while you were stacking wood in your stove. You believe that?"

He shrugged. The fire in the wood stove crackled and popped. A faint smell of smoke tainted the air in the cabin.

"I know a lot about you," I said. "You were a good cop. A good soldier, too—a genuine hero, for God's sake. I'm the last guy who wants to see you get shot. I think you were shafted when the sheriff fired you."

He nodded in agreement. The muzzle end of the Desert Eagle dropped two inches.

"I know where you're coming from," I said. "And to some extent I know what you've experienced. Years ago something similar happened to me. It's tough to get one thing after another piled on your shoulders and not get disgusted. You had more than your share, didn't you?

Korner nodded, and a slight smirk crossed his face. "Yeah, right. Like they say, 'Life stinks.' That your field jacket?"

He pointed at my sun-faded olive drab coat. Only the spots of cloth once covered by embroidered patches and cloth badges remained the original color.

"It is," I said.

"You wore a patch on your right shoulder?"

I nodded. Knowing he was alluding to the insignia indicating I had served in combat.

"Vietnam?"

"Yep."

"Some other badges, too."

"Yeah, I picked up a few do-dads over the years."

"You been around. Officer?"

"Not at first, but I got there eventually."

"In Vietnam, you were on the ground?"

"Oh, yeah. Didn't spend much time in the rear with the beer."

He nodded and gave a look of understanding only another soldier could offer.

"So what do we got here?" he asked.

"No big mystery, kid. Only two choices." I shook my head at the futility of the situation. "Look, this is all but over. No one is going anywhere. I'll give you a reasonable deal if you cut your losses and do it the easy way. You know you can't skate on this."

He nodded again and lowered the gun another couple inches. It looked like I'd made a little headway.

"You put a man into the hospital," I said. "He's okay now, bruised up, but he's alive and well."

He shrugged. "Good. I had nothin' against him. Things just got outta hand."

"When I learned about you from your former CO and your parents, I disliked how you were treated by the system, and I actually got to like you. Hell, if you hadn't pulled this dumb-ass stunt, I might have offered you a job at Prospect PD."

He frowned, and his eyes shifted from me to Rachel.

"You don't believe me?" I snapped at him. "Ask Rachel. She knows me well enough." I turned to her. "Would I do that?"

She nodded and whispered. "Yes, I think he would."

"So, call it quits now," I suggested. "I'll take you in like a gentleman, and Rachel goes home to her family."

He closed his eyes for a second and let out some air. That was a bad move on his part, but I took it as a sign of trust.

"I know," I said. "I can guess how you feel about her. She was nice to you. She cared about your side of the story. Well, so do I. But abducting her was a bad choice. Now you've got to make it right."

He looked like he might start to cry and wiped the corner of his eye with the back of his hand.

"The FBI has jurisdiction on the case now. I can't answer for them, Darrell, but I'll let them listen to what I propose—at the same time you hear it. If the agent in charge can agree to what I want, then you can make your decision. Mind if I make a phone call?"

"You have a phone?" His eyes widened, and the muzzle of the

handgun elevated slightly.

"Yeah, same one I called you on."

A few seconds passed in silence. "Okay... Go ahead," he said. "Take it out—slow-like. What pocket?"

"Right bottom jacket pocket. Okay?"

He nodded.

"Right. Nice and slow now."

He nodded again. I called Oliveri.

"Ralph, listen carefully. I don't want to have to repeat this, and I don't want to make Darrell promises I can't keep. I'll tell you and him what I think is reasonable. Something in everyone's best interest, and something that makes co-operation worthwhile. You tell me if you can swing everything. Agreed?"

"Yeah, okay, Sam. Start talking."

"One, you process the arrest in Prospect—no Blount County personnel present. Two, Darrell gets his choice of lawyers. I plan on suggesting one. Three, we arraign him in Blount County, and after that he does the pre-trial confinement up in Knoxville near your office. Again, no Blount County cops who he used to work with get involved. Last, you do all this in the state courts—no interstate flight, no Federal charges. Let the lawyers work out a deal if they can." I turned and looked directly into Darrell's eyes. "That work for you?"

"I don't know," he said. "I got to think."

"Ralph, Darrell reserves his decision. How about you?"

"Yeah, we can agree to that. You didn't promise him a walk on anything did you?"

"Negative on the walk. He knows this cannot go away. I just think a good deal can end this now and avoid any unpleasantries."

"Unpleasantries? Jesus, Sam."

"I take that as a yes, Ralphie?"

"Yeah, yeah. Just do it."

I focused back on Darrell. He and I sat less than three feet apart, the Desert Eagle still loosely pointed in my direction, his back facing a window. Outside the window, I watched Harlan Flatt crawl up to within thirty yards of the cabin and lay prone in the snow, his baseball cap turned backwards and his scoped Remington 700 trained on Darrell's back.

"You said there was another choice?" he said.

"Yes, I did. Two more actually, but I don't like to think about those."

He wrinkled his brow, but waited for me to continue.

"You could reject my offer," I said. "You only abducted Rachel because of an affection you felt for her. So you let us go, and I take her home. But you decide, like Butch Cassidy, you'd rather be in Bolivia, and you try to shoot your way out of here. Of course, we do what the Muslims couldn't do—we kill you."

It became obvious Darrell wasn't a Butch Cassidy fan. His frown deepened, and the muzzle of the Desert eagle raised an inch—now back to where it started. That didn't make me a Darrell Korner fan.

"A dead son would make your mom and dad real happy, wouldn't it?" I said.

His face relaxed, and he shook his head slightly.

"Less attractive still," I continued, "is the idea that you kill both of us and then try the Butch Cassidy act. But I don't think you're a real bad guy. Killing innocent people isn't in character for you."

"I could use you two as hostages and demand a car…or a chopper." His voice held a note of defiance.

I half way expected a little argument.

Time for me to act cool and smile for the cameras.

"Yeah, maybe on TV you could. In real life, as soon as you stepped outside, a bullet would hit your head before you could pull the trigger. That's not an option. Get over that one."

He began to look frustrated and puffed out more air.

"You want the opinion of an old cop and soldier who's fully matriculated in both systems?" I didn't give him time to speak. "I'll give it to you anyway. Take deal number one. You walk out of here with dignity. I'll make sure that happens. Then you work for your best deal. I'll even suggest a good lawyer if you don't have one in mind. What do you say?"

"I told you I gotta think. Now please, sir, shut up."

"Okay, kid, no more talk, but while you're thinking, I have to take my jacket off. I'm sweating my ass off in here."

"Alright, but slow."

I rose up on my knees and unzipped my field jacket. I took it off slowly and dropped it on the floor. In doing so, Darrell saw the holstered Glock hanging on my right hip.

"You have a gun?" He rose up, too, and snapped his pistol directly at my head. "You wanted to kill me."

He sounded disappointed in me.

Chapter Nineteen

"Whoa, slow down, Darrell," I said, trying to smooth him out.

"Down on the floor!" he barked. "Face down!"

I didn't move.

"I said down. Do it!" he shouted.

He didn't seem as upset as I thought he should. And he didn't look convinced he could pull off an escape.

When Korner began yelling, Rachel pushed herself back against the arm of the couch and looked like she just saw Godzilla peeking in her bathroom window.

I shook my head slowly. "Calm down, kid, and take your seat." I spoke with as much bravado as I could muster up. "I don't need to kill you myself. If I wanted you dead, he would have done it long ago."

I flicked my finger toward Harley Flatt. Darrell looked behind him and away from me for the brief moment I needed.

My left arm shot forward with a real purpose. I latched onto the slide of the Desert Eagle, and then with my right hand, slapped the muzzle upward and pried it from his hand. He didn't fight back or even offer a little resistance. That made me happy. Darrell was a big boy.

He opened his mouth to speak, but never made a sound. His anticipation was thick enough to slice with a bayonet.

"What do you say, kid? We call it a draw?" I asked.

He nodded and looked down at the braided area rug on which we sat. It needed a vacuuming, but I doubt he noticed.

Behind him, Harley Flatt ran up to the window and spoke into his radio. In only seconds, three other cops pushed their way inside through the front door.

Without being asked, Darrell stood up and put his hands behind his back to receive the cuffs.

"Easy, guys," I said. "Mr. Korner already surrendered. Everybody wait here for the FBI."

Just after I slapped Darrell's gun, Rachel jumped up and scurried behind the couch. She stood there with her hands protectively raised, her forearms covering her breasts, her face still contorted in fear.

Stan Rose came through the door and took charge of Darrell and the three cops.

I stepped over to Rachel and put my hands on her cheeks. "It's okay now. I'm with you. You're safe. Let me remove the handcuffs."

She didn't speak, but held her hands out like a child reaching for a treat. I took a key ring from my pants pocket, opened the cuffs and held the shackles loosely as she wrapped her arms around my ribs and squeezed.

"Oh, Sam, I'm so glad to see you. Thank you so much."

Someone took the cuffs from my hand. I put my arms around her, squeezed tightly and felt her begin to tremble. When days of stress let go all at once, it's tough not to get a little emotional.

Ralph and Bonnie added to the crowd in the cabin. Stan told two of the cops to secure the cabin when we finished. Rachel cried softly as Darrell began his walk outside.

He looked at us and said, "I'm sorry."

I believe he meant it.

I held Rachel at arm's length, picked up her chin and forced her to look me in the eye.

"Are you okay?"

She nodded. "Yes, I am."

"You're sure?"

"Yes, Sam. I'm okay."

"Did he…?"

She tensed up a little. I felt my jaw tighten.

"No, he didn't." She shook her head. "He never touched me. I'm okay. Really. Just please stay with me."

"Sure, baby, I'm right here."

She forced a weak smile.

Ralph stepped over to us.

"Ms. Williamson, I'm Ralph Oliveri from the FBI. I'll be speaking with you sometime later. But for right now, an ambulance is outside. We'd like you to go to the hospital. Just for a quick check-up. Okay?"

"Sam, come with me," she said.

"I'm right behind you, kiddo. I'll have someone find your shoes and jacket and coat. Put my jacket on for now. It's cold outside."

She nodded and allowed me to help. My big field jacket made her look like a lost little girl. Only the tips of her fingers showed at the sleeves. Rachel tugged at the cuff to push her hand free and as we walked to the doorway, she grabbed my hand and held tightly.

At the doorsill, I looked beyond the porch at the snow and the clearing. A Rural Metro ambulance had pulled down the gravel drive and parked close to the cabin. Behind that, a white sheriff's department SUV sat next to the tree line. When he saw me, Jackie Shuman got out. Two more Prospect police cars pulled up near the cabin and added to the confusion. Behind them, Junior drove my gray Ford in—Pikey still locked in the back.

"It's not a day for you to go walking in the woods barefoot," I said. "Come on up."

Rachel looked into my eyes as I scooped her up in my arms.

Once there, she hugged my shoulders, buried her face into my neck and began to sob. Everything came out at once. No one could blame her.

As I descended the three steps, a sharp pain shot through my bad knee. I hoped it wouldn't cave in. It didn't. Mother Nature acted kindly that day.

Standing in front of the open ambulance doors, I continued to hold Rachel until she calmed down. The two paramedics were patient and solicitous. I placed her on the tail of the rescue truck, and as I bent over, my lower back felt like someone just hit me with a Louisville Slugger. The knight-errant business was meant for younger men.

As the medics began to do their thing, I told Rachel I'd return in two minutes and asked the men to wait for me before they started their trip to the hospital.

I had a lot to do in only a little time. I told Junior to take Pikey

Dillard to the Justice Center and get her arraigned. No judge would be sitting that late in the day, so I wanted him to plead special circumstances and get the man on call for the weekend to come in.

I asked Stan to take custody of my rifle and help Bettye wrap up the department, while I accompanied Rachel to the hospital.

I suggested that since Jackie Shuman was already there, Ralph use him for the crime scene work. He offered no objection.

Before I went back to the ambulance, Bonnie walked over and stood next to me, her hands buried in the pockets of her gray overcoat. A leather purse hung from her left shoulder. I waited a long moment for her to speak.

"That was pretty good work for a back-woods cop," she said. "You think I could learn something from you?"

I noticed a couple of cops giving her the once over. Her auburn hair looked shiny in the fading light.

"I've got a lot of bad habits," I said. "Ralph might be a better guy to watch."

"That's not what he says." She gave me a big smile. "See ya."

"Yeah," I said. "And thanks for the help."

She winked and joined her partner.

One of the paramedics waved to me, signaling they were ready to go. I trotted over, jumped into the back of the truck and sat on the bench seat along the right side. They had strapped Rachel in the gurney with the back tilted up in a chaise lounge position. A medic began taking her blood pressure. She reached over and took hold of my hand again.

"Any girl who holds my hand might end up with high blood pressure," I said. "We'd better wait."

The medic shook his head and smiled.

Rachel smiled and said, "You never quit, do you?"

"Give me a minute to call the office," I said. "When I finish, this nice man can turn his head so you and I can make out before we get to the hospital."

She smacked my arm. I called Bettye.

"Hey, Betts, it's me. Mission accomplished. Everything's okay. We're all on the way home. I'm stopping at the hospital first. Rachel looks fine, but she's going to get checked out."

"She's okay? Really okay?" Bettye asked. "You know what I mean?"

"Yes, I do. She says she's doing fine. I believe her. She's a tough little girl."

"Are you okay? Anyone get hurt?"

"We're just a little cold from this crisp mountain air. Everyone did a great job. Thanks for sending Jackie and the ambulance. You're a good girl."

"Thank you, darlin'. Did you do anything dangerous up there?"

"Nothing Audie Murphy wouldn't have done."

"Remind me to hit you in the head when you get back here."

"I don't think so, but I'll see you later. Oh, the FBI will be using the squad room for a while. Please tolerate them."

"I will. And I'll be here waitin' for you. You behave yourself at the hospital, Mr. Jenkins."

"That doesn't sound like fun, but I'll do my best. And thanks for everything. See you later."

I looked out the back window of the ambulance. Will Sparks, driving his marked police car, followed us. He'd be my ride back to Prospect.

I looked at Rachel and didn't know what to say. The medic had removed the blood pressure cuff, satisfied she was in good condition. And then he actually did look away—out the rear window. But I decided making out really wasn't an option.

"You had a tough couple of days, didn't you?" I asked.

"Oh, Sam, I was so scared. I…"

"I know. I feel responsible. If I hadn't asked you to help with that case…" I shrugged. "I'm sorry."

"No, this had nothing to do with you. That man would have followed me…in Knoxville, at the station, somewhere else. This was not your fault. You hear me?"

"Yeah, I'm listening."

"Hey, you found me," she said. "You saved me. That was amazing. I couldn't believe it when you walked into the cabin. I was so relieved, I…" She stopped. A tear rolled down her cheek.

"I've got to ask again. Are you okay?"

157

She wiped the tear and nodded.

"Honest?" I said.

"Yes, Sam, I'm okay. Honest."

I tilted my head and gave her a questioning look.

"Honest!" she said.

"Sure, kiddo, I believe you. I'm glad."

Less than thirty seconds passed when she said, "Sam, give me your cell phone. I want to call home."

She only spent a few minutes on the phone. From the one-sided conversation I heard, I assumed they were passing the phone around so each of the family members could hear Rachel's voice. She repeated all the usual answers and finally handed the phone back to me. I told Boyd where she would be taken, assured him she was in good shape and advised him to give the doctors about an hour before showing up in the ER waiting room. He seemed willing to comply.

After I hung up, Rachel took my hand again. The three of us then rode to the hospital in silence. Occasionally, as the ambulance twisted down the mountain road, she squeezed my hand and looked at me. Each time the driver goosed the siren to pass another vehicle, the poor kid tensed up and blinked. I thought she needed a drink. I surely did.

* * * *

The crew at Blount Memorial Hospital rushed her into the Emergency Room and shuffled me aside. I waited thirty minutes, but then began to feel like the fifth wheel on a little red wagon. I left my business card with the nurse at Triage and found Will Sparks sitting in his car at the ambulance parking area. He drove me back to Prospect.

I wasn't sure what to expect.

Chapter Twenty

I tapped in my four-digit code at the back door, walked past the squad room where Ralph and Bonnie were interviewing Darrell Korner and stepped into Bettye's reception area. A bunch of the cops milled around, most holding bottles or cans of soda, making it look almost like a Patrolman's Benevolent Association cocktail party. After one man noticed me, they all turned in my direction, and the conversation stopped. Bobby Crockett started the applause. Then another and another, and then all of them stood there clapping. It was gratifying, but I held up my hands to quiet them.

"Hi, guys," I said. "Thank you. I appreciate that, but our FBI cousins are doing business in the squad room." The noise stopped immediately, and I asked, "Does anyone have something to eat?"

There was no food in the office, not even a stale doughnut. But I was famished, and Bettye had been alone—more interested in work than snacks. I handed Bobby a twenty and asked him to go out and find something for everyone to nibble on.

After receiving several pats on the back while walking to my office, I did my best to appear humble and thank everyone concerned for their participation.

I collapsed into my chair, preparing to call Kate, when I looked up to see Stan Rose standing in front of my desk, towering over me.

"Sit down," I said. "You're too damn big to look up at. I'll get a stiff neck."

He dropped into a guest chair and stretched out his legs, dangling a Lakers ball cap on his fingers.

159

"Harley told me what you did," he said. "You've got some balls grabbing for a loaded weapon."

"I used to practice stuff like that."

"Oh, really?" He scowled at me. "In between eating Chinese food and driving your sports car?"

"Stanley, you're scolding me."

I heard the radio squawk at Bettye's desk. Johnny Rutledge called in a one-vehicle motorcycle accident on our end of the infamous 'thirteen curves' of Sevierville Road. Bettye acknowledged the call and dispatched an ambulance.

"Pardon me," Stan said, "but—dumb move. You should have let Harley shoot him."

I shrugged. "I felt sorry for Darrell. He's a troubled soul, Stan. Needs a good shrink more than killing. Of course, if I find out he did something to Rachel I don't know about, I might kill him myself."

He shook his head. "And you two aren't, ah…involved, huh?"

"Rachel and I are friends. Like you and me. Well, maybe a little different, but she's married. I'm married—there's nothing more. We're friends."

He shrugged, possibly satisfied with my answer. Perhaps not.

"Your boy Ralph told me Korner admits to using something called sevoflurane as a knockout drug when he first grabbed her," he said. "Then each night, he gave her a couple dyphenhydramine tablets to keep her groggy so he could sleep some, too. He says he never did anything else. Says he fell in love with her and had to have her with him." He shook his head. "Go figure."

"Huh," I said. "I hope that's all true. She's got enough rattling around inside her head after getting kidnapped. She doesn't need other complications in there."

He got up to leave.

"You okay?" he asked.

"Yeah, thanks. Just hungry."

He smiled, shook his head again and left. Thirty seconds later Bettye walked in and sat in front of my desk, in the same chair Stanley had just vacated.

"Sam…"

I held up a hand. She stopped. I walked around in front of the desk and sat in the chair next to her—as if we were at the movies. I looked at her over my right shoulder.

"Yes, ma'am?" I said.

"I heard what you did, Sam Jenkins. Good Lord, that was brave. Why in hell do you do things like that? Pardon my language, but…"

I stopped her again.

"I did that because the kid needed a break. I didn't believe he would hurt either Rachel or me. Without his gun, no one had a reason to shoot him. That's all."

"How does your wife live with you, Sam?"

"You could ask, but I hear her liquor bill is pretty high."

She started to get up. "Sam Jenkins, if you were mine, I'd…"

"Hey." I pointed at the chair. She sat.

"I am yours, Betts. For eight hours a day, and no, you wouldn't. If you did, you'd feel bad. Now stay here for a minute, please."

I turned my chair. So did she. Now we faced each other. She relaxed and crossed her legs.

"I need to explain something," I said. "Maybe the explanation is more for me than for you, but I still want to make it."

She waited for me to speak. I paused for a long moment, collecting my thoughts. The silence became deafening. The compressor from the mini-fridge sitting on a cabinet against the wall kicked in and sounded like a jet taking off.

"I didn't want you to come with me on this one," I said, "because the last time I asked you to do something like that you were almost shot. I blame myself for causing the trauma you suffered."

She was about to say something. I stopped her again.

"Before you yell at me, listen," I said. "I know you are just as much a cop as me or any of the guys. They know it, too. What I did was for me. I didn't want to put any more stress on me at the moment. I felt responsible for Rachel getting into this mess. That might or might not be true, but it's how I see it. I needed to give myself a break. I had no way of knowing what would happen up there. That's why I took so many people. I'm sorry. I meant no offense. I really needed you here to run things, and I just couldn't subject you to…something else."

She remained quiet for a time, sitting with her hands in her lap. She looked as nice then as she did when she walked in earlier that day, only the stress showed on her face. She stood up. I looked up into her eyes.

"You were very brave today," she said. "You all were. I'm glad you got back safely." She turned and left.

If most men are like me, they probably wish the women in their lives would get mad, yell and then be finished with it. Nevertheless, that doesn't always happen.

I called Kate, explained everything and told her I'd be home after wrapping up the loose ends. Then I called Ronnie Shields. He sounded pleased that we were instrumental in resolving the incident that took place in his city. He asked me to wear my uniform on Monday—fat chance. He'd tell Trudy Connor to make arrangements for a press conference.

Surprisingly, when I looked at my watch, it was less than an hour since I left Rachel at the hospital. My phone rang.

Bettye said Rachel's mother had asked for me, and then she transferred the call.

"Mr. Jenkins, this is Pauline Kiel."

"Hello. Are you at the hospital?"

"Yes. Boyd is with Rachel. Joe and I are waiting with the boys until the doctor says we can see her."

"Good. When I left her, she was doing just fine. You've got one tough daughter. I'm glad she had the opportunity to call you."

"Please thank Sergeant Lambert and Agent Oliveri for us. They called, too. That meant a lot."

I wasn't surprised that they did.

"Everyone here was worried about Rachel. I'm glad things turned out as well as they did."

"I knew you'd find her."

"Thanks for your confidence."

"No. Thank you. Thank you very much, Mr. Jenkins."

"Your daughter calls me Sam. I'd prefer you did as well."

"Well…thank you, Sam. Thanks from all of us."

"You're welcome…Pauline. Enjoy the time with your daughter."

"Good-bye." She hung up.

Three cops walked past my doorway heading for the exit. I heard a chorus of, "Good job, boss. See ya."

I dropped my phone back onto the cradle. "Thanks again, guys."

A yellow pad and pencil lay on my blotter within reach. I pulled it close and began to write, still wanting to accomplish a few more things before putting the complicated affair to bed. At my age, a list of things to do is essential.

Chapter Twenty-One

We sat at the dining room table on Sunday morning with plates full of sweet potato pancakes, sausage links and sautéed apples. I drizzled a steady stream of maple syrup over the pancakes, while Kate sipped her coffee.

"So, you just called his cell phone, and a few minutes later he gave up?" Kate never tries to hide her skepticism.

"He wasn't an evil person, Kats. He's troubled. His head got messed up in Iraq, and then he got fired because he tagged some politico who tried to walk out of the sheriff's office with his drunken son. The kid felt the world pressing down on his shoulders, and he went around the bend. He needs a good doctor, not a police sniper."

"When I listen to this on the news, will I hear that you surrounded the house, called him and he said, 'Whoops, you've got me,' and then gave up?"

"Nothing's that simple." I popped a chunk of sausage into my mouth.

"You're a piece of work, Sambo. When you figure out what you want to be when you grow up, will you call me first?"

"Absolutely, sweetie." I sipped from my cup of black pumpkin-flavored coffee and assumed that segment of the conversation had ended.

"Care to give me a hint?"

"I've made no secret of the fact that I want to be a cowboy, just like Hoppy, Gene and Roy."

She shook her head and grinned. "How's your leg, Hopalong? Weather getting to you?"

164

"Yeah, it hurts like hell. But I'll bet if some good-looking woman massaged it for me, I'd feel a lot better."

"Have anyone in mind, big boy?" She sounded like Mae West.

"Sure do, and you're way up on the short list."

"I'm genuinely honored to be part of your harem, m' lord."

"Snot-nose."

"You said you're going in for a while today?"

"I want to stop at the hospital and see my victims. Then I want to go up to the jail and talk to that kid. I'll be finished early, back by mid-day."

"You probably don't want me to ask, but are you planning on taking a day off any time soon?"

"Yeah. It's a holiday tomorrow. Nobody's working but the guys on the road. I have this pretty well tied up. I can take the day off."

"During your twenty years in New York, you never got this personally involved in a case."

"The victims are my friends. I told you, I feel responsible for their problems."

"And you've always said cops who become personally invested in their victims will end up making mistakes and ultimately burn out."

"Yeah? I said that? What did I know?"

"You never told me much about what you did up there, but everyone said you were pretty damn good at your job. You solved problems and helped people with no emotional attachment. It seemed like the end result was more important than anyone's thanks. You were no more involved with another human being than a mason is to a cement block."

"That was rather melodramatic."

"Remember, sweetie, I sleep next to you. I know when things bother you. You haven't slept peacefully since this began. You might want to slow down a little."

"Sure. There's not much left. I just want to wrap up a few things. After that, it's up to the doctors and the DA."

"Sounds good."

She nodded and took a last sip of coffee. "Are we going out for our traditional New Year's Eve dinner?"

"We've had a big breakfast. How about skipping lunch and then go out for an early meal?"

"I could do that," she said.

"Chinese, Mexican, Italian, something in Knoxville? What's your pleasure?"

"How about the Villa Napoli?" she asked. "We can wish the Cutrones a happy New Year and stay close to home."

"Excellent choice, madam, and just like being back on Long Island. Getting back early is a good idea. I like to stay off the roads on amateur drunk night."

* * * *

At Blount Memorial Hospital, I found John Leckmanski doing much better. The bruises still looked terrible, but the swelling had gone down a little. He anticipated getting released on Tuesday. When I offered to drive him home, he told me someone much better looking than me would take care of that.

I left John, went back down to the lobby and bought a small flower arrangement in the gift shop. Rachel's room was on the third floor, above John, but in another wing. It took some doing, but I found her room. I walked through the open door without knocking and found her sitting up in bed watching television.

She wore a pink jogging suit. Double white stripes ran down the legs and sleeves of the top and slacks. Her white socks and a pair of white Nike sneakers with big pink checks on each side looked spotless. She wore her hair pulled back and tied in a short ponytail. I couldn't see any makeup. The several strands of dark hair falling to the sides of her face and a pair of slightly large, tinted glasses gave her an attractive casual look. She turned when I cleared my throat.

"Hey, kiddo, I came early," I said. "I wanted to catch you in your night gown."

She smiled, but let my glib remark go by the wayside and used the remote control to turn off the television.

"Hi, Sam, it's good to see you." Her smile could sell for a million bucks. "And you brought flowers. You're so sweet. Thank you."

I set the plastic pot on the roll around table next to her bed.

"You left so quickly yesterday. Why did you go?" she asked.

"I was just in the way. And I like to act like the Lone Ranger after my work is done. Besides, Tonto and the horses were double parked in the ambulance zone." I changed the subject. "How are you doing?"

"I'm good now. Last night, I ate dinner. It was…okay. They gave me a pill, so I slept well and still feel pretty relaxed. They're all very nice here."

"Going home today?"

"Yes. Boyd's picking me up at noon. I should be signed out by then."

She said noon. It was only 9:15, and she was still alone. Just when I started thinking Boyd might be a decent guy, I heard that. What kept him? Polishing his suspenders perhaps?

"I met your mom and dad," I said.

Someone who never learned how to speak on a radio mumbled something unintelligible over the PA system. Rachel waited to comment. "I know, they told me. Mom said she called you."

"She wanted to thank me. Wasn't necessary." I shrugged like the modest hero I am.

"Yes, it was."

She looked at me as if I really was a hero. I felt a little uncomfortable.

"Your maiden name was Kiel," I said, wanting to redirect the conversation.

She looked surprised. "It was."

"Kiel is the capitol of Schleswig-Holstein."

"Is it?" She cracked a big smile.

"It's also a bay between Germany and Denmark."

"Wow. I guess I know who to see about European geography."

"You look like your mom—she's pretty, too."

"Thanks. She always has been."

"I think she likes me."

"How could she not?" She laughed silently. It was one of those times when her eyes took on an almond shape.

"She fool around?" I asked.

"Oh God, you're terrible."

"People keep telling me that."

A young man wearing sage green scrubs walked in with a clipboard held under his arm like a textbook.

"Hiiii, Mizz Williamson, how are we doing this morning?" He spoke in a lilting, effeminate voice.

"I'm fine. Thanks, Tony."

"And we're going home todaaay. Great, that's just won-der-ful." He tilted his head like a trained seal. "But we're going to miss you." He sounded like Ross the Intern.

The boy turned to me and extended his hand. "Hi, I'm Tony. I've been looking after Mizz Williamson. Do you work with her at the station?"

We shook hands.

I added a little gravel to my voice and answered. "No, Tony, my name's Vito. I'm in the witness protection program. I'm here to let Ms. Williamson interview me about organized crime in America." Then I grinned like the village idiot.

He didn't.

Tony frowned and spoke seriously. "Ohhh…Well, I'd better let you two get down to business." Then he turned on the bubbles again. "See you soooon, Mizz Williamson. I'll be back to take you downstairs when the doctor signs you out. If you need me, I'll be gassing up your wheelchair."

Tony spun around on his axis and sashayed off into the hallway.

Rachel asked, "Why did you tell him that?"

"He was being nosey."

"He was being nice."

I shrugged. She smiled at me again, another real big one.

"Oh, Sammy." She shook her head. "Sometimes you can be so silly."

It was the first time she called me that.

"Hey, I like your glasses," I said. "It's nice to see a pretty girl wearing glasses."

"Thank you, but I'm afraid I don't look very good at the moment."

"Nonsense. You're beautiful." I began running out of small talk.

Rachel wanted to pursue a new topic. "Sam, I need to talk seriously with you again. If it wasn't for you…"

I held up my hand to stop her. It seemed like I'd been using the hand a lot lately.

"Just another day in the life of your basic all-American hero," I said.

"Well, you are my hero," she said. "And I..." She didn't finish.

We looked at each other for a long moment without speaking. She kept smiling. I needed to think of something to say. If in doubt, look to Bogart for help.

"Of all the police departments in all the towns in the world—you had to walk into mine," I said, with a familiar lisp.

"Oh, Bogey, you're such a romantic." She didn't try to sound like Ingrid Bergman.

"I guess I should be going. I've got a couple more stops to make. Have you seen John?" I knew she had.

"Yes, I went down last night and again this morning. Oh, the poor guy! He's really bruised up."

I nodded. "You should have seen him a couple days ago. He looked like a Halloween mask."

She grimaced.

"Okay, lady, I'm outta here. Call me. Let me know how you're doing. And if you need anything..." I let it trail off. "Hey, I think you look great in glasses. If I ever see you wearing a short skirt and knee socks, I'll kidnap you myself."

"Oh God! You're so bad."

"But all you girls like me."

I started for the door, turned, and stretched my lips over my teeth again. "It's nice knowing a dame like you, angel. Take care of yourself. I gotta go now and find Louie, so we can walk off into the sunset."

She laughed. "See ya, Bogey."

I gave her the gunman's salute. "Here's lookin' at you, sweetheart."

* * * *

Ralph Oliveri borrowed pre-arraignment cell space from the Knox County Sheriff to lodge Darrell Korner until his first court appearance. Their temporary detention facility was located in the City-County Building in downtown Knoxville. It took me less than half an hour to drive there from Blount Memorial Hospital.

When a jail guard brought Darrell into the interview room, he resembled an inmate from Devil's Island. His prison outfit looked like modern hospital scrubs, but the color scheme of wide horizontal white and black stripes definitely said 19th century penal colony.

However garish his clothing, Darrell had been treated well. Because of once being a cop, they kept him isolated from the jail's general population. He ate meals in his cell, had a TV close by and only saw other special prisoners. Under the circumstances, he looked okay.

"You agree to talk to me without your lawyer, Darrell?"

"Yes, sir, I don't care to."

The boy used a colloquialism that could have a double meaning. Good thing I speak the Smoky Mountain lingo and knew he didn't mind speaking with me.

"I'm not here to question you. I'm just here to talk."

"Sir?"

"Talk, chat, shoot the breeze, bullshit. You okay with that?"

"Yes, sir, that'll be fine."

"You have an attorney yet?"

"Yes, sir. My daddy told me he called one."

"The lawyer any good? You know anything about him?"

"Don't know who he is, sir. Haven't met him yet."

I scowled at him to emphasize my next point. "You need a good attorney, and I can recommend one. Best guy in Blount County—Joe Costello. Probably not the cheapest, but what price can you put on your future?"

"Yes, sir."

"I'll call your mom and dad and give them Costello's number. I'll see if they can strike up a deal with him about payments. That okay with you?"

"Yes, sir, that'll be fine."

"Now here's a general question for you. You think what you did made any sense?"

"No, sir, I...I don't know how to explain. I...I'm sorry, sir. There's nothin' I can say to justify what I done."

"Yeah, I understand. Now listen to me. Good lawyers, guys like Costello, understand, too. They know enough to turn this whole mess over and perhaps—just perhaps, get you off without hard time. You hear what I'm saying to you, Darrell?"

"Yes, sir, I hear ya."

"But if you do jail time, a warden will take care of you because you're an ex-cop. But if you don't end up in the slammer, if you just get time in a hospital or even probation with strict stipulations, I suggest you make the most of your good fortune."

"Sir?"

"I'm saying don't screw up when you get the opportunity of a lifetime, damn it. From what I've heard, you were a pretty squared away guy. But after this is over, you're going to have to start from scratch, square one."

Korner sat across from me nodding slightly as I spoke. So far, he showed little emotion, and I didn't know if I was getting through to him.

"Things you had virtually no control over caused you unbelievable grief," I said. "I understand that."

He dropped his eyes and rubbed his right hand over his left, over and over again.

I snapped at him. "Look at me when I'm talking to you, Darrell. Don't hang your head like a teenager caught tapping Daddy's liquor cabinet."

He raised his eyes and stared at me.

"Silver Stars and Purple Hearts don't come cheap, son. The day you won them was only the beginning. The toll they took here," I tapped my head, "continues for a long time—maybe forever. If you go to jail, you'll speak with a psychologist. The shrink they employ there might not be the best, but make the most of what he can offer you. If you get off, it will probably be for psychological reasons, and you'll spend time in some facility with a staff doctor who'll speak with you."

He started nodding again, but kept his eyes fixed on mine.

"If you're turned over to Probation, you'll be obligated to visit a court appointed counselor. I don't know how long those visits will last, but even after the court says you've been evaluated and you're okay to be on your own, go find a good VA psychologist. It won't cost you a dime. Let them show you how to deal with the spiders and scorpions and other demons that crawl around in your mind, making you feel lousy for years. If I can help you, I will. Call me. I'll be around Prospect PD for awhile."

"Thank ya, sir."

His lack of positive emotion was starting to annoy me. "Talkative bugger, aren't you?"

"I guess not, sir. I'm not feelin' too great."

I looked to my right. A black water bug crawled along the floor next to the concrete block wall.

"If you get out on your own, you're going to need a job. This last episode will limit your possibilities. If you need work and have a problem finding something decent, call me about that. I know some people. I might be able to help."

"Thank ya ag'in, sir."

The water bug disappeared into a crack in the glossy enamel, institutional-gray wall.

"One last thing, Darrell. I want you to listen very carefully here."

"Yes, sir."

"Once you're back on the street, there's one rule to live by for the rest of your life: Rachel Williamson is off limits. Understand? No phone calls to apologize. No showing up at the TV station to explain. Don't even watch her on the 6 o'clock news. We clear on that?"

"Yes, sir, I understand, but…"

"No buts, kid. From today on, you forget she exists. I understand how you might have felt, and that's okay. But now you forget her. Leave her alone. She might have been nice to you, but there was never any other connection between you two."

"Yes, sir, I promise."

"I hear what you're saying, Darrell, but let me impress upon you the importance of this. If I ever learn you've tried to contact her, no matter how good your intentions, I'll kill you—like a fucking bug. You believe what I've just told you, son?"

"I hear ya, sir. And yes, I believe ya would…and could. Don't know what it is, sir, but when I look inta yer eyes…ya scare the shit outta me." He closed his eyes and shook his head. "I… Ya just spent all this time tellin' me to get me a good lawyer, make the most of my future. Ya even said you'd he'p me. Now ya say you'll kill me?"

"Nothing personal, Darrell. It's just part of your future. Part of what

I'd have to do."

"I hear that, sir. Sir, is it… Is Miss Rachel…yours?"

"Don't be stupid, kid, Rachel is her own person. She has a husband and two sons. I have a wife and an old dog. She's not mine. But I will look out for her—that's all."

"I promise ya, sir, I'd never harm her. I'll do just as ya say."

I nodded. "Okay. We're good then."

"Yes, sir. We're good."

"Well, I wish you luck, Darrell. Call if you need me." I stood up to leave. "Oh, just for my information, where'd you get the dyphenhydramine and sevoflurane you used?"

"From a girl I knew."

"She work in a hospital?"

"Uh-huh."

"Son of a gun."

Chapter Twenty-Two

At 6:25, we pulled into the parking lot at the Villa Napoli in Maryville. I wore a tweed sport jacket, and Kate decided to wear the little black dress again. She called ahead and made a reservation, but we didn't need one.

In a converted warehouse building, three generations of the Cutrone family built one classy-looking Italian restaurant, something worthy of a strategic spot in South Manhattan's Little Italy.

We entered the front door with another couple right behind us. The owner's daughter, Rose, met us at the hostess station.

"Oh, hi guys," she said. "Happy New Year. Hold on a minute. Daddy said he wanted to see you. Let me get him before I seat these people."

Less than a minute after she disappeared, Nick Cutrone walked up. He was in his mid-seventies, a few inches shorter than me and still trim and dapper-looking. His shiny black hair was combed straight back, and only a hint of gray showed at the sideburns. The old boy's navy blue pinstripe suit must have cost as much as a good used car.

"'Ey, come stai? Sammy, how's it goin'?" he said. "And Katy, va-va-voom! You look terrific! I mean top-shelf, young lady. Why don't you dump this bum and hang out wit' me?"

Nick was not one to hide his emotions.

"Hiya, Nicky," I said.

"Hello, Nick," Katherine said and gave the old gangster wannabe a kiss on the cheek. "As much as I'd like to be your girl, Nick, the bum and I have been an item too long for me to drop him now."

"'Ey, I know what you're sayin', Katy. Good answer. That's why I like you so much. You're sharp. Beauty and brains, right, Sam?"

"You betcha, pal."

"Come on, let me show you your table," he said. "You guys get the best table in the house—my table—table thirty-five."

"Wow, I'm flattered," I said. "You're making me feel like the Teflon Don in this town."

"Hey, Sammy," he said, "John wasn't as bad as you think."

He crossed himself in remembrance of a fallen comrade.

"Yeah, I know, Nick. So, how you been?"

"I'm good," he said, tossing his hands to his sides. "Yeah, I'm good. How 'bout you two? Have a nice Christmas?"

"Yes, we did. Thanks," Kate said.

"Good, good. You both look great. But you, lady, you look better than him. A lot better. You unnerstand what I'm sayin'?"

"Thank you again, sir," she said.

"'Ey, Sammy, I heard your name on the news the other day. You did it again, huh? You're like a local hero, no?"

"You don't leave me much room for modesty."

"Yeah, right. Ha! So, what can I get you to drink? You want a little wine? I'll bring you a special bottle. White or red?"

Kate and I looked at each other. She was indecisive, and I'm easy.

"When in doubt, Nicky—white. How about sauvignon blanc? Nice and cold.

"Good, good. I want you to try this Chateau St. Michelle I just got in. I love it, and it won't break the bank, if you know what I mean."

"Sounds good, and bring yourself a glass. We're in no hurry. Sit and talk a while."

Why did I find myself sounding like a made-man every time I went into that place?

Nick disappeared.

Kate looked at me and said, "'Ey, not bad, goombah. Table thirty-five."

"Yeah, strategically placed, backs to the wall, a quick run to the kitchen and the back door. I'll plotz if there's a machine gun hanging under the table. But I like comin' here. It's like being back in the world."

Nick returned carrying three glasses. His grandson, Vinnie, walked behind him with an ice bucket and the bottle of wine. We gave Vinnie a hello, and like a good boy, he headed back toward the bar when Nick sat down. I poured the wine. We all held up our glasses.

"Salute!" Nick said.

"Cheers," I said.

"A happy, healthy New Year," was Kate's wish.

"So, Sammy," Nick said, "how you like bein' a cop again? Big difference here from back on the Island, no?"

Nick Cutrone was obviously not a native of East Tennessee. From the way he referred to Long Island as "the Island," one might infer he too came from New York. But we in the shadow of the 'Big Apple' allow those from New Jersey to sound like we do—as long as they're not too far from the river.

Nick spent most of his life in Hoboken—Frank Sinatra country. From a ma and pa Italian restaurant and pizzeria downtown, to a chi chi upscale Italian cucina in Tennessee wasn't too farfetched if you compared the relative overhead in each locale.

"Things are nice here," I said. "It's quiet—sometimes. Pretty country. A good retirement job."

"Yeah, but you've been busy," he said. "I read the papers. You found the kidnapped newsgirl yesterday, and you had to kill that Irish broad a couple months ago… Sorry, Katy, I didn't mean…"

"It's okay, Nick," I said. "Things happen."

"Yeah, right. ' Ey you're no slouch, Sam. I know some people who said you were a good cop back home. You're the guy who took off Sonny Masucci, right?"

"Jeez, that's a name from the past. Anthony Masucci—they called him Moon-face behind his back. He was some piece o' work."

"What'd you get him for? Anything big?"

"Loan sharking and promoting gambling at one of the big games he used to run. Peanuts in the big scheme of things, but he got the message."

"Just between you and me, Sam, Sonny was a punk. Yeah, a real punk. I remember him from Hoboken when he was nothin' but a snot-nosed kid. He used to come inta my place actin' like he had all kinds o' juice. He was nothin' compared to his old man."

"Yeah, Nick, I know what you mean. I met Gino once. He treated me with respect, and everyone said he was a stand-up guy. The kid was another story."

Nick looked interested in my opinion of Moon-face Masucci.

"You know, when I executed the arrest warrant for Sonny," I said, "he was home watching a rerun of *The Untouchables*. You believe that? A training film, maybe, huh? A couple of Feds were giving Frank Nitti a hard time on TV, and I took Sonny out in cuffs. Hot stuff."

Before Nicky and I could reminisce about any more of the goombahs from the old neighborhood, Rose came to the table.

"Excuse me," she said. "Daddy, Mr. Sloan from the Chamber of Commerce just walked in with his wife and that other couple. I thought you'd like to see him."

"Yeah, yeah, thanks, Rosie. I'll be right there." Nick turned back to us. "'Ey, I gotta go, but I'll stop back soon. And I gotta tell you—try the Fruiti Del Mare. I had it about an hour ago—delicious! I get all my seafood from that Cajun guy in Knoxville. Fresh every morning. Enjoy!"

Who could refuse a recommendation like that? After two plates of Fruiti Del Mare and another bottle of Chateau St. Michelle, I waved for the waitress to bring the check. Before she returned to table thirty-five, we heard loud voices from the bar. So did everyone else in the restaurant. Vinnie stood next to a nearby table serving a bottle of wine. I walked over.

"Vinnie, you know what that's about?" I asked.

A heavyset man sitting on a stool at the bar poked a finger at another customer.

"Nah, Mr. Jenkins. Alls I know is that fat guy's been drinkin' heavy ever since he got here with Mr. Sloan from the chambah. I think he's arguin' wit the other guy about football or somethin'."

"He's got a big mouth," I said. "I'll see if your grandfather wants a hand."

Vinnie raised his eyebrows. The couple getting the wine looked concerned.

I stepped down from the raised deck of the dining area to the main level and walked to the bar. I moved up behind the loudmouth and winked at Nicky who spoke to him like a Dutch uncle.

Nick leaned close. "Look, sir, I run a nice quiet place here, not some kind o' low-class gin mill. You gotta take the volume down a peg."

"Yew sayin' I'm low class?" The man spoke in a local drawl.

"I'm sayin' if you don't quiet down, I'll call the cops. Unnerstand?" Nick said.

I shifted position so, if necessary, I could hit loudmouth with a quick left jab and follow up with a right to the kidney. Nicky looked at me and shook his head slightly.

I noticed Vinnie step up on my left, followed by his uncle, Tommy, the chef, who tucked a meat tenderizer neatly under his arm and watched how his father handled the customer. The Cutrones seemed to have their act together. I'd watch and if necessary, pick up the pieces and tell the Maryville cops what happened.

"You got any idea who I am?" the loudmouth said.

"Don't know and don't care," Nick said. "But I think you should leave now, capiche?" He sounded very serious.

Finally, Judd Sloan from the Chamber of Commerce stood up and put his hand on the fat man's shoulder. "Come on, Mac, I think we'd better go. No sense makin' trouble."

The fat man drained his low-ball glass and slammed it onto the bar. "Come on, Charlotte," he said to the woman next to him. "Y'all won't catch me eatin' in a place like this ag'in." He wrapped a pudgy hand around his wife's arm and stalked out.

Sloan started peeling twenties from a wad he pulled out of his pocket and placed them on top of their bar bill.

"I apologize to all y'all," he said to no one in particular. Then he looked at his wife. "June, I'm sorry, honey. Let's go."

"Fat son-of-a-bitch!" Nick said quietly.

"Who was that asshole?" I whispered in his ear.

"Some county commissioner from out where you live. I haven't seen him before, but Sloan told me he was bringin' him. Why am I so freakin' lucky?"

"You handled it beautifully, Nick," I said. "Who needs a cop?"

"Yeah, but thanks for the backup anyways. I appreciate it." He turned to his grandson. "Vincent, get me a scotch." Apparently, Vincent

178

didn't move quickly enough. Nick waved his hand dismissively. "Go on."

Vinnie disappeared behind the bar, and I turned to Tommy. "That's a nice mallet you've got there, Tommy. I hope the veal is good and tender." I gave him a pat on the shoulder.

He smiled and walked back to the kitchen.

After the dust settled, Kate and I said our good-byes to the Clan Cutrone and drove east, back to the mountains.

During dinner, Kate shamed me into saving some of my pasta. She never finishes all of the big portions Tommy serves, so we had something in a Styrofoam box for tomorrow's lunch. As soon as we walked into the house, Bitsey's keen olfactory senses homed in on Tommy's use of garlic, and she began doing a Highland fling beneath the plastic bag Kate held.

I gave the dog a small dish of pasta and then deposited the carryout tray in the fridge.

Only nine o'clock and we had the whole evening ahead of us. But after Guy Lombardo died, I promised myself never to stay up until midnight on New Year's Eve again. Kate agreed.

So, I opened a bottle of Taittinger, and we watched a DVD of *Robin and Marion*. Kate thought my idea of watching *Bullitt* was inappropriate for a romantic evening.

By 11:00, we were in bed. By 12:30, we were asleep. The little black dress worked again. I enjoyed my New Year's Eve.

That night Kate got all of my attentiveness. But on the next day at work, two of the other women in my life would require a little more of my attention.

Chapter Twenty-Three

There was no reason for me to be at work early on Tuesday morning. With the holidays officially over and our major incident now officially under the rug, I could bask in my hero status for at least a few days. At ten-to-nine, I walked in and stopped just off Bettye's starboard quarter.

"Mornin', Betts. Happy New Year. How's everything?"

"Mornin', Sam. You doin' all right today?"

Her voice lacked the positive, up-beat tone I'd grown to expect. I walked into my office, took off the uniform coat our sainted mayor expected me to wear to his press conference and hung it on the back of the door. Smells of fresh coffee drifted over from the maker, and I spotted a little white paper bag on the counter next to the pot. My trained investigator's eye drew toward the telltale grease stains—jelly doughnuts. I looked into the bag. Bettye bought two.

I stuck my head out of the office door. "You busy?"

"No. Need somethin'?"

"Yes, can we talk for a minute?"

"Course," she said.

"Like some coffee?"

"Yes, please."

"Doughnut?"

"No, thanks. They're for you."

"Thanks. They look good."

"They end up on my hips."

"Nobody looks at my hips."

She smiled. I fixed two cups of coffee.

"You mad at me?" I asked.

"Sort of."

"Understandable. But I already apologized. You know why I did what I did?"

"I guess."

"Want me to explain again?"

"If you want."

"What do *you* want?"

"I don't want to be mad at you anymore."

"Sounds good. You willing to listen one more time?"

"Okay."

I placed her cup on the edge of my desk next to her chair, turned the other leather-covered guest chair around to face her and sat down.

"Back in October, when I asked you to come with me to the bookshop," I said, "I was impatient. I should have waited, and now regret what I did. I should have taken more help with us to make that arrest. Stan was due here in less than an hour. I hold myself responsible for you almost getting shot."

Bettye is a good listener. She sat patiently looking me in the eye. It wouldn't be easy to lie to her. I didn't really want to, but leaving that option open is just part of what I've done most of my adult life.

"I don't care if you're a woman or a man," I said. "You're a cop. You're my buddy—my partner. But I'm the *senior* guy, and I'm responsible. We work together every day, and I look out for you, you look out for me. I let you down, and I need some time to regroup before I... I don't want to put you in danger again."

"Sam, that wasn't your fault."

"I don't see it that way. I recognize my problem with the patience thing. Sometimes I feel like a bull in a china shop."

"That's not true."

"You're very kind. Look, if you're on your own and something happens, I trust you to handle it as well as anyone else. That's different—I think."

"I do understand," she said. "I wanted to go with you yesterday, not to prove anything to me or to the other people, but because I needed to

181

hold up my end. You saved my life. Now you owe it to me to let me do my part. I need to watch your back. That's all."

That wasn't exactly what I expected.

"Jeez, Betts, I didn't see it that way. I'm sorry. I guess I looked at it in the simpler, more logistical terms you find in a supervision manual. Throw in a little selfishness, and that's me. I'm really sorry."

"It's okay, Sammy. We're fine. I'm not mad anymore. I felt bad, but now we each know. That work for you?"

"Of course it does," I said. "I guess partners just need to know what the book says so they can violate the rules successfully."

She smiled. "Good. Now I'm going to do something politically incorrect. Stand up, Sam Jenkins. I'm goin' to give my boss a big hug."

"I love gettin' hugged by girls with gun belts."

"You're really strange."

"Live with it."

"I can do that."

I got a big hug. She's strong for a girl.

"Okay, partner?" she said.

"Sure, lady. Couldn't be better."

Bettye turned to leave, but hesitated. "Sammy," she had a little extra twinkle in her hazel eyes, "I look at your hips."

"You do?"

"Sure. You've got a cute butt for a guy your age."

"Thanks. I love being a sex object."

"I'll bet you do."

I got through that one successfully, and with only a little white lie. I do care that she's a woman. I've always been overprotective, and I'm too old to change. I might take a bullet someday, but what the hell is chivalry all about?

* * * *

At 9:30, the news people started filtering into the building. The usual county newspaper reporters arrived with their photographers. Three of the four television networks were represented by one of their senior news anchors. Rachel's station manager sent a pretty blonde reporter named Karen Walters, someone I'd met before. The TV cameramen looked poised and ready to go.

Carl Harmon walked through our double glass doors, flipped a salute at Bettye and came directly to my office. Ralph and Bonnie followed him closely.

"Hello, Sam." He extended his hand. "Ralph told me you did one hell of a job up in the boondocks. Good work."

"Thanks, Carl." We shook hands. "Good thing I read that chapter on police work in the boonies."

Carl let that one pass, either because of my genuine hero status or he was already concentrating on carefully phrasing his next statement. Ralph rolled his eyes. Bonnie giggled silently. Maybe I could get to like her.

"Sam, I've got to hand it to you," Carl said. "That information you developed was crucial to our investigation."

It almost looked like making that admission pained him.

"It wasn't just me," I said. "A cop named Junior Huskey came up with the info. He arrested a girl with felony weight drugs—she wanted to make a deal and had something to trade."

"Well, good job by all your people. Really well done."

I thanked Carl again and noticed him stealing a look out my door toward the lobby.

"Looks like this thing is about to kick off," he said. "Want to go outside?"

I took my uniform coat off the hanger, and as Ralph passed by, I grabbed his arm.

"In case you're keeping score," I said, "the skell girlfriend Junior picked up with the pills gave Darrell the sevoflurane. She pilfered it from BMH."

"She the one Junior had in your car up at the cabin?"

"Yeah, the poor but honest hospital worker."

"What are you going to do with her?"

"She promises to work off the debt by ratting out her dealer."

"Lucky you," Ralph said.

"Lucky Knox County."

Bonnie had already followed Carl to the lobby where Ronnie Shields busied himself preparing for the start of his news conference.

After Ralph and I finished speaking, he headed outside, too. I stopped next to Bettye's desk buttoning my tunic.

"My gig line straight, Sarge?" I asked.

She stood up, shifted my lapels a little and straightened my tie. I thought everything was in line, but I guess women just like to fondle me.

"You didn't wear your medals today," she said.

"No, I'm trying to exercise a little humility."

"I didn't think that was possible, darlin'."

"Madam, the liberties you take are extraordinary."

That got me a nice smile. She likes hearing my James Mason imitation.

"I should wish you luck," she said, "but I've seen you do these things before. The reporters need the luck."

"You're such a good girl. See how you just made up for being a wise guy."

I got another smile—enough luck for me.

As I sat in my assigned chair, Ronnie began addressing the assembled multitude.

"Ladies and gentlemen, thank ya fer bein' here today. I'm very happy and proud ta say that through the very fine efforts of our local FBI agents and officers of the Prospect Po-leece Department, Miss Rachel Williamson, who I'm sure y'all know very well, has been found and returned ta her family."

He waited for the brief round of applause to taper off and then beamed like Richard Nixon after he returned from China.

"An arrest has been made," he continued, "and I'm pleased ta say it was accomplished very quickly and easily with no injuries ta anyone. Now, I know y'all must have questions, but first I'd like to have Special Agent Carl Harmon, who y'all recognize as the man in charge of the Knoxville office of the FBI, make a statement. Then our Chief of Po-leece, Sam Jenkins, will say a few words and answer all y'all's questions." Ronnie extended his hand toward Harmon. "Carl."

After Harmon delivered an eloquent statement, praising his agents and acknowledging that an officer from PPD developed the crucial information leading to the arrest and rescue, he turned the program over to me.

184

"Good morning, people," I said. "Just like the mayor, I'm glad to see you here this morning. It's so much easier to put out correct and timely information when we get together and share it. Now, let's take this incident from the beginning."

A couple people shifted in their chairs. Two flashguns popped, and I saw the reporters poised to write.

"The morning of the assault on Mr. Leckmanski and the abduction of Ms. Williamson had the Prospect PD in high gear. I'd like to thank every member of my department for giving up their personal time to come back on duty and assist in the search and investigation.

"I quickly realized that to carry on an investigation of this importance, resolve the situation as rapidly as possible *and* provide the citizens of Prospect with the protection and service they pay for, I needed assistance. Therefore, since kidnapping cases are a specialty of theirs, I contacted the FBI. They had the personnel, technology and expertise to do a job in the best interests of Ms. Williamson. After the FBI took operational control of the case, one of the officers in this department, Davis Huskey, Jr., developed intelligence and exploited it, leading a joint force of FBI, Prospect Police and THP personnel to locate and arrest a subject and bring Rachel Williamson safely home. Questions, please."

A big sandy-haired anchorman who had been a pushy pain-in-the-ass on previous occasions jumped to his feet with a question.

"Chief, is it true that you took several Prospect officers to the cabin before notifying the FBI?"

I knew I could count on that rat-bastard to break my chops.

"No, sir, that's not true. Your information is faulty. We arrived at the scene first. However, I contacted Special Agent Oliveri, the lead investigator on the case, before leaving this department. Because of logistical difficulties late on a Saturday, mobilizing a team from Knoxville could have been possible, but would have taken too much time. It was already afternoon—we lose light quickly in January."

Any idiot knows that, pal.

"I wanted to be in place before nightfall," I said, "so I took seven officers with me. We located the cabin and secured the area. Agents Oliveri and Rowatt were airlifted to the scene by a state police helicopter. When they arrived, Oliveri took command." I finished my statement with a theatrical scowl. "Next, please."

I wanted to sound and look dismissive. Perhaps someday the big schmuck would learn how to act around Sammy.

A good-looking redhead in her late-forties from another network asked, "How did you communicate with the subject, and was he cooperative?"

I smiled at her so she'd think only Big Sandy was in the doghouse. "We first used cell phones. Then, we spoke face to face, and yes, he was cooperative. We had no trouble with him at all."

She smiled back.

The blonde from WNXX raised her hand and stood up next.

"Chief, isn't it true that you entered the cabin and then disarmed the subject, wrestling the gun from him?"

I assumed she spoke with Rachel, the short girl with the big mouth.

"Well, it wasn't as dramatic as all that. I spoke to the subject on the phone. Since I started the dialogue with the subject, Agent Oliveri asked that I continue the negotiations. I entered the cabin, where the subject and I talked at length, and then he surrendered. There was no physical confrontation involved. I took the handgun from him. He didn't resist. It was all over quickly. Ms. Williamson was unhurt and had been well treated.

Next, a newspaperman in a wrinkled sport jacket and open collar jumped up.

"What was the kidnapper's motivation in abducting Rachel Williamson?"

"I think that's an aspect of the case the prosecutor would rather I not speculate on at this time. The subject has cooperated with the DA and admitted to both the assault and the kidnapping. Perhaps his motivation will come out at trial."

The remaining questions were all inconsequential, and I answered them with the appropriate mumbo-jumbo. In ending my portion of the dog and pony show, I again thanked the Prospect cops, the FBI personnel and even the troopers for the use of their chopper. Ronnie took the program back and closed it like the talented ringmaster he is.

When I returned to the office Bettye asked, "Do you enjoy bullying reporters?"

"Did I sound like a bully? I don't think so. I just like to keep these things focused and on track. Control is very important."

"You sounded like a bully to me."

"Hey, be nice to me. I've got to go eat my doughnuts."

* * * *

I barely started my second cup of coffee and my first jelly doughnut when Moira Menzies called from the DA's office.

"Do I need you to come down here, or can we talk on the phone?" she asked.

It sounded like I'd be subjected to one of her perpetual snits.

"Hello to you, too, Moira. I'm here and listening—speak."

"Two FBI agents arraigned Darrell Korner this morning. Your friend Oliveri wrote him quite a sweetheart deal. You have anything to do with that?"

"Why would you infer that?"

"Because Korner's lawyer said you visited his client this weekend in the Knoxville jail. He said his client now wants Joe Costello as his counsel. The kid also told his lawyer you told him to see a shrink, and if he got away with no hard time you'd help him find a job."

"That sounds dreadfully benevolent. Maybe I should be a social worker."

"Maybe you should keep your smart mouth in low gear. The lawyer told the boy you shouldn't be trusted because cops are infamous liars. Korner assured the lawyer that you were not a liar. He said you not only offered advice and possible assistance, but you were honest enough to threaten to kill him if he got within a mile of Rachel Williamson. You're Korner's goddamn hero, for God's sake. What the hell were you doing, Sam?"

"Tell that shyster, whoever he is, Darrell is very perceptive. I am not a liar. Look, Moira, Darrell and I had a friendly chat. I didn't question him as an investigator. I talked. He listened. What's the problem with that?"

"Prospect PD wraps up a case the Feds had trouble with, and you expect me to believe Junior Huskey came up with all this on his own?"

The sounds of Moira's snit escalated to full-scale anger.

"Junior's informant broke the case."

"We'll get to him later," she snapped. "Then you tell your defendant to sack his lawyer and get the best defender in the county. Does that make any sense to you?"

"Listen, what Darrell Korner did was reprehensible. You can imagine what went through my mind each day we hadn't found Ms. Williamson. But I learned that Korner had been a pretty good guy before he did all this. After checking on him some more and then talking with him, I believe he's not totally responsible for his actions."

She snorted. "Maybe that social worker thing is a good idea."

Now I was the one getting pissed off. "Here's a kid, Moira, who goes to war and gets forced to see and do things young people should not have to see or do. Then he comes home a hero, resumes his job as a conscientious public servant and through no fault of his own, becomes another victim of a corrupt political system."

"That's melodramatic."

"Yeah? Nuts! Remember the straw that broke the camel's back? What the hell was he fighting for?" My own snit began dominating the conversation. I heard my voice rising. "Something like that might tend to screw up a guy's head, goddamnit. There was no good reason for what he did. You know all about levels of culpability. He needs to be handled by a talented therapist."

I looked up and saw Bettye standing at my doorway. I must have been louder than I thought.

"And how about your victims?" Moira asked, down shifting her snit and getting more RPMs.

"Leckmanski is doing well. He's hurting, but he'll fully recover. He's a cameraman. He's covered wars and major civil unrest all over the world and knows what goes with the territory. John's a big boy and a good man. Ms. Williamson says she's fine. She told me she was neither hurt physically nor molested in any way. She's a tough kid, too."

"Nice of you to speak for them."

"Then ask them yourself, damn it. And think about this," I said. "Darrell, the third victim, is going to pay for his actions one way or another. He understands that. He knows the system. No one is getting away with anything."

"Sam, please stop with the phony Mizz Williamson formality. It's pretty common knowledge you two are an... uh...item. Anytime something creeps or flies in Prospect, she gets the story long before anyone else. Makes a body wonder why."

"You know what, Moira? At my age, I'd be totally exhausted if I got laid as often as some people think I do. There is no *item*. Do we need to go further on that subject?"

She didn't answer the question, but sighed audibly and continued. "Let's talk about your second defendant. Junior Huskey arraigned this Pikey Dillard late Saturday. I understand you'd like a deal involving probation for her?"

"She provided the information that led us to find Darrell's cabin hideaway. No Pikey, perhaps no clearance of a kidnapping for another day or two or more. Would you want to be Rachel for those extra nights?"

"Okay, point taken. But she had almost six hundred pills. What did you have in mind?"

"She still owes us the pill dealer in Knoxville, and talk is cheap. Tell her she has to produce for Knox County narcotics and set up a couple of buys. If that works out, couple those cases with the tip on Darrell. How about five years probation with drug and alcohol conditions, no chance of time off?"

"Lord have mercy, you don't want much."

"Come on, you're just saying that so I'll think I owe you a big one."

"You will, and I'll remind you, mister."

"I thought you might."

"Last thing," she said. "Your third defendant, the mechanic Swaggerty. He was in here with his attorney bright and early today. The lawyer wanted to see if I'd offer a deal. And I did. For a quick plea, I wanted one year on each count to run concurrently, then five years parole with no less than eleven months, twenty-nine days jail time. But the lawyer wanted to start with negotiations for good behavior time, and Swaggerty stopped him, jumped on my first offer. The lawyer objected and wanted to talk more. Swaggerty told him to shut up. He used those words. Swaggerty said he was messing with his life. Your defendant looked scared, Sam."

"He's obviously guilty. Maybe he needs to repent," I said.

I heard her expel more air than a burst balloon.

"No, Sam, he looked petrified. You know what that's about?"

"Who knows what goes on in Elrod's mind? The guy's a head case, an antisocial miscreant. Maybe he found religion, and he's got the fear of the Lord in him."

"Sure, Sam, that must be it." She hung up without saying good-bye.

Ah, Jenkins, you do have a way with the ladies.

Bettye was still standing in my doorway. I looked at her a second time and grinned. "Hi there."

She shook her head and returned to her desk without comment.

My original cup of coffee had gotten cold, and I refuse to drink cold coffee. I poured another and finished both jelly doughnuts—that would hold me until lunchtime.

Ronnie had forced me to wear a uniform, subjected me to speak with a group of reporters, and I'd been brow-beaten by a female ADA. That was no way to treat a local hero.

After all that work during the morning and the company business I transacted over the weekend, I felt entitled to most of the day off. I put my feet up and read from *Dead Certainties* by Simon Shama for almost an hour.

When my clock struck noon, I walked across the square and ate lunch with Mr. Lum. After a plate of Mongolian chicken, I stopped at the real estate office to see Glenda Mae Waddell.

Just before 1 p.m., I came back into the office to take over the desk while Bettye ate her salad and read a romance novel with a guy who looked like Fabio on the cover, embracing a woman who looked like Brenda Starr.

When Bettye returned to her desk, I walked around feeling like a little kid looking for trouble. I walked to the rear door, stared at Earl Biggins' garage and watched Logan Mapes change the oil on a city pick-up truck. Nothing else was shaking outside.

I returned to my office for another date with Mr. Shama and his story of the intertwined lives of General James Wolfe, the author Francis Parkman, and others. But that didn't last long. Out of boredom, I made a mistake that led me into a messy situation, but inadvertently to an important bit of intelligence.

Chapter Twenty-Four

After less than half an hour, I tossed Simon on my blotter and walked around again looking for something to do, but found nothing. Rather than starting up a meaningless conversation and getting Bettye annoyed by disturbing her, I decided to spend a couple hours riding along with one of the patrolmen. I checked our roster for a likely chauffeur.

"Betts, would you tell Junior to come in and pick me up? I need to do a little road time and blow the cobwebs out."

"Okey dokey, darlin'."

Davis "Junior" Huskey was pushing thirty-years-old. He'd worked for Prospect PD for almost seven years, and for the time I'd known him, he'd been a nice kid, enthusiastic, honest, and smart enough to be given those extra jobs that eventually make some road cops good investigators. Fifteen minutes after Bettye called him on the radio, Junior walked into my office without knocking.

"Howdy, Sam. You doin' aw rot today?"

"You sound up-beat and full of yourself today. Solving that big case gone to your head?"

"Shoot, no. I'm still the same modest, but handsome young man I always been."

I shook my head. "As your den mother out there would say, 'Lord have mercy.'"

He stood there grinning like a child on Christmas morning.

"You up for a partner today?" I asked. "I've got a case of the 'willies' and need to hit the road."

192

"Sure, boss. Stick with me, an' I'll show you how us real cops do it."

I exaggerated a laugh. "Just remember, kid, I've got more time in a PD men's room than you have on the job."

"Shoot," he said.

From two o'clock on, we patrolled, roamed around, wrote a traffic summons for fifty in a thirty-five-mile zone, which also netted Junior an additional ticket for two bald tires, and because the driver showed an attitude and opened his big mouth once too often, a third for having a dirty license plate.

We met the two other patrolmen on duty and shot the breeze for a few minutes with each of them. Then at 3:30, the call most patrol cops dread came over the radio.

The lovely voice of Sergeant Lambert said, "501, Unit five-zero-one, active maternity at 1175 Osborne Road off Prospect. See Mrs. Myers—daughter's in labor.

I grabbed the mike. "This is 501, we copy. And thanks a bunch, honey."

She didn't skip a beat keying the mike. "Prospect headquarters to 501 and all Prospect units. Refrain from using unauthorized language on the radio. Prospect headquarters out."

Feeling appropriately chastised and dismissed, I said, "If she hadn't just bought me two jelly doughnuts, I'd get her for that."

Junior laughed.

We'd been parked in the lot of a small strip mall half a mile south of the town square. Junior drank from a plastic bottle of Mountain Dew, and I held a half-empty cup of coffee. He screwed on the cap to his soda, but I had nowhere to go with my coffee. So, I opened the window and with great panache, tossed the remaining coffee into the lot—or so I thought. I hadn't seen the man walking past our car, only six feet from the passenger's window, when I threw the hot liquid. Splat—about five ounces of coffee hit him directly in the crotch.

"What the hell?" he bellowed. Junior flipped on the blue lights and hit the siren as we peeled out of the parking lot.

"Yahoo!" Junior yelled as the car fishtailed slightly before streaking off down the road.

"Take it easy, kid. Maybe the ambulance will get there before us. We're heading for messy business."

"Got him good with the coffee, didn't ya, boss?"

"No doubt the mayor will get a call on that one."

Thirty years ago, I would have laughed all the way to our call. Today, there's nothing like a big faux pas to give a supervisor a little humility.

We roared up Main Street, drove counter-clockwise around the town square, north again on Main and over the Crystal Creek Bridge where Main Street changed names to Prospect Road.

As we charged north, I noticed a ratty blue Toyota go through a stop sign at one of the side streets. The description rang a bell.

"Didn't Pikey Dillard drive an old blue Toyota with a crumpled front fender?" I asked.

"Yep," he said and blasted the siren to get a slow-moving farm truck to pull over. "Ugly li'l car."

"I didn't see the driver, but I'll bet it was her car that ran the stop sign back at Fred Hanson Road. She's probably still driving with that suspended license."

"I'll go check it out," Junior said. "Sit on her house when I got me an extra minute."

"Good. Lock her ass up. Put more pressure on her to produce for the narcotics guys."

"Boss, ya got me doin' real po-leece work ag'in."

Another half-mile and Junior turned left onto Osborne Road. The whole trip took less than five minutes, and we pulled up in front of number 1175, a neat, brick-faced ranch house with a carport.

I hung my badge on the pocket of my sport jacket as I exited the cruiser.

I said, "Grab the first aid kit. I'll be inside," and trotted up to the front door to meet a woman in her mid- to late-forties, while Junior popped the trunk.

"Someone in here about to deliver a little bundle of joy?" I asked.

"Yes, sir, my daughter is. Right this way." The expectant grandmother seemed calm enough.

I started walking through the living room, heard the front door slam shut and then re-open again right behind me. I turned to see Junior holding the big orange first-aid kit.

In the main bedroom, lying on a queen-sized bed, we found a very pregnant young lady with a belly the size of a Volkswagen Beetle. Her face showed the expression of a tortured POW. I took off my coat, began to roll up my sleeves and turned toward Grandma.

"How close are the contractions?" I asked.

"We called the doctor when they was two minutes apart. He said when they's a minute come to the hospital, and he'd meet us there. She ain't gonna make it to no hospital now, is she?"

"Doubt it. The guy you talked to a witch doctor?"

"I guess," she said, shaking her head.

"Okay, there's an ambulance on the way from Maryville, but we'll figure the kid might not wait. Get me a shower curtain to put under her, a big clean pot with a cover and a few bath towels," I instructed.

I knelt next to the pregnant girl.

"You're in good shape, young lady. Hang in there for me, and we'll do this together. You feel the baby coming out?"

"*Yeees! Oooh!!* Damn!" She spoke with the inflection only an expectant mother can create.

"Enough said."

I stepped into the bathroom to wash my hands.

"Boss, you want me to boil some water?" Junior asked.

"Why, you want a cup o' tea?"

"No, don't y'all need hot water?"

"You watch too many cowboy movies, kid. Do me a favor. Move some of the living room furniture out of the way so the medics can get their gurney in here without a hassle."

"*Oooooh!* Damn it! Damn it!" The young mommy needed to be heard again.

Grandma returned with the plastic curtain. We rolled the girl over and covered the mattress.

"What's the pot for?" Grandma asked.

"Afterbirth. Got to keep it nice and clean. The doctor will want to see it, and I'd rather let him cut the cord in the hospital," I said. "I assume her water's already broken?"

"It has, uh-huh."

I heard the front door open and close again.

"Where's my wife?" someone asked Junior.

I looked toward the bedroom door.

"I called my son-in-law," Grandma said.

A young man dressed in the uniform of a carpet cleaning company stood in the doorway.

"What's happenin', Lucy?" he asked his mother-in-law.

"She's havin' the baby, John, any minute now."

"Folks," I said, "She's going to need a little more help than I can give by myself. Grandma, help take her panties off."

"Hey, wait a minute," the young father said, "you cain't look at my wife with no panties."

"Chrissake, son," I said. "It's kinda difficult for the baby to come out while she's got her drawers on. I promise not to look. Swear to God. Now come around here, and hold her hand. Grandma, you hold the other."

Mrs. Meyers did the honors, and her daughter was now logistically ready to begin the delivery.

The girl looked in so much pain, I was afraid she might kick me in the head.

"Okay, Mom, take a deep breath, and give us a push."

She did, and it was a big one. It's amazing how Mother Nature teaches women what to do.

"Oooooh! Ooooh, Lord have mercy!"

"Try again. I see the top of a little bald head."

Ooooh! God, this hurts! *Ooooooooooh!*

"Halfway there, baby. Once more and it's a touchdown."

"*Ooooh,* Jesus save me!"

"All done," I said.

When nature cooperates, delivering a baby takes less time than telling the story. That was a good day for amateur obstetricians.

The slippery little critter rested on my forearm. I stroked his throat and gave his cheek a pat. Zowie! He let out a scream a UT fan would be proud to hear at the big game against Florida State. I wrapped him in a bath towel, attended to the rest of the necessary logistics and handed the little boy to the new mother. We smiled at each other. The baby gurgled.

A hi-low ambulance siren disturbed the otherwise tranquil neighborhood. I wiped my palm on a towel, turned to the father and extended my hand.

"Congratulations, Pop. He's a neat lookin' kid. Best of luck."

I heard Junior open the front door. Two paramedics, a man and a woman wearing Rural Metro uniforms, came in pushing a folding gurney.

"Hi, guys," I said. "Ready to take over?"

They grinned and nodded.

"Yes, sir," the female said. "We'll take it from here." She quickly looked over the mother and child and then turned back to me. "Good job—thanks."

I stood up, felt a substantial pain in my lower back and tried to stretch it out. Having little luck in the self-chiropractics area, I called, "Junior?" I didn't see him. "Junior?" I called again and stepped into the living room, still wiping my hands on the towel.

Junior had taken Grandma aside, where he stood pointing to his head. I heard the conversation.

"Ma'am, could I trouble you for an aspirin?"

"Certainly, son," she said. "Lotta tension here today, ain't there?"

* * * *

Back at the PD, Junior and I walked through the back door feeling like gun-toting obstetricians. Bringing a new life into the world gives you a good feeling. All smiles, we walked up and stood in front of Bettye's desk. I held up my hand showing her four fingers.

"Number four," I said. "A healthy, bouncing baby bubba, thanks to the Huskey-Jenkins OB-GYN services."

"I heard. Congratulations, gentlemen. They gonna name the baby Samuel Davis?"

"I hope not," I said.

"Uh-huh, me, too," Junior added.

Then Bettye made her motherly 'mad' face and looked over the tops of her little glasses. "Honey?"

"What?"

"You called me *honey* over the radio, Sam Jenkins."

She calls me Sam Jenkins when she scolds me.

"Sorry. Sergeant Honey."

"Okay, darlin'. Apology accepted."

I winked at her.

How could she get mad at me?

She smiled. "What do you mean, number four?"

"I delivered three others back in New York."

"Well, for goodness sake."

"Messy business." I shook my head. "I don't know why you girls do it willingly."

She chuckled. "Sam, that was a nice thing you two did."

"Yeah, feels good, too." I looked at Junior and slapped him on the shoulder. "Good job, partner. Thanks for the ride." I looked at my watch. "Now you're on overtime. Don't work too hard."

"See ya tomorrow, Sam, Miss Bettye." Junior walked out with a Cheshire cat grin spanning his face.

"Hey, kid," I yelled at his back. "Don't forget to track down Pikey Dillard. I want to see her in cuffs again."

He waved over his shoulder and disappeared through the back door.

Chapter Twenty-Five

My world changed drastically during the early days of January. With the Elrod Swaggerty and Darrell Korner sagas closed, the Smoky Mountain winter once again weighed heavily on my shoulders.

All traces of Christmas had disappeared from the landscape, and Baby New Year vanished on the second of the month.

Life in the Smokies once again became tranquil. Or is the correct word boring? For the cops in a small town, the mild winter, the long days and the lack of action made the work tours seem forty-eight hours long.

On Tuesday, January 9th at 2 o'clock, Rachel called sounding happy. She planned on taking another week off and enjoyed simply waiting at home to meet her two sons when they returned from school. She even anticipated Boyd coming home from the office shortly after five each night. Maybe she wanted to be a good wife and polish his suspenders.

She began calling me each morning. If she didn't, I'd call her early in the afternoon. Basically, we spoke about nothing. Rachel could rattle off small talk with a charm I can't duplicate. We spoke of rented movies, the few TV shows worth watching and current events. She always laughed at my foolishness and fed me opportunities to say clever things.

But these diversions didn't come without a ration of invasive thoughts slamming around inside my head. I felt my emotional attachment to Rachel growing out of proportion—something capable of disturbing my mental tranquility. I had experienced enough brain upheaval from the life I'd lived to think one more issue wouldn't matter much to me. But I couldn't anticipate where Rachel envisioned our friendship going, and I didn't want to cause her future pain. I valued what we had and could probably stop drinking easier than just flipping a switch to turn off our relationship. And it wasn't my business to tell Rachel what to think. Or was it?

The logical thing to do might be discuss it with my wife. But I've never brought home my problems or quandaries before and dropping that bomb on Kate didn't look like a good icebreaker. I've never been a Renaissance man looking to share his troubles and cry on a pretty shoulder. Sometimes Life is a card game. I held back two and tossed in three.

On the following Monday, as Bettye and I muddled through the lackluster, monotonous existence cops without significant action in their lives experience, I thought about Pikey Dillard.

Junior hadn't been able to catch her driving, and I hadn't received a call from the Knox County narcotics cops she promised to introduce to her on-call drug dealer.

At noon, I drove to Howell's Pub for lunch, ordered a large barbeque pork sandwich, a pint of black and tan and engaged in a rousing conversation with Reggie Smethurst about Northumbria and northwest Yorkshire.

By two o'clock, I felt bored beyond expectation and stood at the back door of the PD hoping the sky would fall on the parking lot so I could run outside and save someone from Mother Nature's wrath and quiet an overwrought Chicken Little.

At 2:15, a gold Lexus SUV pulled up and slid into one of the spots reserved for visitors to the police department. Above the Knox County plates and the RX350 model designator, a magnetized facsimile of a pink looped ribbon clung to the tailgate. The driver's door opened, and Rachel Williamson swung her legs out and stood on the blacktop. She hung a black Fossil handbag on her shoulder, walked toward the rear entrance of the building and climbed the four steps.

I did an about-face and walked down the hall to the reception area. Standing next to our file room, I watched Rachel approach Bettye's desk. As far as I knew, the city of Prospect was completely quiet. There seemed to be no newsworthy reason for Rachel to be here without calling first.

Bettye stood up. Rachel stepped around the desk, and they hugged, parted, held hands for a second and then spoke for a few moments. I wondered what that was all about.

Being an insensitive clod, I needed to think about that. Bettye had known Rachel as long as I did. While they always seemed friendly, I associated this behavior with something close girlfriends would share. Finally, my astute male mentality inferred that they were two intelligent females, close to the same age, who had been subjected to a severely traumatic incident. I chalked up this sharing of emotions to their mental health being in better shape than mine had ever been.

Rachel smiled at Bettye, pointed toward my office and walked to my door. I met her half way there.

"Hi," she said. "Might I come in?"

I extended my arm, ushering her through the doorway. "Of course you might, madam. And how might I assist you today?" I used my posh London accent and showed her the smile I practice in the mirror.

"You're ridiculous," she observed.

"And you love every minute of it."

We came to the side of my desk together. She put her hand on my upper arm and began to rise up on her toes. I put my hand on her back and bent down to allow a kiss on my cheek. Even with high heels, Rachel is six inches shorter than I am.

"How are you?' she asked.

"I'm great. Don't I look beautiful?"

She slapped my arm.

"A better question is how are you doing?" I said. "I missed my morning phone call."

"I'm okay. You know, getting by. I'm sorry I didn't call. I wanted to come and see you. I want to ask you something."

I frowned. "Sounds serious."

"Come on," she said. "Sit. Talk to me."

She took a step to the armchair in front of my desk and sat first. I looked at her outfit, a black pantsuit with a thin pinstripe, white blouse with the pointed collars turned over the lapels of her jacket. The top two buttons of the blouse were open, showing a short double strand of pearls. As usual, her makeup and dark brown hair looked perfect, an overall lovely picture.

But as we teetered on the brink of what I thought might be a serious conversation, she looked a little tense. The happy, confident aura that usually made her even more attractive seemed to be missing. It wouldn't take Dr. Phil to surmise something might be troubling Mrs. Williamson. I wondered what happened over the weekend and why she came to see me.

"Is something wrong?' I asked. "You look a little, oh, I don't know, a little less bubbly than your usual self. And you never mentioned driving down to see me. What's up?"

"I don't know, Sam, I've been thinking about something for the last couple of days."

She paused and finally sighed before speaking again. Her shoulders relaxed and dropped an inch.

"I think I need to do something for you," she said. "I'd like you to let me do a show about you—something for *Sunday in Knoxville*. You and I could talk for a whole half hour."

I hesitated longer than usual to make one of my usual inane but humorous remarks. My face must have showed a quizzical look, so she continued.

"Sam, what would have happened if you hadn't found me and…saved me? How can someone minimize that or ever forget it?"

I wanted to remain focused on our conversation, but a fly, trapped in the building for who knows how long, soared into the room and buzzed past us.

"Rachel, sweetheart, that's what I do. Not all the time, of course, but it just seems that I can usually get lucky and make things come out okay. I could never let something happen to you and then wait around while someone else tried to fix it."

She looked at me, but didn't comment. I hadn't said anything confusing, so I continued.

"No one comes into my town and harms my friend and should expect me to sit back and watch what happens."

"You don't like to watch things happen, do you? You like to make things happen."

"Better than standing around wondering what *just* happened."

"Am I your friend, Sam?"

"Silly woman. Of course you are, and I'd like to think you always will be…a special friend." I smiled. "I don't want to be just another middle-aged police chief in your Rolodex."

"No, Sammy, you're more than that, and you know it. And I've told you so." She took a turn at smiling. "You're my best buddy and the one who saved me. And I have no idea how I can ever thank you enough."

I raised my eyebrows twice and tried to look lecherous.

"Oh, you can be so stupid." She shifted in the chair and crossed her legs, left over right.

I tried to interject an appropriately self-effacing comment, but she stopped me.

"No, don't say it's nothing. Don't say something funny or stupid. It's the most important something in my life right now. I want to explain, but I don't know how to say what I want to say—what I *have* to say. What are we going to do, Sam?"

Tears began to well up in the corners of her eyes. I needed to do something. I hate watching women cry.

"Wow, that's a relief," I said. "I thought you came here to warn me never to call you again." It wasn't the best line I've ever thought up.

I watched patiently, while she took a tissue from her purse and carefully dabbed the corners of her eyes avoiding the makeup and wondered how women could do that without a mirror.

"Hey, I know what you can do for me," I said.

"What?"

No doubt she expected a serious answer, but I was looking for a smile.

"The next time I see you, wear your glasses. I told you, you're gorgeous in glasses."

She tried to ignore my attempt at humor, but broke down and gave me a good laugh.

"Oh, please! Besides riding in on your white horse and scooping me up in your arms, you can always make me laugh."

"That's me, baby, Groucho Marx with a gun."

I looked down and noticed her left shoe dangling from her toes. That's the kind of thing that can…I refocused on the conversation.

"Sam, I want you to do that show with me. I want everyone watching to know who you are. I want to tell people about you, what you've done in your life, what kind of police chief they have in Prospect. If I tell everyone your story, I can find out even more about you myself. This might be the only thing I can do for you. Please let me do it."

"I think we covered enough about my part in the rescue at the press conference. I might have a big mouth at times, but I prefer to keep a low profile for most of my life."

She started to speak, "Sam, I..."

I held up my hand.

"I know how much effort you'd expend to do this. Most people would love to be on TV with you. They'd be flattered. I am flattered—a lot. But I'm also kind of funny. I don't like to be the center of attention. Can you understand that?"

"Yes, but..."

My hand went up again. The fly landed on my brass desk lamp.

"But I won't let you off the hook," I said. "Can I suggest something?"

"Yes, of course."

"Good. You'll be satisfied. You can do something nice for me, and I'll even answer more questions about my sometimes infamous past. It won't be anything for publication, but you might get another laugh or two."

Rachel frowned and sat forward aggressively. "What are you talking about? You mean you won't let me do what I want?"

I halfway expected her to throw a temper tantrum.

"Hey, when I met your mom and dad, they didn't seem like the kind of parents who spoiled you rotten. No, I won't do what you want."

That remark got me a serious frown.

"Being on TV like that would make me uncomfortable," I said. "I'd feel like a circus act, probably behave like an idiot and damage your ratings." Then I smiled and took hold of her hands. "But you can make me happy by going to lunch with me again. I thought our last lunch was terrific. I'd love to do something like that. Pick a time that's good for you. We can spend an afternoon talking, and I can get a bunch of envious stares from the guys who see me with a beautiful woman. That work for you?"

"That's not what I wanted."

"Poor baby."

She wrinkled up her nose. It's something she does when I don't cooperate, and she wants me to know I've made her unhappy.

"I should fight you on this," she said. "But I'd never win. And if that's what you want, okay. But I need you to know, I think you're impossible."

Her smile came back, and she didn't pout from not getting her way. I guess Joe and Pauline had done a good job raising their daughter.

"I'd like to just sit and talk with you," she said. "If buying you lunch is the only way I can do that, okay, I'm ready."

"I said go to lunch with me, not buy me lunch. There's a difference. I'm an old-fashioned guy. When I take a girl out, I buy the lunch."

She scowled at me again—several times in one day. The fly fell off the lampshade and died on my desktop.

"Smile," I said. "I'm introducing you to the Jenkins' method of compromise. We talk about it and then do it my way. I always get my way. Remember, I'm a lot bigger than you."

"I've noticed. Can I call you tomorrow to make a date? I'm going to the station for a meeting, and I'll check my schedule. I want an afternoon when we won't be interrupted. Is that okay?"

"It is. I'll be waiting. Now, answer a question for me?"

"Sure."

"Are you really doing okay with what happened? I know you have someone to talk with and help you sort everything out. Is that going well?"

"I don't have a simple answer. Yes and no and yes. How's that?"

I shrugged.

"I've already seen her a few times. She's very nice and helpful, but as you probably know, I'm the one who must ultimately help myself. I'm doing okay, but I wish I didn't feel the… complications all this caused. I'm trying. I'll be okay. I think a nice lunch will help. It's a good start."

"Well, I'm wonderful company. You just have to get past my quiet modesty."

"Terrific. You're my favorite middle-aged police chief. I love your

205

company and can't wait for our next lunch."

She stood and put the expensive purse over her shoulder at sling arms. I got up from the chair parked next to hers. She looked up at me and gave me another dazzling smile.

"That's the kind of smile your audience expects," I said. "How does it feel having millions of men in love with you?"

She put her free arm around my back and gave me a squeeze.

"Thank you, Sam. Thank you so much."

"Good seeing you today, Shorty," I said. "I'll talk to you again tomorrow. Don't forget me!"

She wrinkled her nose when I called her *Shorty*. "I won't. And I'm glad I came." Rachel turned and walked from my office.

On the way out, she stopped at the reception desk, touched Bettye's forearm while she spoke on the phone and waved good-bye. Bettye put the phone down and stood up. They gave each other a little peck on the cheek, looked genuinely glad to have seen each other, then Rachel left.

I felt a little confused. For a guy with such a high opinion of his intelligence, I sure wouldn't want to take a quiz on women.

I walked out and looked at Bettye.

"You ever have a nice conversation with someone, think you said all the right stuff, but when it's over you get the feeling you screwed up?"

"What happened?"

"I don't know that anything happened. Nothing bad anyway. I'm really not sure what Rachel wanted. She looked sort of sad. A little confused maybe. She told me she wanted to do a TV show about me. She's only out of the hospital a week, and she wants to go back to work next Monday. I don't want to be the subject of a TV show. You understand, don't you?"

"I guess so. I understand both what you say and how she feels. You saved her from a terrible ordeal. She looks at you as the man who saved her life. You might remember that I have a reason to feel that way, too?"

"Yes, I remember. But you didn't want to do a TV show about me or paint my portrait or... hell, I don't know what. You thanked me. I guess I'm supposed to say even that wasn't necessary, but I'm glad you did. That was enough."

"Sam, I've known you for six months now. I think you're one of the smartest men I know—smart about bein' a policeman. But when it comes to women, you're as dumb as a stump."

"Huh?"

"Sayin' thanks is enough for you, right?"

"Uh-huh."

"You ever think it's not enough for Rachel? Maybe not enough for me?" Her volume elevated, and she sounded a little agitated.

"No, I didn't. But I see where you're going with this. Without a big explanation, I guess my sensibilities and frame of reference is...a bit different."

"Sam, just after you prevented me from getting shot...to death maybe, I remember sittin' here while you were flittin' around the office, and I found myself just wantin' to look at you. After someone saves your life, Mr. Sam, dumb-as-a-stump, Jenkins, you really can't help but feelin'...a bit closer to them than you did the day b'fore!"

Her voice had risen to about eighty decibels. And she wasn't finished with me.

"I'm sure you'd like me to say it's because you're just as cute as the dickens, but I'm too old to be swoonin' over some big good-lookin' guy I'm not married to."

I felt my eyes pop as she scolded me.

"I guess you've lived through some violent times in your life, Sam Jenkins. That's not true for either Rachel or me. When someone saves your life, you big fool, it's pretty damn special!"

Tears begin to show in Bettye's eyes. She tried to fight them off but wasn't having much luck.

"Dumb as a stump, Sam! Dumb as a damn stump!" She turned and walked off to the rest room.

What had I done? I saw myself as a clean-cut all-American boy and a genuine hero when I had to be. Wasn't that good enough?

* * * *

Ten minutes later, Bettye came back to her desk where I'd been sitting in her absence. I looked at her for a few seconds. She seemed composed.

"You okay, kiddo?" I asked.

"Sure, darlin', I'm fine. Thanks," she said, "and I'm sorry for gettin' so upset."

"No need to be sorry. I should probably apologize to you—again. Even though I've been diagnosed as dumb as a stump, and that sounds serious, maybe I can plead insanity and get off the hook."

"I'm sorry I said that, Sam. I truly am."

"Don't apologize. It might be true. At least you didn't hit me in the head with a night stick."

She smiled. "I need to ask, Sam. What did you tell Rachel?"

"I told her I felt uncomfortable about the TV show. I really didn't want that, but I figured she wanted to do something. So I said she could take me to lunch. I'd pay, of course, but she could pick the place and time. That's nice, right?"

Bettye sighed and rolled her eyes like she was talking to a little boy who just couldn't get anything right that day.

"Sam, I know when you guys do favors for each other, you buy a lunch and think everythin' is paid back, and all's bright and shiny. I've seen y'all do it. But damn it, Sam, Rachel is not Ralph Oliveri or Jackie Shuman. Taking her to lunch, actin' all nice and sweet and funny and charmin' may be the worst thing you could do. Don't you understand?"

I shook my head. "No."

"Sometimes I wonder, Sam Jenkins…sometimes I just wonder!"

That sounded like I'd gotten into trouble again. Sometimes I just couldn't win.

Back in my office, I held private services for the fly. Later, I went home. Kate had no reason to chastise me. Guess again, Jenkins.

Chapter Twenty-Six

I parked the Crown Victoria, walked over the gravel driveway and under the sweet gums and tulip trees that months ago had lost their leaves. The air felt almost cold. I smelled the layers of decomposing foliage in the dense grove of dogwoods adjacent to the gravel.

Taking a deep breath made me anticipate snow, but the WNXX weatherman never mentioned any during the last forecast. At twenty-past-five, the thermometer still sat at around fifty degrees. Things warmed up after the last snow. The sun had disappeared below the horizon an hour earlier, but there were still a few birds, cardinals and chickadees flying about, resting on the branches of the big Leyland cypress trees near the house.

As I hit the concrete apron in front of the garage, the wide overhead door began to rise. The interior door to the laundry room swung open, and Kate stood there leaning on the doorframe. Bitsey made a dash through the garage, over the concrete and stopped in front of me, wiggling all over. She looked like the star of a Mighty Dog commercial. Kate walked out with a sexy swing of her hips, but nowhere the amount of wiggle Bitsey could generate.

"Hi ya, Sambo," she said, "Who gets a better welcome home than you?"

"Well, you could be wearing a flimsy negligee and holding a bottle of real champagne—not the cheap stuff I usually buy."

"Later maybe. Right now you've got an enthusiastic dog, and I have a dinner that will make your ears wiggle."

Kate stood next to me as I crouched down petting a dog in perpetual motion. She wore a pink angora sweater that accentuated all the curves I love to fondle and a pair of washed-off jeans, just a bit too tight for a conservative but beautiful middle-aged woman. Her salt and pepper hair looked perfect.

"Come here, momma," I said. "I've spent a hard day fighting crime, and I need a hug." I rose to my feet.

Katherine put her arms around me and squeezed tightly. "Hello, sweetie, I've missed you."

"I've missed you, too, love. Good to see you."

All that affection took place as a barking Scottish terrier ran rings around us.

After a sufficient amount of bonding passed among us, our happy threesome adjourned to a warm and well-lit kitchen.

"Are you drinking, sir?" she asked.

"Yes, ma'am, I is."

She poured several jiggers of Canadian Club Classic 12 into a small pitcher, added two more shots of red vermouth, then dropped in a few ice cubes and stirred.

I wondered, if you make a Manhattan with Canadian whisky, should you call it a Toronto?

Only moments later I said, "Cheers."

We clicked glasses. Kate gave me a long, soft kiss and asked, "So, how was your day?"

"Well, I didn't shoot anyone, didn't have to torture a confession out of an arch criminal, and I didn't conquer a gang of drug-crazed hooligans. But I did get totally confused by two women."

"So I heard," she said.

"What?"

"Bettye called. She thought she might have been a little critical of you and wanted me to treat you accordingly."

"Huh? Bettye called you? Just now?"

Kate nodded and sipped her drink.

"Now I know how old people feel when their doctors and children talk about them like they're not in the room. Remind me to look up *conspiracy* in my law books."

"Don't get testy, Samuel. She meant well. And just thought I could further her discussion with you…on what you two were talking about."

"Uh-huh."

"And help you understand a woman's perspective on this."

"Uh-huh."

A Johnny Mathis CD was playing on the stereo. It's hard to get annoyed with women when Johnny sings his love songs.

"And how I might be able to help you formulate your own perception," she said.

"Huh?" I noticed a definite pattern developing in my responses.

"Come on, sweetie. Let me show you what I've made for dinner."

Kate is wise in the ways of manipulating me.

She lifted a pan cover, revealing medallions of pork tenderloin simmering in a sauce of white wine, diced onions, garlic and red currants. The side dishes were baked pears with ginger, red cabbage with onions and blueberries and wide whole-wheat noodles. A bottle of dry Riesling waited in the fridge, and a loaf of multi-grain bread, ready to be toasted, lay on the kitchen counter. Nero Wolfe could eat his heart out. We might have been the only two detectives fed epicurean delights like those, but my cook was better looking than Fritz Brenner any day.

Over dinner, Kate again explained and elaborated on some of the things Bettye wanted to emphasize. She ended by saying that when it came to women, sometimes I *was* dumb as a stump, but I shouldn't take that observation the wrong way.

She flattered me by saying any girl could easily fall in love with the likes of me, so I should act accordingly and not turn on too much charm when dealing with the opposite sex, especially someone I recently rescued from a kidnapper. That was not only flattering but also a sufficient warning—for the likes of me.

Between bites of the pork tenderloin, she said, "Besides noticing our obvious anatomical particulars, do you think you'll ever understand that women are different than men?"

"Of course you're different. That's why… Why lots of things. I know that."

"That was eloquent."

I stuffed a forkful of noodles into my mouth and chewed slowly for a moment to think of a snappy comeback.

"Bettye told me all kinds of things I could have thought about. Jeez, I'm not ambassador to the female race. Can't you girls be satisfied when I save your world and then go about my business?"

"I think dumb as a stump covers it." She took a long sip of the Washington state wine.

"What would you have me do, Miss Psychotherapist?"

"Well, Mr. All-American Hero, you've successfully guided two women through fairly traumatic experiences." She wiggled a fork around in her salad bowl.

"It's what I do, little Darlin'."

"Wanna listen or do your stand-up comedy act?"

"Oooo."

She finally ate a bit of salad and thought for a moment.

"You know women aren't ashamed to show emotion."

"Uh-huh." I nodded and washed down a piece of pork with a sip of wine.

"You, on the other hand, never show emotion…at all."

"Never?"

"Unless you're getting passionate, you wouldn't get excited if…" She stopped speaking and then added a little base to her voice in a feeble attempt to imitate me. "Uh, Kats, seems that I just cut off my right hand. Hurts like hell, but I put it in a plastic bag and stuck it in my back pocket. If you're not busy, would you drive me to the ER? I might have a problem shifting and won't be able to sign the insurance forms."

"I take that as a compliment."

"You would."

"What's your point?"

"You spend at least eight hours a day with Bettye. In today's vernacular, she's your workplace spouse."

"Uh-huh." I returned to my eating, willing to listen.

"I've about given up trying to figure out your relationship with Rachel. I hear what you say, but I look at her and don't think she's the same as Ralph Oliveri."

"We've been over this. You have nothing to worry about."

"Maybe she does. Maybe Bettye does."

"You think I'm a potential masher?" I said that with a smile.

"There's the stupid thing again."

"I'm listening to you be intelligent, but don't get smart."

"Despite the differences in your ages, Sammy, I think either of those women could easily fall in love with the likes of you." She sipped her wine and got a twinkle in her big browns, indicating I could expect a snotty remark. "I can't imagine why, but I suppose they could. So, lover boy, be solicitous of their emotions, their feelings, and don't turn on too much charm when dealing with the opposite sex, especially those who you've just rescued from the jaws of evil. Don't complicate their lives."

"Somewhere hidden within that might have been a little flattery."

"Just a little."

I swallowed the remainder of my wine. Kate wrinkled her nose and blew a kiss across the table.

Having been thoroughly beaten to the mat by two formidable women, and as Nero Wolfe would say, *confounded* by a third, I decided to pour myself another glass of wine and retire to the living room to watch Jeopardy before clearing away the dishes.

In the category of famous policemen of the 21st century, the answer was: Sam Jenkins. "What is dumb as a stump, Alex?" would have been the correct response.

My wife switched off the soffit lights in the kitchen and sat down next to me on the love seat.

"So, Katherine, my dahling, do you mind much if I go to lunch with the attractive female celebrity who's been the subject of our conversation?"

"Of course not, Sammy. I think she needs to talk with you. You might not completely understand why, but you can do the right thing and make her feel better. I have every confidence you'll be just as perfect as you need to be. Rachel had a terrible time, and you saved her. She needs to thank you—let her. She's nice, isn't she?"

"Yeah, she's a good kid." I took a long breath and let it out slowly. "You know, you girls make me feel like a dolt. Have I done this all wrong?"

"No, sweetie, you didn't do anything *wrong*. You just don't understand women as well as you think and can do things better."

"Pfui!" That, too, was something Nero Wolfe would say.

Chapter Twenty-Seven

At quarter to one on Thursday afternoon, after taking half a vacation day off, I left work to meet Rachel for lunch at Chesapeake's in Knoxville. I pulled off US 129 and drove east on Cumberland Avenue through the UT campus, past gas stations, pizza joints, bookstores, kiddie gin mills and restaurants that were lucky if they lasted more than six months in that neighborhood.

Turning left on Henley and right on Summit Hill brought me to the entrance of Chesapeake's parking lot. At five-to-one, I backed into a spot diagonally across from Rachel's Lexus. I locked the car and straightened my tie, using the side window of the Ford as a mirror.

Wearing a tan corduroy sport jacket, one with leather patches on the elbows, gray slacks, an off-white Tattersall shirt and a tweedy, brick red woolen tie, I thought I looked dreadfully English. I toyed with the idea of introducing myself as Nigel Stoat-Marten of the BBC, there to interview Rachel Williamson.

I yanked open one of the heavy oak doors and entered the restaurant lobby. In front of me, a glass-fronted cold case from some long forgotten fish market, acted like a greeter. Atop the cabinet, a blackboard with the day's specials written in Day-Glo chalk stood next to a display of several brightly painted float buoys and two plastic blue claw crabs. Around the room, several large paintings of boats and other bay scenes from the Chesapeake tidewater region decorated the walls. I scrapped the Nigel idea before I stepped up to a podium and spoke to a seriously efficient-looking blonde hostess.

"Hi, my name is Jenkins. I'm meeting a Ms. Williamson."

No sense in sounding overly familiar with a locally famous but married woman.

"Yes, Mr. Jenkins, she arrived a few minutes ago. Follow me, please."

With me in tow, the hostess wove her way toward the back of the restaurant. I won't say the place was jam-packed, but more than eighty percent of the tables were occupied, and at least a dozen people sat on stools at the bar and a few small round tables in the lounge.

We passed stuffed and mounted fish hanging on the walls. Brass ship's clocks, barometers and telescopes punctuated the areas that needed additional decoration. Nets hanging from the ceiling beams and floor columns added to the waterfront atmosphere. Nautical prints occupied strategic places on the dark, wood-paneled walls.

At the very last table in the house, Rachel sat in a dimly lit area with her back to a section of glass brick wall. Softened daylight crept in, creating a cozy atmosphere in the alcove. It looked like the perfect place for a famous person to have her lunch. The backlighting showed her almost in silhouette. Hard for fans to recognize her and stop by to say hello.

Rachel stood as I approached. The hostess pulled out a chair on the opposite side of the table and told me to enjoy my lunch. I pushed that chair back in and took the seat to Rachel's left so I could have my back to a wall and look out toward the crowded room. Behind Rachel, a three-foot-long, gaff-rigged skipjack sat on a narrow hunt table. Near that, an assemblage of fish netting, a weathered oar, and a shiny copper and brass diver's hardhat made the place look like a maritime museum. Over my shoulder a stuffed yellow-fin tuna looked down at me from his spot on the wall. I began to feel a coastal sensory overload, but resisted the need to say, "Yo ho ho. Shiver me timbers."

Rachel smiled as we sat in the heavy captain's chairs. She wore a pale blue leather suit with a straight skirt and an Ike jacket over a pearl gray turtleneck. The leather looked as soft as cashmere. Casual but business-like.

"Hi ya, doll-face. What's a nice girl like you doin' in a joint like this?"

Great line, Jenkins. Really original.

"Hi ya, Bogey. Seen any Maltese falcons lately?"

For the first time, I felt a little uncomfortable being alone with Rachel. Maybe my two female coaches had caused an apprehension about my ability to do the right thing—if I could figure out what the right thing was. Leave it to a couple of women to make a self-sufficient, confident guy feel like a stick of used chewing gum.

She rose up a little and stretched to give me a quick kiss on the cheek.

"I like your outfit. Very classy. And sexy at the same time."

"Thanks, it's sweet of you to say that. You look good, too. I always like the way you dress."

"Yeah, I had good luck at the Salvation Army yesterday."

She laughed. It sounded genuine. Why wouldn't it? I'm funny as hell when I try. Her smile made me happy.

Rachel put a hand on my forearm, but quickly removed it when the waitress came to take my drink order. She'd already gotten a glass of white wine, still almost full. I ordered Chesapeake's own micro-brewed porter.

Michelle, who introduced herself as our server, came back in a flash with my beer.

"Are we ready to order?" She sounded impatient.

"Haven't got a clue," I said. "Can you give us ten or fifteen minutes, please?"

Michelle left, obviously unhappy that I broke the rhythm of her act.

Rachel pointed at my beer. "That's really dark. Is it good?"

"Sure. Try some. See if you like it." I pushed the glass close to her hand. She took it and ever so carefully brought it to her lips, almost as if afraid something might pop out of the rim and bite her. She took a sip, smiled and ended up with a little tan foam on her upper lip.

"Ooh, that is good." She sounded surprised. "It's very creamy and...nice. I don't think I've ever seen Boyd drink beer. He usually drinks martinis."

"Martinis are good."

She wrinkled up her nose and made a face. She didn't agree.

After placing my glass back on its coaster, she extended her hand and laid it on my forearm again. Perhaps she didn't want me to drink any more.

Hidden speakers in the restaurant had been playing a medley of Glenn Miller songs. *Moonlight Serenade* just finished, and *A String of Pearls* began.

"That's great music, isn't it?" I said. The uneasy feeling of moments ago began to fade away.

"I love big band music," she said.

"I'll bet your mother taught you to do the Lindy."

"Yes. She did. How did you know?"

I shrugged. "I'm a detective. I know everything."

"Ha! Do you like to dance?" She sounded like a schoolgirl.

"I'm not much of a dancer."

"But you like the music?" Her voice still sounded enthusiastic.

"Love it. Makes me sorry I missed World War Two."

She tilted her head and stared at me. I guess looking to see if I was serious.

"I think you mean that, don't you?"

"Oh, I don't know, maybe. I guess so. Those were interesting times."

"And you're an interesting guy."

"Who, me?" I said.

"You don't want me to tell the people out there about you, but you'd better tell me about yourself."

"Sure. You already know a lot. But I'm a pretty simple guy. I started out there and ended up here. And now I'm having lunch with you. Life's good. What do you think?"

She picked up her glass, held it with both hands and took an imperceptible sip. I remember thinking the gesture looked incredibly feminine. I, on the other hand, took a long pull on my tall glass of porter, decreasing the volume considerably. I probably looked like a lush.

Rachel set down her glass and gave me a no-nonsense look. Something common to reporters and cops looking for answers.

"Not good enough, mister. Start talking, or I'll get out my rubber hose. You rolled over once before—do it again or else."

"Wow, that's pretty scary—or maybe not. I hear some people can really get into that kind of stuff."

"Oh, yuck! You're weird. Start talking, buddy—you promised."

"Did I?"

Rachel gave me a pleading look I doubt any man on the planet could resist.

"I feel like I should be lying on a couch and you should be wearing your glasses and holding a notebook," I said.

"You're going to need prompting, aren't you?"

I shrugged.

"Let's get back to where we left off the last time we had lunch."

I lowered my eyebrows and made my version of a suspicious look. "Okay."

"To relax, the average man plays golf, goes fishing or watches sports," she said. "You told me how you got your kicks playing cops and robbers at a big police department and jumping out of airplanes and scuba diving for the Army. The closest thing to conventional recreation you liked was sailing. Most of those things are not relaxing. Explain, please."

"I guess I had different role models as a kid."

"Did you play sports in school?"

"I was pretty good at baseball. Could hit a fastball and had a pretty good glove at second base."

After my statement, I drank some beer and smiled. I guess she wanted to hear more.

"Do I need a winch to drag things out of you?"

"Stick around, kid. You'll see me in action."

The wine Rachel had been gingerly sipping suffered a drastic reduction in volume. I guess she drinks when frustrated. So do I.

I received a temporary reprieve when Michelle came back with her order book at the ready. Even celebrities and their pals couldn't impede that girl's appointed rounds. Rachel ordered a house salad with grilled salmon and low-fat dressing. From memory, I hadn't looked at the menu yet, I choose the char-broiled swordfish with fire roasted vegetables, served on a bed of rice pilaf, with a side dish of Spinach Maria. I'm usually easy, but generally hungry.

Rachel finished her first glass of wine. I downed the remainder of my beer and ordered two glasses of whatever she was having. It turned

218

out to be a crisp and fruity California chardonnay.

We spent a long time over lunch. She asked more about me and my life before Tennessee. I learned about her time at college, her husband and her two sons. Close to three o'clock, Michelle took our plates away and brought us two more glasses of wine.

"This was nice," Rachel said. "I really enjoyed myself. Thank you, Sam."

"It was nice, but I'm the one who should say thanks. How often does a kid from Brooklyn spend half a day with a famous TV star?" I gave her my shy little boy smile.

Without skipping a beat, she ignored my question. "Sam, the other day I told you I'm not having an easy time with things."

When Rachel gets serious, she has a habit of looking at the table and turning her wine glass in slow circles.

"I am getting past the trauma of being abducted. That's easy. I get lots of good advice how to handle that." She snapped her mouth closed, sucked in a big breath, then blurted out, "What I'm having the big problem with is *you*."

What the hell have I done now?

"Explain and help me out," I said.

"I find myself thinking about how you walked into the little cabin while that man held a gun on you. You winked at me and sat down and talked to him like he was someone you met at a bar."

"That was just an act. In a situation like that, you have to make the guy holding a gun think you don't care if you live or die. You can't let him see a soft spot."

She shook her head dismissively. "Anyone else would have told their sharpshooters to kill that man. You took the gun from his hand and had him taken out in handcuffs. Do you know how amazing that looked?"

Talk about an ego booster!

"I didn't think he needed killing. He needs a good head shrinker and a lot of medication. Maybe someday he'll come up for air and be able to function again without all those obstructions in his brain."

I found myself thinking back to that snowy day and the little cabin in the woods. Rachel kept her eyes locked on mine.

Wayne Zurl

"Things you see when you're a soldier at war can do bad things to your mind," I said. "I saw him as a victim of sorts himself."

In the background, the CD changed, but the decade remained the same. Vaughn Monroe began singing *Racing with the Moon*.

"Your men took him out alive and unhurt." Rachel spoke with a new intensity. "And you smiled at me, and I knew everything was okay again. You carried me to the ambulance and made me feel like a little girl. It was the first time I felt safe in days. I can't get that out of my mind. I'm thinking about you a lot, Sam. About that time and about the other times, too, when we've seen each other and...just talked. Sam, I think I..." She didn't finish her thought.

I felt uncomfortable with how the conversation had turned, but found myself at a loss for words. Rachel however, was on a roll.

"You once told me I'm the only girl you'd ever leave home for."

Jenkins and his famous big mouth does it again.

"Did you mean that, Sam?"

"A guy can dream, can't he?" I put my glass up to my lips and wanted to drain it in one gulp. I settled for a more reasonable, but sizable, sip. I remember giving better answers on the witness stand.

"Sam, I'm beyond day-dreaming, and it scares me. I wake up and feel you—just like when you held me in that cabin and carried me. I feel how you were warm and strong and made me safe again."

Mel Torme started singing *I'll Be Seeing You.* Michelle streaked past carrying a tray of dishes. Rachel tucked a few dark hairs behind her right ear. Her eyes looked like shiny brown gemstones.

"Sam, if you asked, I would run away with you today. I wouldn't care where we went, just so you could hold me again. That feeling of safety was like a drug."

I managed a smile and said, "I can understand how you feel. Now I need you to understand how the things you've said make me feel."

She pulled her chair up an inch closer and sat forward, taking hold of my hand and looking like she expected an answer to change the world. I remember being grateful that most of the other customers left earlier.

"You know that I needed to find you," I said. "I've told you that. A simple thanks and a hug was all I wanted."

She blinked and squeezed my hand, making me feel like some kind

220

of heroic nitwit. I wanted to drain my glass of wine and start drinking hers.

"What you've told me is overwhelming, flattering and more tempting than you can imagine." I took a deep breath. "I can't pull rank on you because you're not a cop, but as the senior member of our partnership, I claim my right to make you listen to me."

She moved her hand and sat back slightly. Her expression changed, and not for the better. I felt sure she expected a letdown.

"Only a totally senseless guy wouldn't conjure up exciting fantasies about running away with you. I'm sure my future holds a dream or two about what could have been. Rachel, I…"

I found myself dangerously close to using the L word.

"I have a wife whom I've loved for more than forty years. And you have a husband who genuinely cares for you. And two boys who I think are really nice kids. And I know they love their mom."

She sat forward again, squeezed my forearm and looked back into my eyes.

I managed another smile. "When we first met, I thought you were a knockout, but there was something else very special about you."

She smiled, too, for the first time since the conversation turned in that serious direction.

"You were confident, smart, and you seemed so happy. Unless you were content with your family, your job and life in general, I don't think those things would have shown through as they did."

Rachel's eyes glassed over, and she shook her head. She reached for her purse and put a hand inside.

"I'm really flattered that you would consider making me an important part of your life, Rachel, but I think you have something better right now."

"Oh, Sam." A small tear rolled down her right cheek. She swallowed with difficulty. "I feel so foolish. Excuse me for a moment." She dabbed her eye with a tissue and stood up.

I stood, too, and as she began to turn away from the table, I reached out and touched her forearm.

"You be sure and come back when you're ready. Don't leave me here," I said.

"Yes, I'll be back. Just give me a minute, please. I think I'm about to lose it."

I sat down, drained the last of my wine and felt a great blue funk wash over me. I remembered the old Chinese proverb about the man who saved another person's life and became responsible for them forever.

Speedy Michelle popped over to my side and asked if I wanted more wine. Actually, I wanted a pint of vodka on the rocks, but I settled for the check, which I paid before Rachel walked back to the table and sat down on the edge of her chair.

"You okay?" I asked.

"I am, and I'm sorry. I…"

I held up my overused hand, and she stopped speaking.

"Did I lose a friend today?" I asked.

"Oh, God, no," she said, shaking her head. "No, Sam, you didn't. No, you found a much better one…and a smarter one."

Maybe I'm not such a dolt after all.

"Good. Some friends you just don't want to lose." I shrugged. "Anyway, someday we might change our minds. Have I ever told you Corfu is beautiful? We could get jobs as olive pickers. What do you think?"

"I think you're crazy," she said with the lovely smile that made her the sweetheart of East Tennessee. "But that's what I like most about you."

"Let's go, partner." I offered her my arm.

Outside the restaurant, we looked at each other. I had no idea what to say next. She did.

"Walk with me for a while."

I nodded.

We turned right. She held my left arm, and we walked slowly up a quiet street full of old brick townhouses.

"I feel silly…and a little embarrassed," she said.

"Don't. I've been silly all my life, and you don't come close. You were honest. What could be better than that? Besides, you made an old man feel special today. Look at this as your contribution to the wellbeing of a senior citizen."

"You're pretty funny for a tough guy."

"Yeah, it was a toss-up when I went looking for a second career—police chief in Tennessee or stand-up comic in the Borscht Belt."

She laughed. *If women only knew what they could get out of a guy with nothing more than a genuine laugh.*

A Knoxville PD sector car went north on Broadway with its lights and siren working. Neither of us looked.

"Seriously, lady," I said, "I'm only a sidewalk psychologist, but I do know a lot about post-traumatic stress. Ask the woman you're seeing. You don't get out of the woods easily, but you're doing great. You'll be fine—real soon. You're a tough guy yourself."

We came to a corner, turned left, walked another hundred feet, turned left again and found ourselves back at the driveway entrance to Chesapeake's parking lot. We walked to her car, and she clicked the remote entry device on her key ring. The lights of her Lexus blinked.

"Thanks for lunch," I said.

"You paid."

"Not what I meant."

"I know." She grabbed my tie, pulled me closer and gave me a long and not very platonic kiss.

When we parted, I blinked and let out a breath. "Wow, it's nice to be kissed by a tough guy."

"That's what I thought," she said.

"Yeah, well…uh…I'd better be going. I've gotta find a cold shower before too long."

She laughed again and then got serious.

"Sam, I'm only going to say this once more because I think you'd like it that way. Thank you. Thank you so very much—for everything—for then and for today."

"Just one thanks would have been enough, but this was sort of special."

She touched my cheek. "Bye, Sammy."

I wondered if that was a final goodbye.

"See ya, doll-face," I said with that familiar lisp.

I turned and took a couple of steps across the lot. Less than half way to my car, I heard her call.

"Hey, Jenkins, you still owe me another ride in your sports car."

I did an about-face. "You're right, I do. We'll have to go up into the mountains next time."

"I hope you don't expect me to keep doing you favors until I get pay-back for what you owe me."

"Then I guess I'd better ante up. I know I'll need something from you in the future. Can't let you think I don't pay my debts. Next time you're coming to Prospect call me. I'll put the top down and be waiting."

"Okay, I will. It's an Austin-Healey, right?"

"Yeah, an Austin-Healey—the big one."

We waved and went our separate ways. I headed back to Prospect and more unfinished police work.

Chapter Twenty-Eight

At 4:05, I walked back into Prospect PD.

Bettye swiveled around in her chair. "You look a little stressed out. Everything okay?"

"I wasn't sure for a while, but, yeah, everything's fine. She'll be perfect—sooner than she thinks. Mission accomplished, I guess."

"You're a good guy, Sammy."

"Yeah, that's me, a real Boy Scout."

Bettye smiled. I smiled back and retreated to my office. With utterly no ambition to do anything productive for my last hour at work, I sat behind my desk, put my feet up and began reading *Dead Certainties*. In the middle of the second page, I fell sound asleep. Perhaps a refresher course in stress management might help me.

Moments later, I found myself waking up in the bedroom of a villa on Corfu with Rachel Williamson next to me.

Dreams sometimes make things very convenient. When I awoke, my face was smooth, lacking any of the usual morning stubble. My hair was combed, and I tasted an absence of morning-mouth.

Rachel turned over and looked at me. Her makeup was all there, and her hair only looked a little tousled. She smiled as I touched a finger to the cute little dimple in her chin. She kissed me several times, got out of bed and walked to the open French doors that led to a balcony. I followed and felt the pleasant breeze on my skin. Rachel rested one arm on the railing, cocked a knee slightly and placed a right hand on her thigh. Every curve of her body looked smooth and sensual; a model never posed with more elegance. Stepping closer, I felt her hand warm against my chest. As I began feeling more than a little amorous, the scene switched to the road beneath our villa.

We were dressed: she in a simple shirtwaist dress and sandals, and I in corduroy slacks and a shirt with the sleeves turned up above my elbows. We looked like two people from the 1940s, holding hands and walking down a narrow gravel road, among rows and rows of olive trees.

In the background, I heard clear but soft music. Glenn Miller and the Army Air Force Band provided the sound, while Johnny Desmond crooned the lyrics to *Long Ago (and Far Away)*. For me, it was 1944.

Our walk took us down the road until we overlooked the blue waters where the Adriatic meets the Ionian Sea, the boot of Italy barely visible to the west. We descended an easy path to a pristine and deserted beach, left our clothes on the sand and walked into the cool clear water. When we reached a point where the sea covered most of Rachel's body, she put her arms around my neck and her legs around my hips and...

In any book on Greek mythology we learn that Poseidon, Hercules and Odysseus all came to Corfu and found themselves girlfriends. I wondered if they, too, went skinny-dipping.

I felt Bettye take the book from my hand. I opened my eyes for a moment and watched her mark the spot with a scrap of paper and lay the book on my desk. She gave my shoulder a gentle shake.

"Sam, darlin', it's after five o'clock. Time to go home."

I looked up at Bettye and saw her smiling. She was close enough to get a faint smell of perfume. I blinked and smiled back.

"Thanks, Betts. Obviously I dozed off." I felt a little embarrassed.

She patted my shoulder. I swung my feet to the floor.

"Good night, Sam." She turned and walked out.

"See you tomorrow," I said.

I couldn't help but notice, even in uniform trousers, Bettye Lambert had a really cute butt herself.

* * * *

The air smelled almost like springtime. Breezes from the southwest pushed the scent of Virginia pines toward me at five miles an hour. I could have stood in the driveway longer, but I *really* needed a drink.

Bitsey met me at the front door. She sniffed my leg, said, 'Boof' and jumped up onto the love seat. I walked into the kitchen.

"Did you have lunch or go three rounds with George Forman?" Kate asked.

"What a charming sentiment. Do I look that bad?"

"Uh-huh."

"I don't handle stress as well as I used to."

"Want a drink?"

"Would the Pope say a Hail Mary?"

"Time for the big guns?"

"Why not? Fire away."

She poured a double shot of Laphroaig into a short glass and gently dropped in two cubes.

Kate handed me the glass. "Cheers."

"Slainte," I said.

"So, how's Rachel?" She spoke while filling a footed goblet with merlot.

"I think she's doing fine. Has a good therapist, good attitude." I sipped the single-malt. "Going back to work suits her."

"Not exactly what I meant. How are you two?"

"We two are peachy. She never mentioned that TV show nonsense. Although in a place like Chesapeake's, she should have ordered something more than a salad."

Kate set her glass down and gave me her hands-on-hips pose. "Stop dancing, Sammy. I'm not one of the bosses you snowed for twenty years."

"That was terribly parental of you."

"And quit practicing Transactional Analysis. Answer my question, don't dissect it. I'm not going away."

"Everything's fine… What was your question?"

"Oh, for God's sake. Is she in love with you? And how about you?"

"She has a husband and two kids. The husband wears suspenders and may be kind of a jerk, but I don't have to live with him."

"And?"

"And you know better." I sipped the Scotch and rattled the cubes. "I'm home too often to be having an affair."

"Yes, you are."

"So?"

Kate picked up her wine again, and I half finished my drink. Bitsey walked into the kitchen, looked at us and must have sensed a little tension. She did an about-face and retreated again to the couch.

"I'm not saying I suspect you of infidelity," Kate said. "But don't be obtuse. She's obviously attracted to you, and she is a beautiful woman."

"And so are you. Has there been a problem before? There are lots of good-looking women out there. I've met a bunch. And while I'm not immune to thinking they're attractive, I don't take those thoughts anywhere."

"Sam, I always considered myself lucky. You never did the bar scene after the five-to-ones like so many other guys. You always came home to me. If I never said it before, here it is now. I appreciated that."

"Thanks. I'd hate to think all those years being true-blue went unnoticed."

"But listen to what I say now, okay?"

"Sure."

"When you retired, your entire world changed. Sorry, but without the badge, you lost a lot of the juice you walked around with for so long. I assume that was a big shock to your system."

I nodded.

"Then for years, you were just Sam Jenkins, the guy next door, not Lieutenant Jenkins, leader of super-cops."

I shrugged and let the last trickles of whisky slide down my throat.

"Now, like Gene Autry, you're back in the saddle again...at Prospect PD. And in your traditional way, you often do the impossible and never slow down. Big ego booster, huh?"

"And your point is?"

"I'm gettin' there, cowboy. You're right back being the old-fashioned hero you always were. In this case, you rode into town with your shootin' iron on your hip and saved the school marm from the local gunslinger."

"Sounds like a good movie."

"Stop."

"Whoops."

"You're not a kid any longer, but a big good-looking hero might still appeal to a younger woman. You can't scoop her up off the railroad tracks and just drop her off on Main Street, thinking you didn't affect her."

"I'm not trying to make her fall in love with me. I don't need that kind of ego trip."

"You might not have to try too hard. You're a lovable guy. And God knows you're often the best-looking guy in the room. But look what you just did for her. Sam, you can't be her hero and then just kiss your horse and ride off into the sunset."

"I'm not an idiot, Kats." I tossed my old cubes into the sink, poured out more Laphroaig, and added new ice. "You want more wine?"

"Yes, please."

I topped off her glass.

"She and I are squared away. How about you and me?"

Kate was about to take a sip from her glass, but looked up, only moving her eyes.

"We're good," she said.

"Sure?"

"Sure."

"Show me."

She set her glass aside and stepped away from the kitchen counter.

"Come here, cowboy. How about a hug from the bar girl who pours your glasses of Red-Eye?"

"I've always had the hots for silver-haired saloon girls." I took the necessary steps forward.

"You better." She put her arms around my neck.

"Always have. Always will. And don't be lookin' fer me ta git outta Dodge any time soon. I still got me some outlaws ta catch."

Chapter Twenty-Nine

On Friday, after enough rest to recharge my stress battery, I went back to work and promised Bettye I wouldn't fall asleep at my desk again.

We settled in for another boring day. But Bettye let me answer the phones and talk to the sector cars so I wouldn't feel like a prisoner in solitary confinement. And she kept busy doing some filing that might or might not have been necessary.

I contemplated going down the street to Primo's Gym and working out for an hour but decided against it. If I got changed and started building up a sweat, the mayor would only call and catch me screwing off on company time.

I called Moira Menzies and asked what Pikey Dillard had done to work off her debt and provide the narcotics cops with an introduction to her unofficial pharmacist. Moira suggested I telephone a Knox County detective named D. L. Showalter for a progress report.

When I called, I found D. L. working days and in the office.

"So far," he said, "I'm not impressed with Pikey's performance."

"I was afraid of that. She's got the makings of a real bullshitter."

"I hear that. She named a small-time pill head as her volume dealer. That sounded wrong—surprised me. I didn't believe a word of her story. My partner and I both know this guy, and we doubt he could handle a sale of five-hundred Oxy at one time. That's just way over his head."

"And she claims he's her only supplier?"

"That's what she says. Look, you know the drill. I wanted her to make one big buy then go back and introduce one of us to the dealer as a friend who wants to do an even bigger score and strike up a long-term relationship. My partner's a girl. I figgered she'd be best to pull it off. After that, we could cut Pikey loose and work the dealer ourselves."

Showalter explained that historically Pikey's pill pusher bought and used various drugs, but only sold enough to finance his habit. That's prevalent with junkies, hypes and other assorted dopers around the globe. They buy twice as much as they need for short-term use and sell half at a profit so their drugs cost them less or nothing.

"We went out with her twice," he said. "Each time she promised to cop five hundred hits. But each time she came back with no more than a dozen. Miss Pikey wants us to believe in bad luck. She says her piss-ant supplier sold off most of his stash each of those days to some other big dealers."

"Amazing how these two-bit hopheads think cops are imbeciles," I said.

"I wasn't happy about wastin' two nights with her, but when she lied, I wanted ta smack the shit outta her."

I laughed. "I know the feeling."

"My honest opinion," he said. "I think she's just stringin' us along, playing us—stallin' for time. We'll take her out once more, but I don't have any hope of scorin' more than ten or twelve pills. She ain't worth what she wants from ya."

I thanked D. L. and hung up, feeling frustrated and annoyed. But I knew I could trust Moira Menzies, Daughter of Darkness, to evaluate Pikey's efforts and results and treat her accordingly.

In the interim, I still hoped Junior Huskey would catch Pikey driving with a suspended license. After the pressure of another arrest and a few hours in pre-arraignment confinement, maybe she'd muster up the enthusiasm to introduce Showalter or his partner to a true volume dealer.

At ten minutes before noon, I got in my car and started heading to Howell's for lunch. I could easily kill an hour talking with Reggie about what Manchester United, the Sterling Blades or the Tottenham Court Hot Spurs were doing in the world of European football.

I pulled up to a stop sign across from Finn's Paint and Decorating Center. Two vehicles drove past slowly, and I waited patiently, listening to XM radio, tapping the steering wheel in time to The Drifter's version of *Up on the Roof.* As an ancient Ford pick-up cleared the intersection, I looked toward the paint store and watched Pikey Dillard walk out, carrying a white plastic shopping bag.

I first assumed she intended to go home and paint her walls and ceiling black. Then as she opened the door on a battered and sun faded, electric-blue, twenty-year-old Toyota, I thought, 'Eureka' and decided to let her drive a short distance before ruining her day.

There were no cars behind me. I blocked the corner until she started the engine and drove off. After following her for more than a half mile, I flipped on my red and blue flashing grill lights, attempting to pull her over on a stretch of quiet road. At first, she sped up from forty-five to sixty miles per hour. I looked carefully for another person in her car but didn't see a second head. This kept up for another half mile, and I wondered if she was trying to outrun me. Then she slowed down, turned into a side street and stopped. I got out of my Ford and walked over to the left side of her car as happy as a kid with a season ticket to the Ebbets Field home games. She rolled down the window.

"Oh, it's you," she said.

"Yeah, it's me. Did God come down from on high and tell the Commissioner of Motor Vehicles to reinstate your license?"

"Do what?"

"You heard me. Neither deal we made, nor the piddly little buys you've made with the Knox County narcs, entitle you to drive around with a suspended license."

"Oh, man, you're, like, not gonna write me a ticket, are ya?"

I noticed the flimsy plastic bag she carried from the paint store lying on the passenger's seat. As often happens, the contents of these bags don't remain inside for very long. The quart-sized paint can she carried was more than half-visible. I saw no label or markings on the outside.

"What's in the can, Pikey?" I asked.

"I, like, came out of a paint store. Whaddaya think?" She bristled with bad attitude.

"Let me see it."

"Why?"

I wanted to smack her.

"Because I've got the next twenty-five years of your life in the palm of my hand. If you persist in pissing me off, I just might revoke any deal we made and tell that good-looking blonde DA to send your ass up the river. That a good enough reason?"

"It's, like, just a freakin' can o' paint. You're, like, so anal."

"Yes, I am. Now give the nice policeman the freakin' can of paint. Like, okay?"

"Man, why are you breakin' my shoes here?"

"Are you going to show me the paint can? Or am I going to lock your ass up for a suspended license, impound your car—which will cost you two hundred bucks to get back—and get a warrant to open the can? Am I seeing resistance here for some damn good reason?"

"Look man, I'm workin' with Detective Showalter. He told me to make a buy and bring this stuff back to him."

"Oh, marvelous. I'm so glad you're helping us fight the forces of evil in Southern Appalachia. You're a real super-heroine. Might I assume from your statement that there are drugs in the can?"

She didn't answer. Another overwhelming need to smack her engulfed me. But I resisted.

"Okay, last chance… Give me the paint can."

"Oh man, you're, like, a real prick, ain'tcha?"

"Oh, man, like, yeah," I said. "And I can't help but think you're a world-class moron."

I took the can into custody, cuffed Pikey and secured her car. Then I called Bettye on the radio to say I'd be transporting a female prisoner. Bettye asked for my mileage and gave me an official time check in case Ms. Dillard later claimed I took a detour and engaged in some fabricated inappropriate conduct.

Five minutes later, Pikey and I walked through the back door of the PD. Once up front next to Bettye's desk, I said, "Hey Miss Bettye, look who's here again. Our old friend Pikey Dillard's come back to pay us a visit. Are you overjoyed like I am?"

Bettye just looked at me.

"Book her, please—suspended license for the moment. Then call someone in from the road to watch your desk so you and I can have a chat with Pikey. I believe we may be a while."

Bettye went through the booking formalities and then called in PO

Joey Gillespie, her favorite pinch-hitting deskman.

We settled into the squad room. I shackled Pikey to a desk, and the three of us sat down for a long wintertime chat.

"What am I going to find in the can?" I asked.

Pikey invoked her right to remain silent.

"When I call D. L. Showalter, will he tell me this buy was part of his deal with you?"

Still no response.

"You're too young to remember Monty Hall," I said. "But I'd suggest you start thinking about that old game: Let's Make a Deal."

"You'd do that again?" She finally spoke.

"I don't know. I owe you something for Darrell Korner. But then you owe me lots for not charging you with stealing the sevoflurane and dyphenhydramine from the hospital." She looked at me with surprise. "The stuff you gave Darrell. Of course, it wouldn't stretch the imagination to call you an accessory to assault and kidnapping, would it? And you can't claim to be nuts like Darrell might do."

"Did Darrell tell you that?"

"I didn't need Darrell to find out all about you."

"Oh, man, I guess I screwed up again."

"Yeah, you think? You know, Pikey, you've really got to work on that moron thing."

She pursed her lips in disgust for a few seconds. "So, like, whadda y'all want now?" She looked from me to Bettye. Finding no ally in Bettye, she focused back on me.

"Life is just full of interesting twists and opportunities," I said sarcastically. "You only have to know how to recognize and exploit them."

She looked at me as if I had two heads.

I thought about clarifying my philosophical statement. "See them and use them." That worked. "How about we see what's in the can and take it from there?"

Pikey blew out a little air and shrugged in an attempt to communicate her frustration.

I took out my pocketknife and pried out the blade that doubled as a bottle opener and screwdriver. I wiggled the blade around the ridge of the can top until the lid popped up. As I suspected from the lack of weight, there was no paint inside the can. I did find a plastic bag with what looked like another five hundred Oxycodone—the same type of pills I watched Will Sparks count only days before.

"Son of a gun," I said, "Can I assume the shit bird you told Showalter about is really just the small time pill-head everyone thought he was?

Pikey looked up at me through her false black eyelashes as she sat pouting.

"I'll be damned, but I'd bet a pair of tickets to a UT–Alabama game that your real dealer is right here in beautiful downtown Prospect. Am I getting close?"

"Do ya really, like, really, have ta try your hand at all this comedy? Or could ya, like, stick ta bein' a cop?"

I couldn't look at Bettye but sensed she snickered.

"Oh, I'm shocked that you can't appreciate this lighthearted approach to my chosen profession. Okay, let's cut the comedy and do some math. Follow me closely here, and you'll see the magic in what might happen."

Pikey tilted her head and squinted, indicating she might not believe my next statement.

"A charge that could net you twenty-five years in jail is being held over your head. The DA agreed to release you ROR to work with the Knoxville cops, but you're just jerking them off."

She stared off into space, seemingly to convey her displeasure with my remark about her honesty.

"Meanwhile, in another part of town," I continued, "I find you buying five hundred more Oxycodone. Similar crime, but *a different* twenty-five years. Damn, but even a high school dropout could add those two up and get fifty years. I could even make my life simple and forget about your part in Darrell's kidnapping and assault spree—if I wanted to be a nice guy. Hmm, what to do...? What to do?"

She screwed up her mouth, again trying to convey her displeasure.

"But that's a big 'if', don't you think?"

She dropped her eyes and again stared at her black nail polish.

"Before we got here, you called me a prick," I said. "You're not the

235

first, so I didn't take offense. But just to show you I'm not, how about for old time's sake, you and me being such good friends, I'll throw out the two suspended license charges. I know it's a few hundred dollars in fines for the city, and they can use the cash, but hell, you don't need a license in jail anyway. And in the big scheme of things, that's just a little chicken shit."

Bettye seemed happy to let me monopolize the conversation.

"So," I continued, "I figure we're even now for you ratting out Darrell. But we still have those pesky fifty years suspended somewhere over your head."

Pikey turned her look of annoyance into a serious frown and glared at Bettye who represented the kindly mother to my nasty father figure. Unfortunately, Bettye still didn't offer the girl any comfort.

"Let's say you want to behave yourself in the joint," I said, "and you pay a lawyer to make an application to get you out in one third of those fifty years. I don't have my calculator handy, but I'll bet that would be sixteen years and eight months. Damn, now you're pushing forty and just getting out of jail. When I was a kid there was an expression, 'Life begins at forty.' You know what?"

"What?"

"That's a bunch of crap. You'll be spending the best years of your life behind bars. You know, in prison the guards won't let you keep your ear studs and eyebrow pin. You don't get to dye your naturally blonde hair black. You'll have to forget about all this Goth bullshit, and once again, you'll be the pretty Miss Pikey that Darrell Korner fell for."

Surprisingly, I held her attention, and she listened without any more of her facial theatrics.

"I just hate to paint a dismal picture for you, Pikey, but remember what I once alluded to? I sure hope you don't mind having love interests named Bertha, Lulu and maybe even Marsha for the first ten or fifteen years you're a guest of the state.

That remark got her eyes to pop.

"We can help you, Pikey, but there won't be any walk this time, and the dealer I want is right here in Prospect."

After much talk, thirty-three minutes later, I said, "Pikey, we've screwed around here for half an hour and made no progress. Do you want to make a deal and save yourself all kinds of grief, or do I just send you into the system and watch you go down the chute?"

Bettye interrupted. "Pikey, I know him." She pointed to me. "You made a big mistake when you lied to him. He takes that personally. He will not give up until either you do what he wants or you're sentenced to more time in jail than you want to think about. Just get it over with. Tell him about the dealer, and do what he wants. You can't win."

Pikey waited almost thirty seconds before answering. I started to lose patience. Bettye looked more tolerant than I felt. But we waited.

Finally, Pikey spoke. "What do I gotta do?"

I jumped on the opportunity. "I'll get you flash money to buy more drugs. You go back to the dealer and set up a buy for another five hundred Oxycodone. I know it's right after you bought the last load, but tell him you gave those to your cousin in... I don't know, pick a place—Johnson City. Tell him the cousin wants the next pills on consignment and will give you half the money up front and half after the supply gets sold—all at a profit to you. So, you'll need five hundred more tonight or tomorrow. Then leave the door open for a third buy, maybe a thousand more on Saturday morning. You know, inventory for the weekend."

"You can get that much cash?" she asked.

"Don't worry about it."

"Damn."

"Can this guy handle that volume?"

"I think so."

"Okay, you ready to do this?"

"Oh, man, I don't know. This is, like, dangerous. If he thinks I'm the one who ratted him out, I'm in, like, big trouble."

"You're in bigger trouble now. I'll put you with a local narcotics cop who knows his business. In his world, this deal is small time."

"I think you're gonna get me killed."

"Hasn't happened to anyone I've worked with yet. And I've been in business since long before you were born."

"Yeah, but, like, I gotta say I got a cousin in Johnson City?"

"Yeah, that sounds good."

"But I, like, *don't* have a cousin in Johnson City."

I shook my head in moderate disbelief. "It's okay. We'll forgive you for lying."

Bettye took care of the necessary paperwork and called Moira Menzies to tell her what we were up to.

I called Blount County CID.

Chapter Thirty

"Hey, Jackie, you know a narcotics guy I can trust to do a good job?"

"Uh-huh. Whut's up?" Shuman said.

"I need a handler to take a girl out and buy some heavy-weight pills. Having a wad of flash money would make my life easy. He can also have the girl and try to turn her once we're finished."

"Whatcha got goin'?" he asked.

I gave him the twenty-five-cent story.

"Damn, yer a busy guy."

"It's the same snot-nosed kid who flipped on Darrell Korner. I picked her up with five hundred more Oxycodone. She's agreed to make two more big buys from the same dealer, a guy who works at Finn's paint store—name's Larry J. McMillan."

"Who?" Jackie almost yelped.

"Larry J. McMillan. He works at Finn's Paint and Decorating Center here in town."

"Sam, Larry J. McMillan's the guy Darrell locked up for DUI when he ended up punchin' out the county commissioner. Larry J's father is Finnbar McMillan. He owns the store, and he's the commissioner from that Prospect area. Don't y'all know nuthin' 'bout your local legislators?"

"I know the governor and the representatives in Washington, but I never remember the local guys. You're not kidding, are you?"

"No, sir, I ain't kiddin'. Same two players from Darrell's story. Damn, Chief, y'all kin 'spect the shit ta hit the fan with this one."

239

"Hey, they've got to be able to take a joke."

"Lord have mercy. Y'all better plan for the worst."

"I always do."

"Didn't ya ask Darrell who he punched out?"

"I was kind of busy at the time, and it didn't concern the kidnapping. Remember?"

"Yeah, I know."

"Now, how about that reliable narco guy I need?"

"Ya need ta talk with Rocky. Hang in there while I git 'im."

Jackie disappeared for a few minutes. Rocky turned out to be Detective Rockwell Sipe. Later, I met him and Jackie Shuman at the Justice Center where I learned Rocky spent two years with the Loudon County Sheriff before signing on at Blount County nine years ago. The bearded Rocky wore an FDNY baseball cap, sport shirt and blue jeans. A half-dozen tattoos covered his lower arms. After a few minutes of conversation, Rockwell sounded as competent as some of the better narcs I'd known back in New York.

Later that afternoon, Rocky, Pikey and I sat in my office.

"Look, miss," Sipe said, "I know the Chief's heard enough lies from ya. I ain't even gonna start listenin' ta no bullshit. You got one chance ta make a buy and get a favor from us. If the first buy poops out, you're done, far's I'm concerned. I ain't givin' ya no three strikes like those Knoxville boys."

Pikey sat in a guest chair listening and hanging her head but didn't offer any opposition to Rocky's plan.

"You score five hunnert pills tonight," he said, "and another five hunnert or a thousand tomorra, or you're goin' ta jail. End of story. Personally, I think the Chief sounded conservative when he estimated two twenty-five year sentences. You got popped with five hunnert schedule two narcotics—twice. Far's the law's concerned, you're a bona-fide dealer. With that aggregate weight, it's class A felony stuff. I'd push for twenty-five to life—times two." He let that idea sink in. "Now, you with us or what?"

Pikey's eyes bugged out. She must have been thinking about the shock of fifty years to life. She'd be over seventy-two before she could hope to hit the bricks again. It seemed like her mind was ticking away at warp speed, and she looked scared.

"Okay, okay," she said. "What do you want me to do?"

Rocky Sipe and I agreed on a plan. Pikey would go to see Larry J and show him some of the flash money. She'd set up a buy for 8 p.m. that night—five hundred Oxycodone. She'd agree to pay a few bucks more than her last purchase because of the short notice. That's how the trade works. During the initial meeting, she'd push him to agree on a second buy for early Saturday at the old price.

On Friday night, Rocky Sipe called me at home. He said Pikey picked up another five hundred Oxycodone. Not bad for short notice, he thought.

Just before lunchtime Saturday, he called again and said Pikey scored a second load, this time five hundred Vicodin which is the commercial name for Hydrocodone with a little Acetaminophen thrown in to spike the performance of the first ingredient.

McMillan assured her the substitute was close enough for government work, and her customers would be overjoyed with either drug. Pikey didn't argue. She knew the pill-head crowd.

Rocky Sipe led Pikey through those buys like a dog handler training a smart puppy. Everything went like clockwork.

At least I found my winter boredom once again interrupted. I met Sipe after the second buy to go over the next phase of our work. By two o'clock on Saturday afternoon, when Stan Rose and I sat down with two of bowls of hot and sour soup from Wah Lum, my week officially ended.

On Sunday morning, Rocky and I took Pikey to be arraigned—again. Instead of five years probation, a little jail time popped up in her future, but much less than she deserved.

With Pikey's statement, the aggregate fifteen hundred and eighty pills—Oxycodone and Vicodin—were all attributed to Larry J. McMillan.

Rocky Sipe worked a little magic, and a lab technician promised he'd have a complete report by 10 a.m. Monday. At noon on January 15th, he and I appeared before a judge requesting warrants.

The judge saw the name of the defendant and raised his eyebrows two inches. He read the name of the business we wanted to search for additional drugs and began getting heart palpitations.

But he signed both warrants. Before I left his chambers, I called Stan Rose who, along with four Prospect cops, Jackie Shuman and Rocky's partner as the technical advisor, waited outside the paint store.

They executed both warrants before the judge, his clerk or any other potential whistle-blower could alert Finnbar McMillan about our intentions. Before I left his chambers, the judge stared at me with more than a moderate amount of annoyance. Actually, his expression left me wanting to look in a mirror and check if I showed symptoms of the pox.

* * * *

Rocky left the Justice Center to meet the arrest team at Prospect PD, while I stayed around for a powwow with Chief Assistant DA Moira Menzies who had accompanied us to the judge's chambers.

"You really rubbed his nose in that, Sam" Her usual bitchy demeanor showed through like a lighthouse on a moonless night.

"I thought he'd be impressed with my efficiency."

"You knew all about Larry and Finn McMillan's involvement with your boy Darrell Korner, didn't you?"

"Why do you think that?"

"But that's all meaningless to you, of course. And that's why you're the sweetheart of the local politicians. Did you really have to imply the judge couldn't be trusted?"

"You look much younger when you smile. All these frowns don't do you justice. And I've heard they can permanently wrinkle your forehead."

"Will you shut up?" she said.

I smiled just to aggravate her a little more.

"I never doubted his honesty," I said. "I just figured I'd give him a big share of plausible deniability so he could throw the blame on me."

"Please don't imply I'm an idiot."

"Pfui. Your inference is twaddle." I used Nero Wolfe's words again. "You're one of the sharpest lawyers I know. And I'm no witling. But I wouldn't allow Judge Myers to pass the paperwork to someone *else* who could alert one of the McMillans before my cops hit the paint store. The old boy should send me a fruit basket as a thank-you."

"The more I see you in action, Sam, the more I am amazed at what you get away with."

"Moira, every day when I shave, I'm thrilled with the guy who looks back at me from the mirror. How many other cops can say that?"

"Goodness me, Buford Pusser is alive and well in Blount County."

"See ya in court, Counselor. As always, it's been a pleasure workin' with ya."

"Oh…nuts!"

"Gee, you're starting to sound like me."

* * * *

When I arrived at Prospect PD, Rocky Sipe and his partner had already counted up all the pills my search team confiscated. I found Larry McMillan sitting in the squad room, Stan Rose busy processing his arrest.

After that, I walked up front by Bettye and saw a heavy-set man of around fifty sitting in the reception area. He looked familiar.

"Hi, Sarge," I said. "Someone I should meet?"

She stood up. So did our visitor.

"Chief, this is Finnbar McMillan. His son was arrested for possession of controlled substances."

McMillan took a step toward us. I recognized him as the loudmouth who created the disturbance in the Villa Napoli on New Year's Eve. I wished Tommy Cutrone had brained him with the meat mallet.

"Excuse me for a minute, Sergeant. I've got something to do in the back."

Before I turned, I watched McMillan's face drop.

"Have a seat, Mr. McMillan," Bettye said. "The Chief will be with you shortly."

I walked back to the interrogation room where Rocky Sipe and his partner hung out.

"The kid's old man is out front," I said. "I assume he's here to negotiate a walk for his boy. My advice to you is don't get involved. Stan will finish the arrest package and take the kid to arraignment. I'll have him call you from the Justice Center. Maybe the kid will play ball to work off his nut after he's hopelessly stuck in the system. Anyway, he's all yours. I'll see if I can brush off the father. Stan's already got his numbers for the reports so if the arrest disappears, someone will have to answer for it. Let's see what happens."

The two scruffy narcs sat in armless chairs, tilted back on two legs, their feet resting on the small metal desk. Sipe's partner looked about twenty-five with a dark beard and a ponytail.

"You're really enjoyin' this, ain't ya?" Rocky asked.

"Less than you think, but no one's going to walk on this one, I guarantee that."

"Damn, I wish I had me a lock on my job."

His partner locked his hands behind his head and grinned.

"I'm too old to care."

The narcs laughed. I walked up front again. Bettye introduced me to Finnbar, the paint man. The three of us entered my office and closed the door.

"Now, Chief," Finn said, "I believe there's been one big mistake here. I'd appreciate it if I could take my boy home, an' we'll all jest forget about this."

I thought about Darrell and Rachel and the landslide Finnbar McMillan inadvertently started a long time ago. I swore silently and resisted the urge to slam him between the eyes with a blackjack.

"There's no mistake or misunderstanding, Mr. McMillan. Your son is going to jail for selling narcotics—lots of them. It all looks very clear to me. He's not going anywhere except to arraignment, and if a judge thinks he qualifies for bail he'll be able to go home—for a while anyway. Be patient."

McMillan squinted at me. "Don't I know y'all from somewheres?"

"I don't think so. I've got a common face."

He didn't look like he believed me, but he shook his head and didn't come up with the connection at the restaurant.

"Now looka here, Chief, Sergeant, if y'all want, I kin call the chairman of the county commission, the county mayor or somebody mebbe higher up, an' they kin call Mayor Shields about this. That way someone could take the responsibility from all y'all's shoulders. You unnerstand?"

I was so pleased he included Bettye in his statement. At least I knew he wasn't a sexist pig. She needed recognition, working so much overtime and all.

"Sure, we understand," I said. "But I'm not looking to shrug off responsibility onto someone else. I don't want Ronnie Shields put into an awkward position."

"So, we're all set here? Larry J kin come home with me?"

"No, sir, Larry J's going to jail. There's nothing anyone you know can do for him. Your son's here, and all your political friends are immaterial to me. Now, is there any other business we have to transact?"

"Oh, I'm sure there's somethin' kin be done, Chief. I think I unnerstand ya now. Yessir, I shore do. I shoulda anticipated this myse'f and not wasted y'all's time. Okay, bottom line it fer me, what's it gonna take fer my boy ta walk outta this with me—rot now?"

"I'm a reasonable guy, Mr. McMillan, but the law's the law." I took a step closer and lowered my voice. "What did you have in mind?"

Finnbar McMillan took a wad of hundreds that could have choked a wooly mammoth out of his pants pocket and began fanning through them.

"Do I start countin' an' wait fer ya ta say stop, or do I assume y'all are goin' ta hold me up fer ever'thin' I got here?"

"Mr. McMillan, are you telling me that you're offering *part* of that money to let your son go? Sergeant Lambert here is my partner, you know." I shrugged. "There's *two* of us listening to you."

"Goddamn it, man, this is ten thousand in hunnerts! It damn well better be enough fer both o' ya!"

I said nothing, but held out my hand and grinned like a glutton. He slapped the wad of cash into my palm. I handed the money to Bettye. Her eyes looked as wide as saucers.

"Do I need to count it?" I asked.

Finnbar shook his head.

"You don't want a receipt, do you?"

McMillan spoke through his teeth. "Spare me the jokes, please."

"Okay, Finn, old buddy, no jokes. You can join your kid now."

"Good."

"Yeah, good. You're under arrest, just like him, you bastard. Now turn around."

I had taken the cuffs from my waistband and held them ready to use.

"Goddamn yew!" He took a single step closer to me.

I grabbed him by the throat with my left hand and pushed him back over my desk with my right. I hit him so hard and so fast everything on my desk scattered. I tightened up my grip on his neck and pushed him down harder.

"Roll over, you fat bastard, or I'll crush your wind pipe."

He tried to nod his head. I loosened up a little. He didn't fight but tried to turn over. I let him. Then I cuffed him and yanked on his pants belt, pulling him to his feet.

"You're under arrest for bribery of two public officials. You have the right to remain silent, the right to an attorney, blah, blah, blah. Do me a favor, and keep your fat mouth shut because I don't want to hear a word you have to say."

"I got one thing ta say ta yew, mister," Finn sputtered, "I'll have yer job after this—count on it!"

"No, you won't, asshole. I have a contract with the City of Prospect to work here for five years. After that, I'll be too old to give a rat's ass what they or you think. Now, let's go and show sonny boy what kind of a hero his daddy is."

I sat Finnbar in a squad room chair and used a second pair of cuffs to lock him to the desk. I wanted the fat prick to feel great discomfort with his hands cuffed behind his back.

"Sorry to interrupt you, Stanley," I said, "but this gentleman is another customer. Keep an eye on him for a few minutes while I take care of some things. I'll be back shortly to do his paperwork."

Stanley grinned, shook his head and probably guessed the identity of my new detainee.

* * * *

"Bettye, I'll be tied up with our new friend for quite some time. Would you call upstairs and tell Ronnie what happened? Don't take any crap from him. Tell him I've gone crazy, and if he wants to speak with me or if he comes down here, you're afraid I might get violent."

"You want me to say all that?"

"You're much more circumspect in these matters than I. Tell him whatever you think is appropriate to get the best results. Use your intelligence, guided by experience. I trust you."

She smiled. "Okey dokey, darlin'."

"After you speak with Ronnie, call Rachel. Welcome her back to work and give her the poop on this new fiasco we're involved in. Let's make sure she gets a jump on this story before the other stations."

"Wouldn't you rather call her?"

"I think she'd like to hear from you. I'm a little busy right now."

Bettye chuckled. "I think that'll work out just fine, Sam. Just real fine."

* * * *

Two hours later, I sat in the side chair at Bettye's desk.

"Sammy, you can get downright mean when you're mad, can't you?"

"I can, but I don't…very often."

"Well, I'm glad for that."

"Yeah, guys my age have to watch their blood pressure."

"What should I do with the ten thousand dollars? I'm afraid to just leave it in the evidence closet."

"How about two tickets to Bora Bora? I'll have Stan watch the PD, while we're on the beach sipping drinks from hollowed out pineapples."

"You might think I'd know better than to ask, wouldn't you?"

"By now…yeah. But I have fun when you do."

"Someday I'll get you for things like that, you know."

"Yeah, some day. Maybe. I'm not as quick as I used to be."

She offered a smile bright enough to light up a coalmine.

"Somehow, I don't believe that."

"Thanks."

"How did you engineer this arrest?" she asked.

"I didn't engineer it. It just happened. I didn't do anything but respond properly to the circumstances. I'm just a product of my po-leece training."

"Am I supposed to believe that?"

"It's the truth. Nothing but a coincidence. I'm a victim of circumstance."

"Do you believe in coincidence?"

"No, but you're too young to be as cynical as me."

She wrinkled her nose and stuck out her tongue. I frowned.

"I wonder what Darrell Korner will think when he hears what you did to the people who caused him all that grief?" she asked.

"Only one way to find out."

"You'll tell him?"

"Sure, why not?"

Chapter Thirty-One

On Tuesday morning, I asked Joe Costello to meet me at the Knoxville jail so I could speak with Darrell Korner. We checked in and walked to the interview room together. A lanky redheaded jail guard brought Darrell in, still looking like a Devil's Island inmate.

"What do you say, Darrell?" I said.

"Hello, sir. Mr. Costello." He nodded twice and sat in a scarred-up oak side chair.

"Are you familiar with Larry J or Finnbar McMillan?" I asked.

"Sir, I believe you know I am."

"Yeah, I do."

"What's this all about, Sam?" Joe asked. He sat on the opposite side of the table next to his client.

I took several sheets of paper from the inside pocket of my sport jacket, unfolded them and pushed them across the table to Darrell and his lawyer.

"I thought Darrell would be interested in seeing copies of these reports. I assume he still recognizes them from when he worked as a cop."

Darrell began scanning the paperwork: two arrest reports and prosecution worksheets. Together, they told the complete story.

"Yes, sir, I sure do." He didn't look up but continued reading.

Costello stood up and read over his client's shoulder. "Lord have mercy, Sam. You arrested Finn McMillan for felony bribery?"

"And his kid for Sale One."

"Why'd you do this, sir?" Darrel asked.

"Because they were guilty, and it needed doing. You think I've got some other agenda here?" My answer sounded curt.

"Beats me, sir." He didn't seem to take offense. A slight smirk crossed his lips.

"You're gonna catch some flak over this, Sam," Joe said.

"Yeah, well, I'll dig out the old flak jacket from my footlocker."

Darrell, the ex-soldier, smiled at the reference. "Sir, I cain't say I'm not sorry to see them—the pair o' them—arrested. I guess I should say thank you."

"I'm not looking for thanks, kid. I'm just glad to show you that occasionally there is a little justice in the world. And I've recently learned to never again deny the existence of coincidence."

"Yes, sir, I hear that. Thanks anyway."

"How are things going for your client, Joe?" I asked. "Any idea what the disposition of all this is going to be?"

"We haven't ironed out all the wrinkles yet, but I'm doing the best I can for him. Darrell will be okay."

"Good for you, Darrell. Have faith in this guy. Your lawyer's almost as clever as me."

That got a grin from Darrell and a nasty comment from Costello.

"You know what you want to do when you're out on your own again?" I asked Darrell.

"Haven't come ta that bridge yet, sir."

"I hear you've got a pretty snazzy '85 Super Sport you rebuilt. I guess you're good with engines and cars."

"Yes, sir, I'm not too bad."

"I think you might be able to get a good deal on an auto repair shop in Prospect in about eleven months and twenty-nine days if you're around and interested."

* * * *

The next weekend, Katherine and I made a spur-of-the-moment trip two hours over the mountains to Asheville, North Carolina. We ate in a great Indian restaurant, looked around in a bunch of antique shops and artsy gift boutiques, went to a crafts fair and then on Sunday, drove south a few miles to visit Carl Sandburg's home in Flat Rock. For lunch, we ate a brick oven pizza at the Flat Rock Bakery. Late that afternoon, we arrived home again.

I made a pitcher of Manhattans, and Kate forced me to play Scrabble with her and get horribly beaten. The woman knows thousands of obscure two- and three-letter words the rest of humanity forgot long ago.

In spite of my horrific defeat at the gaming table, I enjoyed a nice weekend.

Repeatedly, I promised myself I'd exercise restraint whenever I saw Rachel Williamson. Being friends sounded good. Being more than friends did not. Exercising willpower was really a necessity.

On Monday morning, I walked into work an hour early, took two brass gun hangers and a few wall mollies and hung my re-creation of a rifle made in Prospect, sometime around 1790, on the wall behind my desk. On my first try, it looked level. I stood back and admired my handiwork. Then I remembered what I said to Rachel when she asked to see one of the guns I made.

My little voice spoke to me again, "Jerk!" he said.

Then another voice grabbed my attention.

"My, you're in early," Bettye said, as she passed my door.

"Mornin' Betts. Have a good weekend?"

"Yes, sir, I surely did."

She took off her coat, hung it on the rack behind her desk and walked back into my office where I stood looking at the long rifle.

"Well, that's new." she said. "My papaw had an old gun like that. Says it was his great, great grandfather's. Where'd you find this one?"

"It's not old. I made it about a year ago."

"You made it? Go on. Well, I never. Can I see it?"

"Sure, I'll get it down."

THE END

About the Author

Wayne Zurl grew up on Long Island and retired after twenty years with the Suffolk County Police Department, one of the largest municipal law enforcement agencies in New York and the nation. For thirteen of those years he served as a section commander supervising investigators. He is a graduate of SUNY, Empire State College and served on active duty in the US Army during the Vietnam War and later in the reserves. Zurl left New York to live in the foothills of the Great Smoky Mountains of Tennessee with his wife, Barbara.

Zurl has won Eric Hoffer and Indie Book Awards, and was named a finalist for a Montaigne Medal and First Horizon Book Award. He has written four novels and more than twenty novelettes in the Sam Jenkins mystery series.

Author Links:

Author website: http://www.waynezurlbooks.net
Twitter: http://www.twitter.com/#!/waynezurl
Facebook: http://www.facebook.com/waynezurl

Other books by the author at Melange

From New York to the Smokies
A Leprechaun's Lament

www.ingramcontent.com/pod-product-compliance
Lightning Source LLC
Chambersburg PA
CBHW050502260626
47157CB00004B/1154